The Recipe *for* Love *and* Friendship

Shirley Jump

FOREVER

New York   Boston

Copyright © 2017 by Shirley Jump
Preview of *The Secret Ingredient for a Happy Marriage* copyright © 2017 by Shirley Jump
Reading group guide copyright © 2017 by Shirley Jump and Hachette Book Group, Inc.

Cover design by Elizabeth Turner
Cover copyright © 2017 by Hachette Book Group, Inc.

Forever
Hachette Book Group
1290 Avenue of the Americas, New York, NY 10104
forever-romance.com
twitter.com/foreverromance

First Edition: July 2017

Forever is an imprint of Grand Central Publishing. The Forever name and logo are trademarks of Hachette Book Group, Inc.

The publisher is not responsible for websites (or their content) that are not owned by the publisher.

The Hachette Speakers Bureau provides a wide range of authors for speaking events. To find out more, go to www.hachettespeakersbureau.com or call (866) 376-6591.

LCCN: 2017935995

ISBNs: 978-1-4555-7200-7 (trade pbk.), 978-1-4555-7201-4 (ebook)

Printed in the United States of America

LSC-C

10 9 8 7 6 5 4 3 2

To the friends who have become my sisters over the last few years, supporting me and lifting me when my spirits were low— Kathy, Amanda, Marci, Karen, Tina, Melanie, Carrie, Sally, and Bruce (who is an honorary sister). You all will never know how much that meant to me and how you have been my strength when I thought I had lost mine. Love you guys.

ONE

The primrose were blooming. If there was one thing Bridget would remember about that spring, it was the way they bloomed, small but proud and bright, like they were determined to show their happy faces even as winter's gray lingered, making one last feeble attempt to overpower April's promised sunshine.

She stood on the back porch while people hovered inside her house, talking in hushed tones with somber faces. Her heels pinched at her toes, black shoes she'd bought and set on a shelf in her closet. Worn today, for the first time, shiny and tight and mean.

She inhaled deep breaths of the crisp, fresh air. She'd always thought spring smelled like hope. Like promises of great things around the corner. In elementary school, her desk had sat by the wide crank windows at St. Gregory's, and every spring, the breeze would drift into the room, riffle her papers and books, and tease her into going outside. As soon as the bell rang at the end of the day, Bridget would run for the door, eager for the long walk home that she dreaded when snow filled the streets. Today, the air didn't smell like hope at all. Instead, it seemed too harsh, too angry.

Good old-fashioned Catholic guilt, woven into the very fiber of her soul by countless Sundays spent whispering confessions to the shadowy outline of Father McBride, washed over Bridget. She should be inside, playing some kind of macabre hostess. Her mother and her sisters were expecting her, along with the other three dozen people milling around the three-bedroom bungalow with its cornflower-blue paint and crisp white shutters. She and Jim had bought it two years ago. They had still been in the process of fixing it up, about to start the kitchen demo next, when—

Bridget turned back to the house, to the place where all her hopes still resided, clinging to some life raft of delusion. The half of her mind that kept saying everything was fine, that this was all some weirdly realistic dream.

Her mother stood in front of the bay window. Colleen O'Bannon wore a stern expression like it was an accessory to her prim black dress. She motioned to Bridget, that expectant gesture that had brought her four daughters into line a thousand times before.

The rope of muscles in Bridget's chest tightened. She couldn't go back in there. Not now. She slipped out of the shoes, setting them neatly side by side on the porch, then padded barefoot down the wooden steps. The last one creaked, bowing a bit under her weight.

I have to remind Jim to fix that.

But just as quickly as the thought occurred, it was chased by a second one.

Jim can't fix anything. He's gone.

Not just gone. Forever gone.

That thought of *forever* was too big, too overwhelming, too much of a tsunami pushing at her. It made that rope inside her chest twist again and her heart skitter and her breath stop. She couldn't even follow it by the word *dead.* Maybe she could make his death not real, if only she didn't think about it, didn't hear the doctor's voice in her head. *"He's gone,"* the doctor had said, and she'd been in such denial—not Jim, never Jim—that she'd said, *"Gone where? And how? I have the car."* The doctor had given her that sad, sympathetic smile they probably learned in medical school and said a whole lot of things that culminated with *dead.*

None of this was real. She was dreaming the whole thing. The accident, the hospital, the Quincy funeral home with the cloying flowers and the ugly mauve carpeting.

Breathe, Bridget. Breathe. Instead, panic clamped a vise grip over her windpipe.

Bridget charged across the lawn, barreling away from the house, the murmurs, the expectations, and toward the flowerbeds nestled beneath the mottled stone wall, the flowerbeds she had planted just a month ago, when it seemed like everything in her life was as perfect as it could be.

"If we have a baby someday, he or she will see these every morning," she'd told Jim. *"They're the perfect flowers to say good morning, don't you think?"*

He'd chuckled. *"I don't think flowers can say anything."*

"Aye, then you haven't listened to my Irish grandmother," Bridget had said. *"The* sabhaircin *are magical. They protect against the fairies."*

He'd knelt beside her in the dirt, scooping out the musty earth and gently nestling a tender primrose into the ground. *"I thought fairies were a good thing. Like the fairy god-mother in* Cinderella.*"*

"They are. But they're also mischievous little things," Bridget had said. *"So people would lay a bouquet of primroses on their doorstep to keep the fairies from entering in the middle of the night and wreaking mayhem. The fairies love primroses, and if you grow them, it's said that your house will be blessed and happy."*

Jim had kissed her then, kissed her in that sweet spot above her brow, where he would let his lips linger, and he'd inhale the scent of her skin, her hair. It was the kind of kiss that had always made Bridget feel treasured. *"How I love every last one of those legends and superstitions of yours, Bridge,"* he'd whispered. *"You make this practical accountant believe in the impossible, even if all those tales are nothing more than make-believe."*

And now the primroses were blooming and Jim wasn't here to see them and they were never going to have a baby or have a life together. Although that was the same life she had begun to question until—

Her chest heaved, each breath harder and harder to find. Bridget kept moving toward the primroses, toward those happy beckoning white faces, heedless of the dewy grass that some distant part of her mind thought had grown too long.

It's Saturday. Jim will mow—

She crumpled to her knees, her black dress puddling around her, spreading an inky cloth stain across the thick, green grass. Bridget grabbed her arms, tightened her grip, and rocked back and forth, willing the tears to stop, for all of it to stop, for time to reverse. For her to be back here, planting the primroses with Jim, planning for the future she'd always dreamed, while the sun shone and the world spun happily along.

A world that she had created, almost like a writer spinning a tale. Having a baby would fix everything, she'd told herself, over and over again. A baby would mend the wounds in their marriage, bring them together, reknit the connection that had become tenuous in the year since Jim took the job in Boston. The one where he traveled more and stayed home less and seemed to be somewhere else, even when he was sitting on the same sofa.

But every time she brought up getting pregnant, Jim had changed the subject or told her they would talk about it later. Every time she cracked open another circle of birth control pills, she asked Jim if they should start trying. He'd press a kiss to her cheek, promise to talk later, and head out the door on yet another trip.

And now there would be no later.

She closed her eyes, but that only made it worse, made Jim's face dance in the dark space in her mind. She opened her eyes and focused again on the primroses, on their white faces, their yellow cores.

Something twitched in the corner, by the tallest group of primroses and their long, green, finger-like leaves. The flowers trembled, their stems bending. Bridget duck-walked over there, swiping at her eyes to clear the brimming tears.

A hummingbird, so tiny she was sure it was a baby, was caught in a spider web that had been spun between the flowers and anchored into the rough surface of the rock wall. The bird was flying hard and furious, but the web was strong, and every flutter of the bird's green and blue wings wrapped more of the sticky web around its body.

As Bridget approached, the hummingbird's movements became more frantic. "Shh, shh," she whispered, "it's okay. I'm going to help you."

The spider, fat and black, sat in the upper corner of the web, bouncing on the gossamer string like a Wallenda. Bridget reached under the bird and pushed at the web, breaking the strands one at a time. "Don't be scared. It's okay. I've got you now."

The hummingbird stilled, his heart beating so hard she could see it thunder under his gray breast feathers. Another quick swipe and the web was off the bird's wings, but still he stayed. She put a hand beneath him, and the hummingbird eased into her palm, his eyes darting left, toward the spider, then right to her. Bridget flattened her palm and turned toward the primroses. "Go ahead, buddy. Go home."

The hummingbird stayed still for what seemed like a forever moment, watching her, his tail twitching, eyes dark, wary, and big against the blue and green feathers of his head. He lifted off her palm, hovering, wings beating so fast, Bridget could feel the wake. A second later, he was gone, a blur darting toward the trees.

"Don't tell me. You're out here looking for a wee leprechaun to make you some new shoes?"

Bridget turned at the sound of her sister Margaret's voice. No one called her Margaret, hadn't since the day she'd been born, the youngest of the four girls, the one who was the loudest, the most insistent of the O'Bannon daughters. They'd dubbed her Magpie, and the name had stuck. "I just couldn't handle another second in there. It was like..."

"A funeral?" Magpie said; then her face softened with sympathy and she dropped down beside her sister, heedless of grass stains on her navy cotton skirt. That was Magpie. Young and brash and unconcerned with the kinds of things that consumed the rest of the world. Her light brown hair hung in one long plait down her back, like an anchor for the flowy cotton blouse that billowed away from her tiny waist and belled on her thin wrists. She draped an arm over Bridget's shoulders and drew her close. "This sucks."

"Yeah."

Magpie sighed. "I wish I had some kind of good advice for you. Something that would make it all better. But you got dealt a shitty hand, and there's nothing anyone can say that will make it any less shitty."

Bridget tightened her grip on her sister. "Thank you."

"For what?"

"For saying the first honest thing I've heard all week. Everyone else is like, 'It was for the best he went quickly,' or 'He'll be an angel now,' or the worst one of all, 'He'd want you to enjoy your life.' Really? My husband was killed in a car accident at the age of thirty, and I'm supposed to enjoy my life? All I really want to do is crawl into bed and shut the blinds and drink until I forget what day it is."

"Then do it." Magpie gave her a little shake. "I'm serious. And I'll bring the wine."

Bridget laughed. "You're nuts."

"No, I'm not. Mom had me tested." Magpie winked.

The moment of lightness passed in a blink. Bridget put her hands on her knees and looked out over the lawn, but the green blurred in her vision. "Abby didn't stay."

Magpie gave Bridget a crooked, sad smile. "She told me she had to get back to work. Something about her boss being on vacation."

The lie hung in the air, but neither of them called it out. And why would they? If there was one thing the O'Bannon girls excelled at, it was sweeping the truth away and locking it in a closet. If no one mentioned what had happened three years ago, then they could all go on pretending.

But the truth sank its tenterhooks into every sentence, every look exchanged in the O'Bannon family. The "disagreement," as their mother called it—really a full-on shouting match the morning of Bridget's wedding—had culminated in Abby storming out of the reception after telling her sister that she was being blind and stupid. That she would regret marrying that man someday.

Magpie got to her feet and put out a hand. "Come on, Bridge, let's go back inside. Aunt Grace made her crab puffs, and she's upset no one is eating them."

"Because we all got food poisoning at Uncle Lou's funeral."

Magpie hugged Bridget's waist as they walked back to the house. "Look at the bright side. Food poisoning is a totally legit excuse to stay in bed and shut the blinds."

TWO

Bridget did exactly that for the next three days. She closed the blinds, turned on Netflix, and binge-watched *Orange Is the New Black*. A thousand times she picked up the phone to call her sisters or a friend, anyone who could fill the lonely gaps in her days. But in the end, she'd put down the phone and curl back into the pillows.

Every time Bridget tried to think about tomorrow, hell, even an hour from now, she would begin to hyperventilate. It was too much to think about, too much to deal with. Like the sight of Jim's clothes in the closet and his still-dented pillow beside her and the teetering pile of spy novels on the nightstand that she had nagged him a thousand times to put away.

Magpie came by at lunch, followed by their sister Nora at dinner and their mother an hour after Nora left. It was as if the other O'Bannon women had conspired to make sure Bridget was never alone, although Nora barely talked to her and Magpie chattered and paced the room like a caged animal. Two days later, Magpie mentioned a job she had to get to, and just as quickly as she flitted into their lives, she darted away again. None of them mentioned Abby, and not a single one spoke Jim's name.

Their mother foisted food on Bridget like it was a morphine drip. So Bridget ate the soup her mother made and fumbled her way through awkward, stilted conversations about nothing, as Piper and Alex and Red survived prison and Bridget could think of nothing but being back in her bed.

On the fourth day, her mother was there at the butt crack of way-too-early, ringing the doorbell, then knocking, then ringing some more. Bridget swung out of bed, jerked her arms into a robe, and flung open the door. "I'm alive. Please let me sleep."

"Not today. Today you are going to take a shower and do your hair and leave this place." Colleen O'Bannon crossed her arms over her chest and gave her eldest daughter a stern look. It was the look that she'd practiced in the twenty years she'd been a single mother, a single Irish mother at that. "If your ancestors survived the potato famine—"

"I can survive this," Bridget finished. "This isn't the same thing, Ma. Not at all."

"No, it's not." Colleen took her daughter's arms and stared up into Bridget's eyes. Colleen was a good four inches shorter than all of her daughters but had the presence of someone a foot taller. "This is a terrible thing. I know exactly what you are feeling, my sweet daughter. But I also know you will survive and you will be *just fine*."

Indeed, her mother did know. Colleen had watched her husband have a heart attack at the dinner table one Sunday afternoon and buried him a week later, then picked herself up and moved forward with four little girls under the age of ten as if nothing more had happened than a broken dish that needed to be cleaned up. For the next two decades, she had acted as if Michael O'Bannon were there, silently setting a place at the table for him in the cramped kitchen of the duplex in Dorchester every night and referencing him in the present tense.

Just fine had become the O'Bannon girls' motto that summer after Dad died. They'd practiced saying it to teachers and neighbors and church gossipers so often that, if there could have been an Emmy for pretending to be okay, there would have been a four-way tie. *Just fine, thank you.*

Now Bridget was doing it too. *I'm just fine*, she told her friends, her sisters, her mother. She'd even copied and pasted *I'm fine* so she could send it back to every well-meaning text and email. Except she wasn't. She didn't know how to move forward, what to do. Was it because she had grown too dependent on Jim in the three years they'd been married? Had she really gotten to the point where she couldn't make a decision on her own?

"Now, off with you," her mother said as if she'd read her daughter's mind, shooing Bridget toward the master bath. "We're leaving in ten minutes."

Bridget opened her mouth to argue, saw by the tight line on Colleen's face that arguing was pointless, and headed into the bathroom. But even here it was impossible to forget. Jim's toothbrush still sat in the bronze holder between their two sinks; his razor was still perched on the edge of his sink, perpetually drying after one last shave.

I'll be home before you know it, Bridge, Jim had said. *It's just a couple days, and I'll be back. Then I'll take a day off with you. I promise.*

She'd argued with him that morning, storming out of the bathroom, slamming the door so hard that it had shuddered on the hinges. Jim had packed his overnight bag, climbed into a taxi, and left without saying goodbye.

That was the last memory she had of her husband—another fight, another silent departure. The chance to mend that fence had died when a drunk driver swerved across the lanes outside the departure drop-off at Logan, just as Jim stepped out of the taxi.

Bridget fluttered a hand over the razor, the toothbrush, the crumpled towel on the counter. She closed her eyes and drew in a deep breath. Jim was gone, but the life they had planned was still waiting for her. Maybe not with the baby she'd dreamed of having someday, or the future she'd pictured a thousand times, but a life nonetheless. Either she started getting her shit together or she'd end up like Aunt Esther, who had never left the house after her husband died, collapsing of a heart attack thirty years later among a pile of newspapers so high that they smothered her in a makeshift coffin of musty *Globes*.

Bridget could do this.

She had to do this.

The shower blurred her tears and ran them down the

drain with bubbles of almond-scented soap and raspberry shampoo. Her face burned, her shoulders seemed weighted to the ground, but she managed to at least go through the motions of cleaning up.

By the time she emerged, her mother was already standing there, holding a blue and white checked dress and a pair of low navy pumps. A pair of pantyhose that Bridget didn't even remember owning was draped over her mother's arm. "This will do just fine for today."

She bristled. "I hate that dress. And those shoes. And don't even get me started on the pantyhose. Where did you find those anyway?"

Normal people would have been disturbed that their mother had gone through their closet and drawers and then walked into the bathroom uninvited. But normal people didn't have Colleen O'Bannon as a mother.

"A lady always wears hose with her shoes," Colleen said. "And the dress suits you just fine. It's appropriate for where we are going."

Appropriate. That one word raised the little hairs on the back of Bridget's neck. "Where are we going?"

"You'll see." Colleen thrust the clothes at her daughter. "Now, do your face and hair. You can't go out in the world looking like you were blown about by a hurricane."

Bridget wanted to say, *My husband just died. Who gives a shit how I look?* But her mother was giving her that I-survived-this-and-you-can-too look again, so Bridget sighed and nodded instead. It was easier to do what her mother said than to try and figure out what to wear.

Whether to wear the blue dress or her black pants, or heck, pajamas, just seemed like a monumentally stupid decision to have to make right now.

After her mother left the room, Bridget swiped a clear circle into the foggy mirror. Dark shadows hugged the bottoms of her red-rimmed eyes. Her wet, dark hair hung as limp as old spaghetti, and her skin had taken on a pale parchment tone. Okay, so maybe her mother had a point about her looking like she'd been caught in some massive storm.

But when Bridget got out the plastic case that held her makeup, the whole process just seemed so…overwhelming. Too many decisions. Foundation or concealer first? The coral blush or the pink? And the eye shadows…God, why had she ever thought she needed five different shades?

She leaned into the mirror and pressed her palms against her cheeks. *I don't recognize this woman,* she thought. A woman who had lost everything in the space of one rainy afternoon.

She was a widow now.

The word sounded so foreign, so odd. Wid-doh. She tried it out three times in her head, and then whispered it once in the steamy air. *"Widow."*

One whose husband had died. Her husband. Died.
Jim.

She could feel the tears starting again at the backs of her eyes, burning their way to the surface. She swiped at her face with a towel and then shut the case and pushed it to the side. Bridget pulled on the dress and slid into the shoes—ignoring the pantyhose—and then gave her hair a quick once-over with a wide-toothed comb.

She didn't look in the mirror again.

When Bridget emerged from the bathroom, Colleen was standing there, her feet planted, her arms over her chest, and her lips in that thin line of disapproval. Bridget braced herself for the lecture.

"All right, then," was all her mother said. She reached for a handbag on Bridget's dresser, pressed it into her daughter's hands, and led the way out of the dim bedroom and into the light of day.

THREE

There was something about the routine of church that both annoyed Bridget and calmed her. The hard wooden pews, the carpeted kneelers, the candles flickering in the wall sconces beneath painted images of Jesus on the cross and heartbroken disciples. The same setting she remembered from the days when she wore Mary Jane shoes and white ankle socks and wondered if God would smite her for fidgeting in her seat.

Bridget had stopped going to Our Lady Church more than three years ago, until the day of the funeral. Jim was a lapsed Lutheran who would rather read the paper and hit the links than listen to a sermon about loving thy neighbor. She'd lingered in bed with him on Sunday mornings and stayed there after Jim left for golf, feeling decadent and devilish for curling into the soft white sheets instead of heading out for communion.

Plus, Bridget had a complicated relationship with church. An even more complicated one with God. She wasn't so sure He wanted to see her, given that just a few days ago she had cursed him the entire time she'd sat here and stared at the coffin holding her husband, but that wasn't about to stop Colleen O'Bannon from dragging her oldest daughter into the hushed stained glass interior. For penance or peace, Bridget wasn't sure which. Maybe both.

Her mother sent a sharp glance over at Bridget when her step hesitated. "It's time. If any moment is the time to come back, it's now."

Because there'd been a death, and if there was one thing Catholics knew to do when someone died, it was go to church. Except for Jim's funeral, the last time Bridget had stood in Our Lady, it had been in the empty aisle, long after church had emptied out on a Sunday morning, everyone heading off to Denny's or IHOP for pancakes and eggs, while the altar boys shrugged out of their white gowns and hurried to the playground, ignoring their mother's orders not to ruin their church clothes. She could still hear the shouts of the children through the open window, the soft clank of coffee cups being put away in the church kitchen.

You're ruining your life, Abby had said that day, a little over three years ago. *You know that, right? And you're still going to marry him?*

Why can't you just be happy for me? Bridget had asked.

Because Jim isn't who you think he is, Bridget. And you refuse to see the truth. I know things—

Bridget had yelled at Abby, yelled at her to shut up,

to just shut the hell up. Ma had rushed in, dragging Abby away.

Bridget had looked over her shoulder at Jim, who was waiting in the doorway, framed by the sun like his body wore a halo. In that moment, she'd thought he was the most perfect human being she'd ever seen. She'd only known the outside of Jim then, unaware that beneath the dark hair and blue eyes lived a man who was quick to criticize, slow to apologize, and prone to long bouts of with-drawal, pulling into himself like a turtle in a shell. It had been too late by then. A few hours later, the vows had been spoken, the family ties ruined, and Bridget had told herself that looking back would only keep her stuck.

So she'd walked out of the church with her husband, eventually leaving her sister behind, and settled into a life for two. The fissures in their marriage had started that very day. And now...

"You need this," her mother whispered again, and tugged Bridget forward.

Maybe she did. Maybe the incense and flowers and Jesus on the wall would help Bridget find a way to move forward. Sideways. Any direction but staying still. Except just being here reminded her of all of it—her wedding, her sister's words, burying her husband. It all seemed surreal, as if she had been transported somewhere else.

Her mother led the way down the aisle, her handbag tucked into the space between her elbow and her ribs like a football. Her mother wore the same brown Naturalizer shoes she'd worn for as long as Bridget could remember.

Round-toed, kitten heel. Sturdy, dependable, comfortable. She had on a pale gray wool skirt that hung almost to her ankles and a white satiny button-down blouse beneath a navy cardigan. A strand of pearls, the ones her great-great-grandmother had smuggled over on the boat to Ellis Island, sat atop the cardigan. Her mother's dark red hair—once naturally vibrant, now kept that way thanks to a monthly appointment with a box of Clairol—was her only concession to vanity.

Colleen O'Bannon was practical and frugal. And as opinionated as a politician. She loved her native country, loved her adopted home, and loved her daughters most of all.

Her mother genuflected before the altar and then crossed herself and whispered a prayer to God. Then she veered to the right, to the bank of candles sitting against the far wall. Bridget followed her mother but hesitated when she neared the candles. Half were flickering; half were unlit. A glass full of long matches sat to the left of the kneeler.

Her mother knelt before the bank of flames, crossed herself again, and then lowered her temples to her clasped hands. Bridget could see Colleen's lips moving in a quick, silent prayer. Then she lifted her head and gestured to her daughter to kneel beside her.

Go through the motions. Just go through the motions. Then you can go back home and back to bed.

That was all she wanted. To slide back under the white down duvet with the remote in one hand, while Piper avoided Crazy Eyes and Red battled to get her kitchen back, and the fictional world created by Netflix replaced the really sucky one in Bridget's life.

But to get there, she had to be here first. On the day of the funeral, she'd avoided the candles. Avoided as much tradition as she could, feeling like a liar every minute she sat in the church. She'd barely heard Father McBride's words, barely remembered the procession behind the casket.

But now, with her mother staring at her and no excuse like a dead husband ten feet away, Bridget had to at least feign piety. She bent down, left knee on the carpeted kneeler, then the right. The slightly vanilla scent of the wax mingled with the spicy scent of incense in the air. The long match flared when Bridget touched it to another flame and again when it met the wick of a fresh squat candle.

If Jim were here, he'd laugh. *Assuming there even is a heaven, Bridge, how the hell would I see one little flame up there? You'd have to light a bonfire, babe, for me to see it.*

The flame wavered in the slight breeze from the ceiling fans as if laughing at the incongruity of lighting a memorial candle for a husband who'd barely attended church. And her, a lapsed Catholic, pretending for the second time in the space of a week to whisper prayers that were more rote than heartfelt.

She didn't fit in this world, didn't know where the hell she fit right now.

When Bridget's mother rose, Bridget also backed away from the bank of candles and slipped into the pew beside her, behind two old women in matching lime-green hats.

Bridget could almost hear Magpie. *What, was there some kind of sale? Oh, Gladys, get one for you, and I'll get one for me. We'll be twinsies.*

A sound like a snort escaped Bridget. She covered her mouth and feigned a cough.

Her mother gave her the evil eye. "Behave yourself. We're in church."

It didn't matter how old any of them were. When they were in church, Ma treated the girls like there were still five years old. And Bridget wanted to escape, just as she had when she'd been five. And fifteen. And twenty-five. Not to mention she felt like Jesus was staring down at her with condemnation in his eyes. *You didn't save your marriage and now your husband is dead.*

"Will you just look at that Hazel Lockheed," her mother whispered, nodding toward an older woman with a dark brown helmet of hair. "She's sitting there, with a Bible on her lap, as if she didn't leave her husband and take up with the mailman. And that Jeremy Brackett over there. Holding hands—in church, mind you—with that boyfriend of his." Her mother shook her head. "None of that is appropriate. Those people—"

"Ma, I don't want to be here," Bridget whispered. She couldn't take one more second of judgment or gossip. "Can we just—"

"We will do no such thing." Her mother made that pursed lemon face of disapproval. "And you should ask for-giveness for even saying such blasphemy in church. Did you brush your hair before we left?"

Bridget lowered herself onto the kneeler and pressed her forehead to her clasped thumbs. *God, keep me from going off on my mother in church, because we all know that is a path straight to hell.*

Yeah, maybe that wasn't the kind of prayer her mother had in mind.

The dim interior of the church was peppered with color from the late-day light forcing its way through the thick stained glass. The scent of incense and burning wax mingled with the dueling fragrances of L'Air du Temp and Estée Lauder's latest. The whole weird scent confluence should have been called Whorehouse Mixed with Pot Dispensary. That made Bridget erupt in another snort/cough.

All of it seemed so insane. God wasn't listening to her. God had probably given up on her a long time ago. The entire exercise, with the candles, the kneelers, the prayers…so pointless. Like the game she and Jim used to play—Stupid Facts. In the early days of their marriage, they'd take turns finding some random stupid fact to tell the other over dinner, their way of not starting every conversation with "How was your day, dear?"

Did you know, Bridge, that koala bears' fingerprints are almost exactly the same as humans? They're so close, even Columbo couldn't tell them apart at a crime scene.

Manic laughter began to tremble in her chest, rising to the surface. Bridget let out another snort/cough. Her mother shushed her and pointed to the kneeler. More praying, less fooling around. But that manic feeling was bubbling and expanding and she was hearing Jim say,

"Columbo and the Koala," that'd be a great episode, wouldn't it? And then the laughter was there, pushing at her lips, and Bridget knew she couldn't stay in the dim, tight confines of the church a second longer.

She pushed to her feet and scrambled to leave. "Excuse me, excuse me." Where had all these people come from? How come they'd all crowded into her pew? "Excuse me."

"Bridget." Her mother's hushed, angry voice. Any second now, Bridget expected to be told to go back to her seat or she wouldn't get any donuts after church. Every week, it had either been Bridget or Magpie, sitting at the chrome and laminate counter, moping and empty-handed while Nora—the suck-up, the others had called her—took her sweet time licking powdered sugar off her fingers and sucking the jelly out of the center while Abby just hung in the back, alone and apart, even then.

"*Bridget.* Get back here this instant."

But she was already gone, pushing on the hard metal bar, bursting into the sunshine. The laughter escaped her just then, but somehow it had changed into a sob, tearing at her throat. Bridget turned.

And ran.

FOUR

If there was one scent that described the O'Bannon girls, it was vanilla. Not the run-of-the-mill artificial flavoring, but the scent that could only be awakened by scraping the back of a teaspoon along the delicate spine of an espresso-colored vanilla bean.

Gramma had always kept a jar of vanilla beans on her kitchen counter because she said they reminded her of how much work God went to just to create a single beautiful note. So many miracles had to dance a complicated tango, all to create one vanilla bean. The orchid's flower only bloomed for twenty-four hours, and only the Melipona bee could pollinate the buds. Without that bee—or in later years, the intervention of painstaking human cross-pollination—the simple orchid would never become a delicate vanilla bean.

"No two vanilla beans are exactly the same," Gramma had said, "like you and your sisters. Each is unique and beautiful and handmade by God himself."

It had been Gramma who had taught Bridget the joy of baking. It had been Gramma who had coached her granddaughter through the intricacies of piecrusts and cake batters, guided her hand as she'd swirled buttercream and painted sugar cookies. It had been Gramma who had propped Bridget on a metal stool and woven magical tales about mischievous leprechauns and clever fairies, while the two of them mixed and kneaded and baked and decorated. And it was Gramma she'd been trying to hold on to when she'd worked at the shop. Or at least that was what Bridget had told herself for years.

Maybe she was trying to hold on to the magic her grandmother had seemed to embody.

Now Bridget stood on the sidewalk outside Charmed by Dessert and inhaled the familiar, sweet scent of vanilla. It seemed to fill the very air around the little shop, like some confectionary version of the cloud over the Addams Family's house.

She hadn't been here in three years, but everything looked just as it had before. Charmed by Dessert had sat in the same location in downtown Dorchester for three generations, a converted home on a tree-lined block. It was housed in a small, squat white building topped with a bright pink and yellow awning, flanked by a florist on the left and an ever-rotating selection of lawyers and accountants who rented the space on the right. The street was peppered with old-fashioned streetlamps and wrought-iron benches beside planters blooming with flowers.

Once upon a time, Bridget had thought she would

work here until she died, side by side with her grandmother, her sisters, and her mother. Baking pies and frosting cakes and sifting flour into clouds. But then Gramma had died, and Bridget had met Jim and—

Everything had changed.

Bridget had taken a job writing a food column for a local paper, but it wasn't the same as working here. Not at all.

The small silver bell that had once sat on a shelf in Gramma's hutch tinkled as Bridget opened the door and stepped inside. Nora looked up from the tiered cupcake display she was refilling, and her brows lifted in surprise.

For a second, Bridget expected to see Abby behind the counter. But Abby had quit the family—and quit the bakery. She was working at a Williams-Sonoma at the mall, the last Bridget had heard. She used to think Abby was her best friend, but the scene on her wedding day and the ensuing three years of silence said differently.

All these years, she had kept Abby's secret from the rest of the family. And in doing so, she'd lost her sisters. Lost the bond she used to have.

For what? For a marriage that had been fractured for a long time. A marriage Bridget had once vowed to do anything to repair.

"Bridget? What are you doing here?" Nora asked.

"I...I don't know." It was one of the most honest things she'd said in days. All those hours of pretending she was okay, that she wasn't feeling lost and alone and scared.

Hell, she'd been feeling that way for years, but she'd told herself that planting some flowers and getting pregnant would set her world to rights again. Would prove something. To herself, to her family.

"Uh, okay." Nora dusted off her hands and slid the empty tray onto the counter behind her. She looked unsure of what to say, how to act, without the buffer of a funeral and Netflix playing in the background. "Uh, can I get you anything?"

A giant rewind button for my life. "Coffee?"

Nora nodded, her face slackening with relief at having something to do, something to put off the awkward conversation for another moment. She disappeared into the back, returning a moment later with two steaming mugs of rich, dark coffee. "Here." She gestured toward one of the bistro tables at the front of the shop. "Let's...let's, uh, sit for a minute. If you want to."

Now that Bridget was here, she wanted to leave, forget she'd ever walked inside. But where was she going to go? Back to the church? Hell no (and that thought made her whip through a quick mental Hail Mary just in case). Back home? Her house was a mile away, walkable, even in these ugly, sensible shoes, but no. She couldn't walk back into that empty space again because if she did, she'd curl up in that bed and never leave again. As much as she'd hated going to church, she had to admit her mother was right—she needed to get out of that house.

Move forward. Focus on the future. Somehow.

"Why are you here?" Nora said.

Bridget didn't want to say the truth, because she wasn't quite sure what the truth was, so instead she said the first thing that popped into her head. "I was thinking I should get a cat."

Nora arched a brow and took a sip of coffee before she spoke. That was how Nora worked—she thought about her words before she said them. She was the least chatty of the three O'Bannon girls, and the most serious one. Ma called Nora the umbrella of the family, because she was practical and dependable and the calm one in the midst of any family storm. "A cat? Okay. Sounds...good."

"Should I get two?" Nonsense words poured out of Bridget like a leaky tap, filling the too-sweet air in the shop and the empty cavern in her heart and all those questions about *tomorrow* that she couldn't bring herself to answer. "You know, in case one of them gets...lonely? I don't think I could stand to hear one of them crying because it was all...a-alone." Then her voice broke and the river of words jerked to a stop.

Nora covered Bridget's hand and gave it a little squeeze. "Ma made you go to church, didn't she?"

Bridget nodded. She almost cried, thinking how good it was that Nora hadn't thrown her out, that she had reached out and comforted her, and for five seconds not mentioned Jim. Or said anything about Abby. "How... how can you tell?"

"You're wearing that dress you hate, topped with a nice little shawl of Catholic guilt." Nora smiled. "Two cats? Really?"

"I don't know what else to do. I mean, what am I going to do with all of Jim's clothes? And the house? Oh, God, Nora, what am I going to do about all that *stuff*? How am I possibly going to handle it all a-alone?"

Nora's hand tightened on hers. "First, you're going to ditch that dress. No, not just ditch it. Fucking burn it in the backyard. It is uglier than hell."

The curse cut through the air, unexpected from the normally perfect Nora. It seemed to break the tension between them somehow, a crack in the wall. All these years Bridget had spent away from her sisters, her mother, and for just this second, she couldn't remember why. Didn't want to remember why.

But in her head, she heard Jim's voice. *Remember how they hurt you, babe. That's why we were an island, just you and me. Don't let them get close again.*

She wanted to argue back, to tell Jim he wasn't here anymore and what was she supposed to do about that? That maybe he'd been wrong, and maybe if she hadn't shut her family out for all those years, this wall between them wouldn't exist.

Instead, she tugged her hand out of Nora's and put it in her lap. "I hate this dress. I forgot I even had it in my closet."

"I swear, Ma has her homing instinct for outfits that make you look like Doris Day on acid," Nora said. "Remember the polka-dot skirt debacle of 2003?"

That made Bridget laugh again. God, it felt so good to laugh. Just as quickly, a wave of guilt hit her. Jim had just died. His body was hardly cold in the grave. How could she be laughing?

Nora's hand lit on Bridget's arm. "It's okay to laugh and run out of church and eat dessert, Bridge."

"It doesn't feel okay."

"Yeah." Nora sighed. "Maybe it will. In time."

Time. Bridget wanted to slow down the hours as much as she wanted them to pass in a blur. She wanted a second to catch her breath, to absorb what had happened, to accept this new normal. At the same time, she wanted to skip ahead to the days when hearing Jim's name didn't feel like a knife serrating her lungs.

Until then, Bridget had to do something. For so long, her life had been wrapped around the world she had created with her marriage, and now she wasn't sure where to step next. This widow world felt like a minefield. "What am I going to do, Nora?"

"I don't know, Bridge. I honestly don't know." Nora drew in a breath and let it out, as steady as a slow leak in a tire. "What do you *want* to do?"

"Go to bed. And stay there for forty years," she scoffed. "But then I'll become like Aunt Esther, and I don't want to do that."

A little laugh escaped Nora. "Nobody wants to end up buried by the *Globe*."

"I'd at least like to go out under the *Herald*. Better headlines: 'Hoarder Hunched under Heap of *Heralds*.'" The joke made both of them laugh, and the sound lingered inside the shop for a long, sweet moment.

"You know," Nora began, while tracing a circle in the laminate, "you could try getting back to the life you left. You're going to need an income and…well, something to do."

"You mean come back to work here."

"The door is always open," Nora said. "And Lord knows I could use the help, with wedding season coming up."

A wave of guilt washed over Bridget. She'd abandoned the shop, shortly after Abby had quit, and left Nora to run things on her own. Their mother stepped in from time to time, but she was getting older and didn't have the energy to last all day on her feet in a busy bakery. Nora had taken the reins without complaint, relying on a couple of part-time helpers to get through busy seasons.

There'd been a day, when the sisters had started working at Charmed by Dessert, when Bridget had been the chief baker. She'd developed a line of pies that got noticed at a Best of Boston competition and, for a while, put Charmed by Dessert on Must-See lists. Bridget had left the recipes behind when she walked away from the shop, but the pies had never been the same, from what she'd heard and read. Business had dipped a little more each year, and there were times when Bridget could read the stress in her mother's shoulders.

"You had that special touch," Nora went on. "None of us have ever come close to replicating that."

Bridget fiddled with the coffee cup. "I think it was luck."

Nora didn't say anything. The chef-shaped clock on

the wall *ticktock*ed the seconds with a busy wooden spoon. "Do you remember the day you made the chocolate pies?"

The three of them had been together in the kitchen, slipping in and out of each other's spaces like deftly woven braids. It seemed like they'd always been like that, ever since they were little girls, and even as high schoolers working after school, they'd been a team. Magpie had been too young to do much more than wash dishes, which had left the other three in the kitchen. Abby the director, Nora the planner, Bridget the dreamer. "You know what we need on the menu?" Nora had said. "A really good chocolate pie."

"One that's so good, it's better than sex," Abby had added in a whisper.

The three of them burst into giggles, and Ma had admonished them from the front of the store to get to work and stop playing around. They'd blushed and giggled some more, their heads together like three peas in a pod.

"I have an idea," Bridget had said. A vague idea, one that mushroomed into a recipe as she bustled around the kitchen, gathering a little of this, a lot of that. The other girls had drifted away, leaving Bridget to create. Bridget had hardly noticed because the world dropped away when she baked. Her mind was filled with flour and sugar, butter and eggs, cocoa and vanilla. Tastes and scents and measurements and possibilities.

An hour later, she'd opened the oven, pulled out the chocolate base, and then drizzled a layer of salted caramel on top and dropped dollops of fresh marshmallow around the edge. A few seconds with the flambé torch and the marshmallow toasted into gold.

"Your grandmother would be proud," Ma had said when she'd seen the finished pie, her highest level of praise, offered as rarely as comets. To mark the occasion, she'd flipped the sign to closed, gathered her girls around a table, and dished them each a hearty slice. They'd sat at the table and eaten and laughed until their bellies were full and the sun had disappeared behind the horizon.

"That was a great day," Nora said softly.

"It was a long time ago," Bridget said, thinking of all that had been said since then, words that couldn't be taken back, hurts that couldn't be bandaged. "I don't think we can get back there."

"Maybe not. But you need an income now, and we need the help and—"

"Protecting the bottom line as usual." Bridget shook her head and cursed. "Of course."

Nora's face pinched like a shriveled apple. "This isn't about money, Bridget. We're family; we take care of each other."

"You know why I'm not working here." Being here every day would mean being around her mother, and Bridget knew that was a war she wasn't strong enough to battle right now. It would mean dancing that tightrope of *I'm just fine.* "I just can't do it. It's too much on top of everything else."

"Stop thinking about yourself for five friggin' seconds, Bridget." Nora clapped a hand over her mouth and shook her head. Her eyes filled but, in typical Nora fashion, she blinked away the tears. "Damn it. I'm sorry. I shouldn't have—"

"No, you shouldn't have." Bridget shook her head. "You're still Miss Perfect Nora, judging the rest of us screwups. You never do a damned thing wrong. You have the husband and the kids and the perfect house and you run a bakery and probably manage to make dinner every night, too, while the rest of us are…less."

"I never said that, Bridget."

"You didn't have to. You're just this"—Bridget waved a hand—"impossible to live up to Stepford wife. Who seems genuinely surprised that the rest of us aren't as perfect. I stopped working here because I wanted to. Because I was sick and tired of you and Ma and everyone else in the world telling me what to do. And because—"

But no. Those were the words Bridget didn't speak aloud. The family secret that she left buried under a pile of lies. The one thing she ignored because she knew, if she said the words aloud, it would shatter what remaining bridge she had with her sisters.

"I can't do this," Bridget said. "I just can't."

Nora rose and reached for her. "Bridget, wait."

Bridget shook her head and headed out the door and back into the sunshine. She kicked off her shoes, flung them into the grass on the side of the road, and walked home. Barefoot and sweaty. And alone.

FIVE

The thick Sunday *Globe* hit the concrete front stoop with a solid *thunk*. Abby stepped into the dark morning, zipping her fleece sweatshirt closed as the cold hit her. Across the street, Joey O'Brien sat on his bike, his breath frosting puffy clouds in front of his mouth. A cotton messenger bag stuffed with curled papers hung heavy across his shoulders. "Mornin', Ms. O'Bannon."

"Hey, you managed to land it on the steps for once," Abby said.

He grinned. The nineteen-year-old had an affable face with a thick mop of brown hair that tended to droop across his brow. He was too big for the bike, all arms and legs and lanky body, which meant he rode it looking like a skinny Hunchback of Notre Dame. "I've been practicing. You got my tip?"

"Look both ways before you cross the street."

Joey rolled his eyes. "It's way too early for shitty jokes."

"And you are way too old to still be riding a bike built for a twelve-year-old."

He shrugged. "I like the bike. You don't notice the world so much in a car."

Deep philosophy from the paperboy. That was what she liked about Joey. He liked his life, just the way it was, skating by on a part-time job in a coffee shop and the paper route. He said it gave him time to play with his band and spend sunny days in the public gardens.

Abby did the same thing, only she took her peace in the quiet dark of the early morning while Jessie was still asleep, curled into the bed like a bean. Abby pictured Jessie there, one hand spread across the mattress, as if keeping the space warm for Abby's return. She liked that about Jessie, the anchor for Abby's world. She had been the wild one when they'd met, angry at the world, angry at her family, angry at herself. Jessie had smoothed those rough edges with soft words and brown eyes that understood without judgment.

But there was still a part of Abby that craved freedom, like a once-feral cat that purred against the fireplace but still yearned for time to prowl the streets. So she got up early and walked until the sun rose, easing that need deep inside her.

Abby came down the rest of the stairs, stopped before Joey's bike, and pulled a little ziplock bag out of her pocket. "White chocolate macadamia nut."

Joey grinned. "Awesome. They're my favorites."

"That's what you said about the chocolate chip last week and the macaroons the week before."

He shrugged. "What can I say? I don't discriminate

when it comes to cookies." He raised the bag and gave her a nod. "Thanks, Ms. O'Bannon."

"You can call me Abby, you know. I'm not that much older than you."

Joey's nose wrinkled but he tried to shrug it off, as if he thought anyone over twenty-five was ready to sign up for AARP. "See ya tomorrow, Ms. O."

Abby waved and turned down the street. The pavement was shiny onyx, wet from an early morning rain. The streets were dark, speckled with the yellow puddles of streetlamps and the square slash of the occasional lighted window. Abby pulled her hood up against the cold and hunched into the fleece.

She took two rights and a left, past silent cars and shuttered apartments. Then, at the end of the last street, she closed her eyes and drew in a deep breath. And there it was, the sweet, yeasty scent that carried on the air, rising above the warm, rich notes of fresh-baked bread. There was a faint soft white glow from the kitchen behind the plate-glass window of the Maistrano Family Bakery, with one lone figure inside, hunched over a counter, her gray hair spun into a bun under a hairnet, her ample body wrapped in a white cotton apron. The bakery had sat on this corner for sixty-five years, two generations of Maistranos making bread for restaurants throughout Dorchester and Boston. The elderly Maistranos took turns being the early bird, both of them now wizened, hunched, and gnarled. But they could create magic with their hands, still working as efficiently as they had decades ago.

It was their hands that Abby watched. She leaned against the lamppost, the cold forgotten, the time nonexistent, and watched as Mrs. Maistrano cast a handful of flour across the breadboard, like scattering seeds to the wind. Then she nudged a thick pillow of dough out of a glass bowl and began to work it, gently at first, as if they were just meeting.

Her hands eased the sphere into a flattened circle, and then she flipped it, flouring the other side. She pressed the heels of her hands into the bread, harder this time—they were no longer strangers—until it yielded and flattened. Then a flip, another heel press, and again and again, until the bread no longer stuck to her hands and the dough began to glisten, happy, pliable, ready to be whatever she made it.

Abby's hands moved, too, unbidden, twisting and kneading the air. She could almost feel the silky dough in her hands, feel it surrender and soften. She closed her eyes for a moment, and she was there, back in the bakery, with the melodic undertow of her sisters' conversations in the background as the dough morphed into something airy and light. Abby had always been on the periphery, lost in her own world of flour and shortening.

An ache burned in her gut, and she clenched her fists at her sides, but still her fingers itched to move, to be in that bakery. Across from her, Mrs. Maistrano looked up, saw Abby in her usual spot, and gave her a little wave. As she always did, Mrs. Maistrano gestured to Abby to come in and watch. As she always did, Abby shook her head no.

Mrs. Maistrano gave a slow, sad nod and went back to work. She shaped the dough into a long, oblong loaf and then dropped it onto a waiting sheet pan. She set that aside and grabbed the next ball of dough, repeating the process of meeting, kneading, settling.

Abby watched, entranced, as the night began to drop away and the sun inched its way into the sky. The air warmed, and the world began to stir, with people leaving their houses, cars darting down the street, birds calling to each other.

She should leave. Get back before Jessie woke up. But still Abby watched, as the loaves were formed and the biscuits were dropped and the bakery began to fill its windows with golden, crisp treats. Then, when she could stand it no longer, Abby turned away and headed home, walking hard and fast, until she could no longer smell the scent of the bread and the reminder of the family that had abandoned her.

SIX

Magpie waltzed into Bridget's house on Sunday afternoon like she owned the place. Which was pretty much how Magpie did everything—with confidence, flair, and determination. She stood in Bridget's living room, with her hands on her hips and her car keys dangling from one finger, ticktocking a mini Tweety Bird back and forth. "Ma says you have to come to family dinner and I've been sent to make sure you show up."

Bridget thumbed the remote, segueing into the next episode of *House of Cards*. She had at least two days of viewing ahead of her—and if that wasn't enough, there were eight seasons of *Dexter* to fill the void, to add voices to the quiet of the house.

The TV filled up all the spaces that still needed decisions. A stack of bills sat on the coffee table, beside a checkbook she hadn't opened yet. There were twelve messages on the answering machine she had saved, asking her about her lawn service, the quarterly air-conditioner maintenance, the subscription to the *Wall Street Journal*.

"I already texted and told Ma I wasn't going." Bridget hit fast-forward, leapfrogging past the show intro. Images of Washington, DC, whizzed by on the screen. "I have enough lasagna in my freezer to feed the entire state of Wyoming."

"Yeah, well, she figured you'd say that, so she told me, and I quote, that 'a casserole is no excuse to avoid the world.' She told me to tell you that you're lucky she didn't drag you back to church today but she is prepared to do that if you keep on wallowing alone." Magpie put up her hands. "Don't shoot me. I'm just the messenger who happens to be home for a couple days between assignments, so I get delivery duty."

Bridget sighed. She knew her mother—if Bridget didn't show up, Colleen O'Bannon would pack the entire kit and caboodle into her Chrysler sedan and show up on Bridget's doorstep. Far better to go to dinner and leave when she wanted than end up with her family camped out in her bedroom again. "On a scale of one to ten, how bad is it going to be?"

Magpie grimaced. "She made her short ribs stew."

"The one with Guinness?"

Magpie nodded. "She pulled out the big guns."

As in Bridget's favorite dinner, the expensive, time-consuming one that had usually been reserved for birthdays and Christmas when they were young and Colleen was a struggling single mother. *And the Olympic gold for guilt goes to . . . Colleen O'Bannon. Again.*

Bridget sighed.

"I'll drive." Her little sister's grin said she knew the battle was over. "I've got two bottles of Merlot in the car that I'm smuggling in with me."

"Two?"

Magpie grinned. "Yup. I expect Ma to have a total shit fit when she sees them."

"You know you're just asking for a lecture about how wine is only meant for communion and how too much alcohol—"

"Makes for too many bad decisions." Magpie leaned in and lowered her voice to a conspiratorial whisper. "Which is exactly why I'm bringing it. You need to make a few bad decisions."

"Me?"

"Yup. You." Magpie took Bridget's hand and hauled her out of the chair. "Now, come on. Get dressed. I refuse to drive you anywhere looking like that."

Bridget looked down at her pajamas, then back at Magpie's rainbow-hued maxi dress. Her little sister had her hair in twin braids, long plaits trailing along her arms. Her face was bare, but Magpie had the kind of natural coloring and deep green eyes that looked beautiful with or without makeup. "What's wrong with what I have on?"

"You're wearing Minions. As a grown-up."

Okay, so she *was* sporting Despicable Me characters. But the flannel pajamas were comfortable and one of those crazy day-after-Christmas-sale purchases, and honestly, the thought of anything that involved zippers and a bra was too much. "Since when are you the fashion police, Miss I'll Go Barefoot Everywhere?"

Magpie didn't answer. She just gave Bridget the look they'd all inherited from their mother—one arched brow and a half-smirk. "We're leaving in ten minutes. Minions or not. Your choice."

In the end, Bridget changed into a pair of jeans and a pale blue V-neck sweater. She wasn't in the mood for a lecture about her clothing choices. She settled into Magpie's tiny red coupe and held on tight while her sister screamed around corners and down side streets until finally screeching to a stop in front of the triplex where they'd grown up.

The house hadn't changed a bit in more than thirty years. The lime-green paint was starting to fade, paling behind the trio of white porches. Their father had bought the house right after he married Ma and rented out the top two floors. That, coupled with the income from the bakery, hadn't made them rich by any standard but had kept the bills paid. Ma still lived on the first floor with nearly all the same furniture from the day she moved in. Walking into the house on Park Street was like stepping into a time machine that only went in reverse. It even still smelled the same, a warm combination of their mother's L'Air du Temps, fresh baked bread, and ancient history.

The parlor held a pink and white floral love seat and two matching wingback chairs. The chairs sat in the bow of the bay window, centered by an old Singer sewing machine tucked away in the wooden and iron stand. The grandfather clock Ma had inherited from her great-aunt chimed the hour with a deep-throated song. There was a rolltop desk in one corner, where Bridget had spent hours, puzzling over algebra or writing an essay for English. If she closed her eyes, she could still see the four of them, back in the days when their biggest squabble had been over the single bathroom, Nora prim and erect in one of the chairs, reading some extra-credit book, Abby staring out the window and ignoring her vocabulary homework, Magpie on her stomach on the carpet, feet swinging back and forth while she doodled in her notebook. They'd spent hundreds of weekday nights in this very room while their mother whipped up something for dinner and the world rushed by outside the windows.

On the other side of the hall were three doors, one for the master bedroom, two for the bedrooms the girls had shared. Bridget and Abby, Nora and Magpie, because Nora had been the most patient with the youngest and wildest O'Bannon girl. The hall's hardwood floors were still polished enough to reflect every step, the fringe on the edge of the Oriental runner lay as straight as pencils in a box, and every embarrassing dorky school picture was hung on the wall.

Bridget caught the scent of stew, and for the first time in two weeks, she felt hungry. Her stomach propelled her into the kitchen and over to the yellow Kenmore stove that had sat in the galley-style room for as long as any of them could remember. Her mother was in the pantry, searching for something. Bridget grabbed the spoon on the stove and dipped it into the simmering pot. But not fast enough.

"You'll spoil your dinner." Ma reached over and yanked the spoon out of Bridget's hand, setting it back on the spoon rest. "Now go wash up."

"I'm not seven." Though Bridget wasn't sure why she bothered mentioning that fact. No amount of birthdays would stop their mother from telling them what to do, when to do it, and how to do it right.

Her mother waved toward the bathroom. "Go, go. Your sister will be here soon, and dinner is nearly done. I don't want to make Nora wait to eat."

Sister, singular. "Abby isn't coming?"

Ma dipped her head and stirred the stew in a lazy figure-eight pattern. She seemed to shrink into herself, her voice softening, her shoulders slumping. "She...she's busy."

"Did you ask her?"

Ma kept on stirring, in, out, in, out. "Abby will come around when she's ready."

"Yeah, but did you invite her?" Bridget pressed, but the invisible wall had already formed in her mother's features.

"Wash your hands. Nora will be here soon."

Meaning the subject was closed. As usual. Colleen O'Bannon was the master at avoiding topics she didn't want to discuss.

Bridget didn't know why she had even asked. The last time she had seen Abby, they'd been in this very house. Bridget's wedding day. A day that should have been happy and bright and perfect. But what had started in the church had followed them back here, like a winter storm moving inland fast.

46

They'd had a small wedding, she and Jim, and an informal reception back at Ma's house. At the time, Bridget had thought Jim just wanted things to be intimate, easy. But years later, she'd realized Jim had almost no family and very few friends. Eighty percent of the handful of guests at their wedding were Bridget's relatives.

There'd been wine and canapés and bad decisions all around. Uncle Carl got into a fight on the lawn with Ma's friend Ronnie Perez, Aunt Esther was caught stuffing rolls and mortadella into her handbag, and Jim's mother had a nervous breakdown just before the ceremony started.

But then they'd said the words and thrown the rice and Bridget thought everything would be okay. She'd passed off Abby's rant in the church as an anomaly and slipped back into her happy, newly married bubble. Ma had even made a toast, saying that now that Nora and Bridget had found husbands, she hoped Abby would meet a nice doctor and Magpie would settle down with a lawyer and give her many more grandchildren. Then she called over Jim's perpetually sweaty cousin Ned and grabbed Abby's hand.

"You must meet Ned," Ma said, dragging them so close to each other they nearly collided. Ma nudged Abby. "Now don't be shy, Abigail, like you normally are. You're so lovely. If only you'd speak more with men. Show them you're interested and sweeten the pot with some honey. Smile a little."

Abby's face turned crimson. "Ma—"

"Ned here is the perfect man for you to settle down with, Abigail. He's an *orthopedist.*"

Ned had given Abby a toothy grin and reached for her hand. Abby spun out of the room so fast that she knocked over the table lamp. Conversation was suspended, and Ma's face reddened. She stood there for a long second, rigid with fury.

Then Ma had brightened and patted Ned's hand, as if the whole incident wasn't anything more than a fly buzzing around the deviled eggs. "My Abby has always been shy around boys. Just give her a minute. Bridget, please go get your sister and tell her she's being rude."

Ma had always seen the truth she wanted to see, on that day and hundreds of others. But now, looking back, Bridget wondered if maybe she herself had done the same thing in that church.

"Wash your hands, Bridget," Ma said now, in that same tone she'd used three years ago. The one that said arguing was pointless.

Bridget turned on her heel, dipped into the small bathroom, washed her hands, and then took a long time studying her reflection. The shadows under her eyes were less pronounced, and there was color in her cheeks again. Her body was moving on, even if her heart hadn't.

She heard Nora's voice, then Magpie's, then their mother's, the three of them chattering like baby birds in a nest. For a moment, Bridget lingered in the bathroom, her hip against the pink porcelain sink. They were talking about the bakery, about the new scones that Nora had whipped up, and then about two women who made a special trip to Charmed by Dessert every Monday, buying enough scones for the whole office. Bridget realized she had no idea who those customers were, didn't even know the bakery now sold scones—and that she had been out of the loop for so long, it felt a lot like being back in high school again with the girls in the hall speaking in some common code that left her on the periphery.

She came out of the bathroom, and the conversation stilled. Magpie darted away to lay the silverware on the table; Nora turned to the fridge for a water bottle. The cool girls, skittering away when someone outside the clique came upon them. She had left the bakery, and that almost equated with leaving the O'Bannon family.

Bridget debated going home and then remembered she hadn't driven herself. So she reached into her sister's giant good-for-hiding-contraband purse, yanked out one of the bottles of Merlot—a screw-top, thanks to pragmatic thinking from Magpie—and poured a hearty glassful, while ignoring her mother's pursed lips of disapproval at the alcohol.

"What are you doing?" Ma said. She turned to Nora. "Nora, what is she doing?"

Nora put up her hands. "Don't put me in the middle. I'm just here for dinner."

"If you really want to know, Ma, I'm having a much-needed drink. It's been a hell of a day. A hell of a last couple weeks, actually." Bridget took a long sip. The smooth notes of grapes and oak slid through her. From the dining room, Magpie gave her a quick thumbs-up, and Nora used the buzzing of the dryer as an excuse to leave the kitchen.

The others sensed the impending lecture and had the good sense to get out of the room. Bridget, though, was trapped between the bathroom door and the archway to the dining room, with her mother in the space like a concrete barrier.

"When your father died, God rest his soul, I didn't turn to the bottle. I only took one afternoon off from work." Ma stirred the stew, tasted it, added a pinch of salt. "I had you girls to provide for and I couldn't afford to sit around all day and brood. Or drink all night like some hobo on the street."

Bridget bristled. As usual, Colleen had skipped the small talk and gotten straight to the point. The family dinner was merely a ruse to criticize Bridget's decisions. "I'm not brooding. And I'm not a hobo."

That had been one of their mother's go-to doomsday predictions. *If you don't try hard in school, you'll end up a hobo on the streets. If you drink or do drugs, you'll end up a hobo on the streets. If you have sex before marriage, you'll end up a pregnant hobo on the streets.* For years, Bridget thought every homeless person she saw was a high school dropout who drank too much and never used birth control.

"I called the rectory the next day and sent them your father's clothes. Far better to have them warming someone else's back than taking up room in my drawers." Ma bent, opened the stove, checked the biscuits, and slid a giant red pot holder on her hand before pulling them out. "You have had more than enough time to grieve, Bridget. It is time you moved on."

"Time to move on? Ma, it's been two weeks."

Her mother dropped the biscuits into a waiting Pyrex bowl and handed it off to Magpie to put on the table. "And that is long enough. You need to go forward with your life. God has left you alone now, and you need to make the best of it."

"Make the best of it? How the hell am I supposed to do that?"

"For one, you will watch your language. For another, you should find something to pour your energies into. Some kind of altruism. Your father was the one and only man for me, as God wished it to be. As was Jim for you."

One and only man? For God's sake, she was only thirty.

"Aren't you glad I brought the wine now?" Magpie whispered in Bridget's ear as she waltzed by.

Hell, yes. Bridget took another sip of Merlot. "I'm fine, Ma. Just fine. I don't need altruism or a lifelong convent plan or anything else."

"Ma, leave her alone," Nora said as she stuffed the clean dishtowels in the drawer. "Don't you think Bridge has enough to deal with?"

"I'm not giving her anything else to deal with. I'm merely worried about her and giving her some motherly advice."

"Smotherly is more like it," Nora whispered under her breath.

Bridget bit back a laugh. God, she had missed her sisters. Missed the team they used to be, the four of them against the world. Nora had been the one most worried about breaking the rules, and the one who got them caught when they tried to sneak beer into the house one night. But there'd been plenty of lazy walks home from school and hushed late-night conversations about boys. How did she let all of them get away?

Bridget took another sip and then topped off the wine. She was feeling warm already, smooth like the deep-bodied Merlot. "I'm taking some time to make decisions," she said. Except she hadn't made a single decision at all.

Her mother reached over and brushed a tendril of hair off Bridget's forehead. "Why don't we go to the hairdresser tomorrow? Touch up your roots. You'll feel better if you start taking care of yourself."

"Is that the key to getting over losing your husband?" Bridget asked. "Highlights?"

"Bridget Marie, do not get fresh. I'm merely trying to help you. The longer you stay stuck, the deeper the mud gets."

"I can't believe this. My husband has been dead for two weeks, Ma. Two *weeks*, not two years." Bridget threw up her hands and backed away, hitting the table as she did, which jostled her wine and spilled it down the front of her sweater. She cursed under her breath and dabbed at it with a napkin, but that made the crimson stain spread.

Her mother crossed the kitchen and peered into her daughter's eyes. "You are a mess," she said. "You should get cleaned up before dinner and let me soak that in some club soda. Lord knows if I can get the stain out."

Instead of acknowledging what Bridget had said or apologizing, her mother had found yet another fault to pick at. "Good Lord, Ma, it's just some wine. I'm not going to change. It's not like the Pope is coming to dinner."

"No, but someone else is." Her mother gave her a little shove. "So go. Get a sweater from my dresser. Not the orange one—that makes you look all washed out. Get the green one. It brings out your eyes."

In answer, Bridget swallowed the remaining wine in the glass and refilled it. She debated arguing but knew the outcome. Her mother would sigh and pout and mention the wine stain a thousand times, until Bridget finally caved. It was far easier to change her shirt than to argue. Hadn't she perfected that long ago? Go along, and get along, and let peace reign.

Just as she emerged from the master bedroom, in a Kelly-green sweater with a too-tight boatneck, the doorbell rang. Father McBride stood on the doorstep, his black fedora in one hand, pressed to his chest like an apology. "Bridget. So nice to see you. We've missed you at Mass."

Bridget shot a glare in Magpie's direction, but her little sister just put up her hands and mouthed *I didn't know.* "Come in, Father McBride," Bridget said. "My mother made stew."

"And a very fine stew it is, I'm sure. Colleen, you have the most exemplary culinary skills."

Her mother came down the hall, wiping her hands on her apron and blushing like a schoolgirl. "Why, thank you, Father. I'm always so honored to have you at my house." She ushered him toward the table and nodded at her daughters. "Girls, please welcome Father McBride and then sit down so we can eat dinner."

Nora glanced over at Bridget, and they exchanged the why-does-she-still-treat-us-like-children look. "Nice to see you, Father McBride," Nora said.

"Yeah, hi. It's like bringing church home," Magpie added. "Only without all the Latin."

"Margaret!"

"I must agree with Miss Margaret." A wisp of white hair danced on top of Father McBride's mostly bald head when he nodded. He had thin-rimmed glasses that perched on the end of his nose, but his blue eyes sparkled with a hint of mischief. "And I promise to only speak English tonight."

The girls took their seats around the table with Nora and Bridget on one side, Magpie next to the priest, their mother at one end, and the empty plate at the head of the table. "Father, would you say grace for us?" Ma asked.

"Aren't we waiting for one more?" He nodded toward the extra place setting.

"Only if you're waiting to die," Magpie muttered.

"My late husband, God rest his soul," Ma said with a stern glare in Magpie's direction, "is always honored at this table. I could never love another man the way I loved my Michael."

Whereas Bridget was getting the lecture about moving on. She might not have paid the electric bill or cleaned out the drawers, but at least she wasn't still setting out a plate twenty years later.

"That is a noble gesture, Mrs. O'Bannon. I'm sure Michael is looking down on you with love. Now, let us pray." Father McBride bowed his head, waited a beat, and then said a short grace.

Bridget shifted in her seat. Sitting across from the priest was as bad as sitting under the accusatory Jesus painting at church. She mumbled an Amen and reached for the bowl of biscuits, taking one before handing them to Nora.

"So, Father, how are the renovations going?" Ma asked. "It will be so nice to see Our Lady Church restored to its original glory."

"With a modern touch." Father McBride winked. "Everything is proceeding right on time and budget, thank the Lord." He handed the soup tureen to Magpie and glanced up at Bridget. "Your mother tells me you are looking to get more involved in the church. Filling these difficult days with meaningful work."

Magpie choked on her water. Nora dipped her head and acted like putting butter on her biscuit was a job. Ma went on as if nothing had happened, ladling stew into her bowl.

"I haven't decided what I want to do yet, Father." Which was a whole lot better than saying, *Hell, no, I don't want to fill these difficult days with church.*

"We are in need of a Sunday school teacher for third grade. And someone to plan the senior ladies' bus trip to New York City." Father McBride set a roll on the edge of his plate. "Both are worthy causes to donate your time to. Spending more time with the Lord will help ease your pain."

"Right now, I'm using this," Bridget said, and raised her

wineglass. Then she tipped it back and finished it off in one swallow. Her head was woozy, her thoughts a liberating whirl. "Yup. Works just fine."

Father McBride's face paled. He glanced at Ma.

"Bridget Marie, you have had too much to drink. I should have stopped you before you opened that devil's brew. What possessed you to bring it to family dinner?"

"I brought it, Ma, not Bridge. Because frankly, I figured we could all use a little alcohol." Magpie got to her feet. "Now if you'll excuse me, I'm getting a wineglass."

Bridget leaned back in her seat. "While you're in there, Mags, pour me a shot from that tequila Ma keeps in the back of the cupboard."

Bridget had seen her mother angry before. Had heard her yell. But never in her life had she seen her mother's face go from pale to purple so fast. Father McBride clamped a hand over his mouth, covering a laugh. Ma had her fists on the table, the knuckles white.

"I raised you better than this, Bridget Marie. I'm going to allow this one slip because of your recent circumstances, but I expect you to behave with decorum and grace for the remainder of the meal."

"Decorum and grace? My husband *died*, Ma, at thirty. I don't know how to behave when I wake up in that empty bed every morning. How the hell am I supposed to know how to behave here?"

Her mother gasped. Nora's jaw dropped. Magpie raised a little fist of *You go, sister*. "You will not use this language in front of Father McBride."

The priest shrugged and reached for another roll. "Doesn't bother me. I use the word *hell* on a daily basis."

"You're cooler than I thought, Father," Magpie said, and passed him the butter.

The red in Ma's face deepened and her lips thinned. "You are in my house, Bridget. And you will respect my rules."

"Rules like not talking about Abby?" Bridget threw up her hands. All that wine on an empty stomach spun in her head, pushing words out of her mouth before her brain could throw down some brakes. "She's like brussels sprouts at Thanksgiving. Everyone pretends she doesn't exist."

"Your sister made her choices."

"No, Ma, *you* did. She dropped out of this family because you couldn't fit her into one of your neat little boxes of how a good Catholic girl should behave." Anger pushed at Bridget, a tidal wave she'd held back for so long, but now it crashed over the walls of obedience and polite talk that had ruled her life. The judgment, the criticism, all the barriers that had shoved Abby out of the family and kept her on the outside. "You know who that empty seat should be for? Abby. She's alive and well, and the one who isn't here. You keep telling me to move on, and you're still setting a place for a man who died so long ago, I barely remember his face."

Her mother drew in a long breath and then drew herself up, her spine as straight as a steel beam. "You are not yourself, Bridget. Calm yourself."

Bridget shook her head. She was tired of calming

down, of behaving, of living by the rules she'd learned long ago. Where had that gotten her? Alone and widowed and being served up like a sacrificial volunteer to Father McBride. "I came here for stew, Ma, not some crazy grief intervention with my sisters and the local priest." She got to her feet so fast that the chair teetered on its back legs. Then she turned on her heel and started out of the dining room, with Magpie hurrying after her and digging her car keys out of her pocket. At the last second, Bridget turned back and grabbed the last bottle of Merlot for the road.

SEVEN

The quiet meant success.

At least, that was what Bridget told herself when no one came by and her house stayed quiet and still for the next two days. So still, it was as if the air stopped moving and everything sank into suspended animation.

She finished *Orange Is the New Black* and *House of Cards*, moved on to *Stranger Things* and some show with Harry Potter playing a doctor, but none of it took away the quiet. The TV droned and the picture flickered and Bridget tried to make herself do something other than lie in bed.

If she counted going to the kitchen to dish up yet another serving of a mystery casserole left on her doorstep by well-meaning neighbors, then she could almost say she'd gotten some exercise.

Mostly, she lay there in that cold, empty bed and watched TV and thought about her life. Thought about the primroses and the hope she'd once had and the reality she'd been left with.

Death always seemed to twist the truth a little, making jerks nicer in afterthought, elevating the man who tithed once at church to sainthood. In those dark hours when Bridget awoke alone in her bed, she forgot about the fights she'd had with Jim, forgot about the little annoyances that came with living with another person, and ached for his presence beside her. The warmth of his body, the touch of his foot when he rolled over, the soft sound of his breathing. Echoes of their arguments would flutter through her memories, but she pushed them away. What good would it do now to recall all the times they had fought? All the disagreements about their budget, their jobs, their future? She let her mind curl the truth into something palatable and melancholy because it eased the loneliness of that empty bed.

Her phone buzzed, and she considered letting it go to voice mail, another message piling into the digital box. Then Magpie's face showed up on the screen, the one where she was standing in the shadow of a volcano in Machu Picchu or someplace like that. Considering calls from Magpie were about as frequent as meteor showers, Bridget broke her no-calls rule and answered it. "Hey, Magpie. Where are you?"

"Heading to South Africa. I've got a story to do on this little remote village where they harvest these beans that are supposed to make you look ten years younger. Or at least, that's what the editor at *Glamour* thinks. So that's the story I'm writing. While you, big sister, have pissed off everyone. My phone hasn't blown up this much since we found out Uncle Carl was arrested for pissing on the side of Artie Lennon's packie."

Bridget sighed. That little liquor store adventure had even made it into the papers. "Sorry."

"Don't apologize. It's about fucking time you did something other than say yes. So do me a favor." Magpie paused, yelled something into the wind, then came back to the phone. "Get the hell out of that house and do something wild. Unexpected. Hop on a plane or jump in the ocean or kiss a stranger. Just leap, Bridge."

Bridget let out a long breath. It wasn't that easy. She had bills to pay, calls to return, decisions to make. She couldn't just flit into the ether like her little sister. "Have a safe trip, Mag—"

But the phone had already gone dead, and Magpie was gone. Bridget started to roll back into the covers when something caught her eye. She slid out of bed and crossed to the window.

The hummingbird—maybe not the same one but it sure looked the same—hovered above the shrubs outside her bedroom window. Its wings beat so fast that they were a gray blur, but its dark round eyes seemed to hold Bridget's gaze. Like he was expecting something from her.

She blinked, and he was gone. *The wee bird was a sign, Bridget dear,* she could hear her grandmother say. *A sign from the heavens above. You best be listening.*

Listen to what? If there was some cosmic message she was supposed to get, then maybe it should be announced by bullhorn. Maybe it was as simple as the message Magpie had given her—

Get your ass out of that bed and do something. Something other than eat and pee.

Outside, the hummingbird was back at the window, this time darting from the bedroom to the corner of the L-shape of the house, to the dining room, over to the kitchen. It hovered over the greenhouse window, a boxy bump out that had come with the house. Bridget had loved the window, but Jim had said it was a leak waiting to happen.

Bridget slid her feet into a pair of slippers, wrapped a silky robe around her pajamas, and padded down to the kitchen. The sun streamed through the windows, bright and harsh, and it took a second for Bridget's eyes to adjust. The hummingbird zipped from the top of the greenhouse window to the bottom and then crossed to the other side, up, down, side to side.

"Hey, little guy," Bridget said. "Whatcha looking for?"

The bird flitted back and forth, seeming to make a circle around the bright pink plastic flowers sitting in the window, barred to him by glass.

"You're hungry? These aren't even real though. I'm sorry." The bird, of course, didn't answer. He darted away, probably giving up and leaving for more flowery pastures.

Bridget glanced at the fridge, stuffed to the gills with casseroles she'd never finish eating. Her gaze landed on Jim's briefcase and a two-week-old tri-folded *Wall Street Journal* sitting on the tiny corner desk, covering his laptop.

Her phone buzzed, yet another text from her mother asking if she was home.

Good God, the last thing she needed was her mother hovering over her like she would a sick toddler. Bridget texted back, *Just heading out to run an errand,* and then realized chances were good her mother would drive by and check to see if she'd lied.

So she took a shower and got dressed and got in the car and drove through Dorchester, taking each step like eating baby food, slow and steady, without looking back or looking ahead. Just concentrating on the shower, the clothes, the steering wheel, the traffic.

For a while, she drove aimlessly. The supermarket looked too busy, too bright. The park was stuffed with kids and moms. The traffic on I-93 was beginning to choke, filling with people hurrying to lunch appointments.

Across the water, she could see the brick boxes that housed UMass. A little farther south sat Castle Island, just past the pricy condos in Marina Bay. The space between the two was anchored by a massive rainbow-swashed gas tank, with its rumored image of Ho Chi Minh inked into the blue stripe running down the center.

But on the other side of the highway, a small sign seemed to be lifted into the air by huge wooden birds, drawing Bridget off the exit and down a small side road. She parked and looked up at a giant, bright orange birdhouse with a canary-yellow roof. Wind chimes and bird feeders dangled from the eaves like icicles, swaying in the slight breeze from the traffic whizzing by on I-93 beside it.

Little hand-lettered signs in the window promised things like get everything to make your bird friends happy! make your yard "sing!" bring mother nature closer!

The door let out a little *tweet-tweet* when Bridget entered the shop. A bright green parrot called out a croaky hello from a perch set at the end of the first aisle. Then he reached down and flicked a sunflower seed in her direction.

"Petey, you stop that. Be nice." A buxom woman came bustling toward Bridget. She wore a floral maxi dress that bloomed around her hips and skimmed across the floor, and bracelets that sang a happy song. "Good morning! Oh, no, wait, it's afternoon. Good afternoon. How may I ch-elp you?" The woman laughed at that. "Get it? *Chirp* and *help* in one word? That's what makes us Unique Wild Birds! So please, look around, and if you need any ch-elp, just…"

"Chirp?" Bridget supplied.

"You've got it!" The woman laughed and turned away to help another customer, her skirt creating a wake of fabric as she walked.

Bridget wandered the aisles, past the stacked bags of birdseed, the elaborate concrete birdbaths, enough binoculars to stock a Peeping Tom convention, and hundreds of birdhouses, in every imaginable shape, size, and color. There were mini replicas of the White House, the Leaning Tower of Pisa, and even Windsor Castle.

"There's enough here that you'd never have to leave your house to visit the seven wonders of the world."

Bridget turned. A tall man in a dark suit stood beside her. He held two different bird feeders and had a book tucked under one arm. But it was his smile she noticed—nice, warm, friendly.

"How do you know which one to buy?" she asked.

"I don't. That's why I got two."

"You could have asked the saleslady for help. She seems...enthusiastic."

He shook his head. "I refuse to chirp."

Bridget laughed, the sound still feeling foreign and wrong. She sobered and turned back to the long row of bird feeders. They all looked like different versions of the exact same thing. Birds of all shape and feather were pictured on the boxes, but none of them looked like hummingbirds.

"What are you looking for?" he asked.

"I'm good, thanks." She worried her bottom lip and reached for one box, and then another. There were more choices here than in the panties section of Victoria's Secret.

"I don't know much, but I have plenty of opinions." He shifted into her line of vision and smiled again. "And you don't even have to chirp to get my attention."

Wait. Was he flirting with her? Bridget caught her reflection in one of the tiny mirrors. Her face was drawn, her eyes shadowed, her hair flat and limp. She'd whisked on some powder foundation and swiped on a little mascara, just to keep from scaring people, but she certainly wasn't going to win any beauty awards. The late Joan Rivers would have been appalled at Bridget's choice of a pale pink sweater and black palazzo pants with flats. No way this guy was flirting with her. And why was she even thinking that? Jim was barely dead.

"I have this hummingbird in my yard, and I wanted to feed him," Bridget said. Because she really did need help and she wasn't about to chirp. She hadn't felt chirpy in a long time, hell, maybe ever.

"Hummingbirds are something I know a little about. Blue jays and wrens, not so much, which is why I'm hedging my bets with a double purchase." The man held up the two different feeders in his hands. "My mom is into birds and I thought I'd get her something for her birthday. She's got me out there almost every day, helping her fill those feeders. I swear she keeps half the bird population of Dorchester from starving. She says none of us gave her any grandkids, so she's got to love something." He shook his head. "I'm rambling on, answering questions you didn't even ask."

"Well, if I ever want to know about blue jays and wrens, I'll"—Bridget smiled—"ask your mom."

He laughed, a hearty, deep laugh that seemed to well up from inside him. "That's the smartest option. But you mentioned hummingbirds. Those I can help you with. When we were kids, she had a lot of hummingbirds in the house we had on Upland Avenue, and it was my job to fill the feeders twice a week."

She looked closer at him. He was about her age, with salt and pepper hair and dark green eyes, but nothing that spoke of acquaintance. Dorchester's neighborhoods were mini small towns, everyone stacked on top of each other in towering triple deckers that lined the streets like pale tin soldiers. But this guy didn't look like anyone she remembered. "You grew up on Upland? I lived on Park. My mom still has the house there."

That smile again. "We were neighbors."

"You don't look familiar."

"Ah, probably because I was shipped off to Roxbury Latin for school."

The all-boys school in West Roxbury was rated as one of the top five private schools in the Boston area. It was one hell of a step up from the noisy, crowded public schools Bridget and her sisters had attended. She wondered how his parents had afforded the tuition.

"I'm sorry, I haven't introduced myself." He put one of the bird feeders on a nearby shelf and then extended his right hand. "Garrett Andrews."

She shook his hand and realized it was the first time she had touched a man since her husband had died. It was weird, but nice too. Garrett had a firm, warm handshake, over a second after it began. "Bridget Masterson...uh, O'Bannon. No, Masterson."

His grin quirked. "Are you in WitSec or something?"

"WitSec?"

"Witness protection. Considering you've forgotten your last name."

"Oh, no, it's not that. I just...well, my husband just died and well..." She shook her head. Why was she telling a perfect stranger all of this?

"I'm sorry." His gaze softened. "My wife died two years

ago. When something like that happens, it's as if your entire identity is ripped away. Who are you, when you're just one of a half?"

"Exactly," she murmured, and then turned back to the feeders. "So...hummingbirds?"

He took the change of subject in stride. He stepped forward and waved a hand across the displays, like one of the models on *The Price Is Right*. "Okay, you have a few options here. Your standard hourglass shape with the red base, which I don't recommend because bees and wasps are attracted to these little yellow decorative flowers. And it doesn't have much in terms of a rain or ant guard."

"I have to worry about all those things?"

"No. Just get a feeder that does it for you." He picked up two other boxes. "How many hummingbirds do you have coming to your yard?"

"I've only seen one. I think it's the same one."

"Could be. They can be pretty friendly little things." He held up the first box. "This one hangs from a copper swing and has a weather shield. That's really just a plastic umbrella. You can put it in a tree—"

"I don't have a tree close to the house. Is there something I can put on the window maybe? He seems to really like my kitchen window."

"This one would be great for that." Garrett handed her another box. A quartet of happy hummingbirds swarmed the feeder while a family watched from inside, all wearing delighted smiles. *Buy the Window Wonder Feeder,* the box said, *and your family will be entertained for hours!* "It's got

68

a weather guard, a removable ant moat, and holds eight ounces of nectar."

She turned the box over. "Nectar?"

"Hummingbirds drink sugar water. You can make it yourself or"—he gave her a long glance—"if you're not up to that yet, this stuff is already mixed."

She took the red liter bottle from him and scanned the label. "I just pour this in and that's it?"

"Well, not exactly. You have to clean the feeder a couple times a week. Wash it well, so it doesn't get any mold in it. Then refill it and check it every day or so to make sure there's still some nectar in there."

She had yet to get her act together enough to do laundry. The whole thing seemed daunting, overwhelming. "That seems like a lot to worry about. Maybe I should forget it. Or wait until a better time." She reached to place it back on the shelf.

Garrett put a hand on the box, stopping her. "I know right now that even the simple act of picking out a shirt to wear takes more mental energy than you think you have."

Her eyes started to burn. She flicked her gaze to the tiled floor.

"But this will be good for you." Garrett covered her hand with his own. His touch was tender, understanding. Like they were the only two in the world who knew this foreign language of widowhood. She didn't move her hand, not right away. For a second, she let the empathy wash over her, rush in to fill the gaping holes in her mind.

"I don't know." She slid her hand out of his, pretending she needed to brush a hair off her forehead.

"I do." He reached in his jacket pocket with one hand and then slid a business card between her fingers. "There's my number. Text me, email me, call me, any time of day, if you want any tips on hummingbirds or if you just want to talk about how this whole thing sucks."

"I...I..."

"I'm not trying to hit on you. I'm trying to help." He gave her that smile again and nudged the box toward her chest. "Buy the feeder. Hang it up. Because it's okay to let a living thing depend on you again, Bridget."

EIGHT

Colleen O'Bannon folded dry dishtowels neatly into thirds, pressing the edges down with her hands as she stacked them on the kitchen table. When she was done, she pulled freshly laundered curtains out of the basket and started ironing them.

She told herself this was long-overdue spring cleaning, but she knew the washing and folding and ironing was much more. Cleaning and pressing allayed the worries in Colleen's gut, pushing them to the side for a moment.

The dinner the other night had been a disaster. After Bridget left, everyone else had hurried through the meal and petered out soon after. What Colleen had envisioned as a nice evening, a way to bring Bridget out of that self-imposed prison she had created in her house, had ended up as a giant mess.

Bridget didn't understand. Didn't see how easy it could be to slip away from your life and let the shadow of a tragedy blank out everything else. To take one bottle of wine to bed one night and then, just a week later, be sneaking two into the bedroom. And still not finding peace in that cold, empty space.

Colleen hung the pressed pair of white cotton curtains on the rod above the kitchen window and then turned back. Her gaze landed on the empty spots at the table. First, the one at the head where her Michael had always sat, then to each of the other four chairs, once filled with four daughters who kept her house full of lively chatter and bright laughter.

Abby is alive and well and the one who should be here.

Bridget's words haunted the edges of Colleen's thoughts. A sense of failure filled her whenever she thought of Abby, the daughter who had walked out of her life three years ago and stayed away.

Colleen supposed she should reach out. But in her mind, she saw nothing she had done wrong. She'd merely tried to help her daughter, and Abby had rebelled like a toddler refusing to eat broccoli. If anyone needed to apologize, it was Abigail.

Colleen ran her hand along the back of the chair, and for a second, she could see Abby's short brown hair, hear her infectious laughter, see her telling a story with hands that waved as wild as a storm. Abby, so unlike her sisters, her mother. Closest to the father the girls had lost too young. Was that when Abby had begun to pull away?

Colleen prided herself on treating her four daughters the same. Certainly, she'd had high expectations, but what mother didn't? The girls should know everything she had done, everything she was doing today, was for their own good.

When a twig grows hard, it is difficult to twist it. How many times had she heard her mother say those words? A soft upbringing would have left her girls unprepared for life. Yes, she'd done the right thing. And someday, Abby would appreciate that. Bridget too.

Colleen gave the chair a final tap and turned back to the ironing. The pile towered over the laundry basket, hours of work that would probably last until Colleen's legs began to wobble. Maybe it would be enough.

NINE

The chocolate cake had squashed down into itself in the center of the round pan like a rejected lump of coal. Flour, sugar, and cocoa powder speckled Bridget's granite countertops, coated the white stand mixer, and dusted the floor. The acrid smell of burned batter hung in the air, reluctant to leave even after Bridget had opened two windows.

She checked the bird feeder, and it was as full today as it had been the day before, and all the days before that. Even the hummingbird had given up on her ability to make food.

For weeks, Bridget had been feeling...unhinged. Lost. Her husband was gone, her life was a mess, and she couldn't even manage to feed a bird smaller than the palm of her hand.

Bridget yanked a bottle of white wine out of the fridge, uncorked it, and took a long gulp straight from the amber neck, telling herself eleven was the new five o'clock. She perched on the edge of a bar stool, clutching the bottle with both hands.

And cried.

Beside her, the answering machine kept blinking larger and larger red numbers. Deadlines for her column had come and gone, several times over. The stack of mail had grown three inches. On top of the pile of unpaid bills sat one opened envelope and the half-read letter inside. Instead of dealing with all of it, Bridget tossed a dishtowel over the whole mess and took another swig of wine.

"What the holy hell did you do?"

Bridget turned and saw Nora standing in the kitchen, holding a bright red Tupperware container. "Baked a cake." The words hung off the edge of a sob.

Nora took two steps forward and peered down at the mess on top of the stove. Her nose wrinkled. "It looks more like a football that got run over by a school bus."

"Probably tastes like that too." Bridget took another swig of wine and let out a long breath. Was this what her life had come to? Drinking in the morning and crying over ruined baked goods? "I think I forgot how to bake, Nora."

Her sister's green eyes softened, and a smile curved across her face. "Nah, you just forgot the baking powder." She pivoted, pulled open the pantry door, retrieved a small container, and held it up.

"How do you know I forgot that?"

"Because you, dear sister, may be an amazing baker, but you pretty much create a crime scene every time you make anything." Nora swept her hand over the dishes and ingredients scattered down the long counter. "I see everything but baking powder in this...mess."

Bridget sniffled. Good Lord, her kitchen should be condemned. She was a mess, in more ways than her countertops. She thought over the steps in making the cake earlier. "You're right. I did forget it. I guess I thought I knew the recipe by heart and...didn't."

"Don't worry about it. You're entitled to forget something once in a while. You've had a stressful few weeks."

Bridget snorted. "You can say that again." Maybe she should be easier on herself, lower her expectations and stop feeling so stressed by the lawn and the bills. Her husband had died only two months ago. Life didn't automatically restart after something like that.

"Not to mention how you pissed off Ma." Nora let out a low whistle. "No lie, she's wicked pissed. Still."

Which was why Bridget hadn't checked her messages or her texts. She'd heard the pings stacking up, one after another. In the weeks since that debacle of a dinner, her mother had left a steady stream of messages, all saying pretty much the same thing: *You better call and apologize to your mother or you're going to be struck by lightning.* "Maybe that means she'll stay out of my life for five minutes."

Nora snorted. "Yeah, good luck with that. I've never known Ma to stay out of any of our lives for five seconds."

Bridget's gaze went to the window. The primroses waved their happy white faces, barely visible now above the overgrown lawn. A few months ago, she'd thought she had her life all figured out. Her future as aligned and neat as the flowerbeds. In an instant, all that had changed, the straight lines dissolving into wavy, blurred routes that all seemed to lead nowhere. "What am I going to do, Nora?"

For years, Bridget had lived on this island of just her and Jim. But the last two months had left her adrift, lost, craving the bonds she'd had when she was young. The four O'Bannon girls, always together, walking to school like a gaggle of geese, crowding around a jigsaw puzzle and whispering in one of their rooms long after lights-out.

Nora took Bridget's palm and closed her fist over the box of baking powder. The sisters' gazes met and held. "All you have to do is start over."

"What if I can't? What if—"

"What-ifs are like bees in a hive," Nora said. "All they do is keep on buzzing so you don't notice the sweet honey of life."

Bridget laughed. Nora had said just the right thing to yank Bridget off the edge of a good self-pity party. How many times had she heard those words when she was young? They hadn't quite made sense then, and they still didn't now, but the saying brought a wash of warm memories with it. "Gramma had some weird sayings, didn't she?"

"Weirdly true, and weirdly still in our heads three decades later like one of those earworm songs. You can't worry about the what-ifs, Bridge. They'll only drive you batshit crazy. Trust me, I know."

A hint of something more lingered in Nora's words. Bridget tried to reach for it, but her brain was still a muddy thing, and she let it go. Maybe all the wine was making her overanalyze things.

Nora slid onto the second bar stool and plunked the Tupperware on the counter. "And in the meantime, while you're trying not to worry, I brought comfort food."

"Please don't tell me it's another casserole. I could feed all of Ethiopia with what's in my fridge."

"Nope." Nora peeled back the lid. "Kraft macaroni and cheese."

Bridget grinned and inhaled the warm scent of pasta drenched in cheddar cheese sauce. In an instant, she was taken back twenty-plus years. "Oh my God. The forbidden fruit."

"Still the best mac and cheese in the world, though if Ma ever found out we said that, she'd have a nervous breakdown and cut us out of the will." Nora tipped the container in Bridget's direction. "Want some?"

The boxed macaroni was shiny and tempting in all its powdered, processed, fake yellow goodness. Bridget couldn't remember the last time she'd indulged. Jim had seen some documentary on food one day and pronounced they would no longer eat boxed or canned food. Within a week, Bridget had been so sick of salads that she'd snuck out to Taco Bell and devoured four steak wraps in the parking lot, hunched over in her front seat like a heroin addict.

"Hell, yes, I want some of that." Bridget grabbed two forks, handing one to Nora. They dug in at the same time, as if they were nine and seven again and sharing Hillary Colbert's lunch in the shadows of the brick elementary school.

78

They sat like that for a moment, eating in silence, until the container was half empty. "God, that stuff is good. Still my favorite meal, even if it comes out of a box."

"Mine too. I blame it all on Ma not letting us eat school lunch," Nora said. "Maybe if we'd had more junk food, we would have appreciated the homemade manicotti she packed in our lunchboxes."

"Homemade manicotti in your lunch box is never cool," Bridget said. "I always felt like such a dork."

"Thank God Hillary's mom could barely cook." Nora swallowed a bite of the yellow pasta, then got up, retrieved two glasses, and divvied up the wine. "She was more than happy to take our lunches and give us hers."

"I still think we got the better end of the deal." Bridget ate another giant bite of macaroni and cheese. It settled in her stomach like a warm blanket, comforting, familiar. "So, why are you here, besides checking on my baking failure?"

Nora fiddled with her fork. "I . . . I wanted to apologize."

"Apologize? For what?"

"I was an ass when you came into the bakery two months ago, and I should have said I was sorry earlier. I've just been . . . stressed. I shouldn't have pushed you so hard to come back." Nora sighed. "God, some days I think I'm just like Ma."

"First, you are not at all like her. And second, there's nothing to forgive. I was just as much at fault for telling you off. I'm just . . . a mess right now." Bridget swirled the wine, watching the amber liquid roll and tumble in the goblet. That ache for her sisters grew but she knew she wasn't going to ease that—or mend the fences between them—unless she started to open up. "Turns out you were right. I kinda need to get my shit together and find a better job than a column that barely pays enough to buy groceries."

Nora lifted her gaze. "Really?"

Bridget fished under the dishtowel and pulled out the letter she'd received the day before. The page was still folded in threes because all the words she had needed to see were in the first line. "Jim's life insurance policy was canceled six months ago. He hadn't been making the payments."

Nora unfolded the letter, scanned it, and handed it back to Bridget. "So there's...nothing?"

"Honestly, I don't know. I've been afraid to look. I've just been letting all the bills pile up instead of dealing with them. Jim handled all of that. It was just...easier." When had that happened? Before she got married, Bridget had paid her own way, managing her checking account and maintaining a decent savings. She'd more or less stuck to a budget, except for the occasional splurge on sweaters or boots. Then after she and Jim had come home from their weeklong honeymoon in Aruba, Jim had offered to take over the bills while she was writing the thank-you cards.

It's easier for one person to keep track of the budget, he'd said, *and I have the mind for it. I'll just set aside a sum for you every week and then you never have to worry.*

"He made it sound like he was doing me a favor. And I thought he was." Bridget glanced over at the pile. The few inches of bills seemed to tower over her, so many envelopes to open, decisions to make, money to shell out. Jim's last paycheck had hit the bank three days ago. Which meant going forward, there was no more cushion of a second income. And now, no life insurance. Just the funeral alone had set her back fifteen grand, all on a payment plan with the funeral home. Then there was the mortgage, the light bill, the car insurance—

"I'm not surprised Jim took over all the bills and told you it was for your own good," Nora said softly.

"What do you mean?"

Nora picked at the macaroni and cheese but didn't eat any.

"What do you mean, Nora?"

Nora's nose twitched left, right. Like Samantha in *Bewitched*, except the movement signaled some kind of internal debate. "Never mind. I shouldn't say anything. He's gone now and..."

"He was my husband, and it's some kind of unwritten code that you never speak ill of the dead," Bridget finished. God, she was so sick of dancing around words and sentences like they were hot coals. She'd done that all her life. Maybe it was the wine, maybe it was the stress, or maybe it was the shock of Jim's death, but something had started to tear down a barrier inside Bridget that day, and instead of shuffling the conversation into the *everything's fine* pile, she pushed a little more. "Nora, it's okay. Tell me what you wanted to say."

Because every day that went by after Jim's death, Bridget began to face the truth she'd been trying to bandage with a baby. At some point, she'd dropped a stitch in the fabric of her marriage. Somewhere along the way, the threads that had bound them together for three years frayed and Bridget had been too busy pretending everything was fine to notice the unraveling. Even before the primroses had taken root, she'd known.

Nora took a sip of wine, folded her hands, and let out a long breath. "Okay, don't be mad, but I think Jim was a bit of a control freak. He made every decision in your life. Including the one to..." Nora shook her head. Her nose twitched again. "Forget it. I should probably go. I left the bakery in Dani's hands and she's only twenty-two and sometimes panics if we have a bunch of customers at once."

Bridget could fill in the blank herself. Jim had been the one who urged her to leave the bakery. *You don't need them, Bridge. All they do is hurt you.*

She'd left the bakery and left her sister and mother to pick up the slack, right in the middle of their busiest year ever. A one-paragraph mention in the *Globe* had put Charmed by Dessert on people's radar, and business had exploded overnight. Bridget had been working twelve-, fourteen-, sometimes sixteen-hour days. She'd climb into bed, exhausted and covered with flour, and curl into Jim's arms.

I missed you, baby. This is no way to start our marriage.

She'd told him it was only temporary, until they hired some more staff. But the hiring didn't happen, and the hours stretched on, and Jim's words shifted from *I missed you* to *They don't appreciate you.* In the dark of their bedroom, with Jim's lips pressed to her temples, the words made sense.

"Jim wasn't a control freak, Nora," Bridget said. "All he was doing was watching out for me. Protecting me."

"Yeah, of course. I shouldn't have said anything. I'm sorry."

But Bridget's mind whispered doubts around her words. If Jim had truly been protecting her, then where was the life insurance? Why hadn't he told her he had let it lapse?

Just an oversight, she told herself. Something that could have happened to anyone. Either way, he was gone now, and she refused to think of him as anything other than the man she had loved. Even letting any of those other thoughts into her head ran a knife edge along her heart.

"You know there's always a job for you at Charmed by Dessert. I don't want to pressure you, but you said you needed a job, and there's one that you already know." Nora started to get to her feet. "Damn it. I promised myself when I came over here that I wouldn't start in on you again about that. I'm sorry."

Bridget reached for her sister's hand. For a second, it felt like she was reaching for a lifeline. Maybe she was. Her fingers curled around Nora's, and Nora's pressed back. Still there, still her sister.

"Wait, please." Bridget glanced at the pile under the dishtowel again. None of it was going away, and there weren't any fairies coming to leave money under her pillow. Somehow, she was going to have to get herself out of this mess. "I was thinking that maybe...maybe I could work there on a temporary basis. Just a few hours. Until I find something else."

The light in Nora's eyes brightened, and she dropped back onto the seat, clear relief filling her face. How bad *were* things at the bakery?

"Really?" Nora said. "That would be great. It hasn't been the same without you. Having you back there every day would be wonderful."

The last thing Bridget wanted to do was promise forever to Nora or anyone else. Hell, she was having trouble figuring out tomorrow, never mind next week or next year. Right now, her mind could only stretch a few hours into the future.

"I'm just thinking about it, Nora," Bridget cautioned again. "No promises. No decisions yet. If that's okay."

"That's more than okay. The bakery is crazy busy with orders." Nora bounced forward on the stool, making her long brown ponytail swing. Nora wore her hair back so often that none of them could remember what she looked like before. "And you're already experienced, and know how we do things—"

Bridget put up a hand. "Except, if I come back to work, I'll be around Ma more often. And after that family dinner..."

"It's going to be just a tad tense at the bakery." Nora shrugged. "But honestly, Bridge, when hasn't it been tense with Ma?"

"This was different." She'd embarrassed her mother in

84

front of the priest. Talked back, drank wine, and stormed out in the middle of the meal. Each a cardinal sin on its own, but put together—

Tense definitely wasn't the right word.

Nora ate another bite of macaroni. "Still, it wasn't as bad as your wedding. Now *that* was a scene."

"Scene? That was World War Three, O'Bannon style." Bridget sighed.

As one new family had formed, another family had shattered, the sisters scattering to the winds for years. It was ironic that it had taken a death, an ending, to start bringing them together again.

All but one. All but Abby.

The scene on the church steps, when Abby had tried to talk Bridget out of marrying Jim, had only been the preview for the main show that had come at the reception. The bomb that Abby had dropped in Bridget's lap, the secret she had begged her sister to shoulder.

Abby, the most honest and forthright of them all, not afraid to tell anyone off or share her opinion. But terrified of her family finding out why she had bolted from the room.

After that crazy moment with Ned the orthopedist, Bridget had done as her mother told her and gone after Abby. Abby had crawled into her old twin bed in the bedroom the girls used to share, her knees to her chest, facing the baby-blue wall. The posters of Matthew McConaughey and Bradley Cooper had long ago been taken down, but pushpin holes remained in a constellation. A white shelf above the headboard held Abby's softball trophies, her debate team award, a small collection of Beanie Babies, all coated with years of dusty forgetfulness.

The bed yielded with a creak as Bridget sat down and laid a hand on her sister's shoulder. "Ma means well, Abby. And Ned's a nice guy."

"I don't care if he's a saint. I'm not interested in him, and no matter how hard I try to get Ma to see that, she doesn't understand," Abby said, and then her voice dropped to a whisper. "I don't...I don't want a husband. Ever."

In that moment, with her veil pinned in her hair and her wedding dress spreading around her like frosting, Bridget was still wrapped in that bliss of hearing Jim say *I do*. She had pictured their life together since that first date, when he'd swept her off her feet with a picnic along the Charles River. She couldn't imagine wanting to spend her life without a man by her side. And being with Jim just seemed to make things...easier. Why wouldn't Abby want the same?

"That's okay," Bridget said, tabling the argument for a time when Abby wasn't so upset. "Aunt Mary never got married, and she's perfectly happy."

"I mean..." Abby's gaze held Bridget's. A second passed. Another. "I don't want a man. At all. Ever. I'm not...I'm..."

Abby's green eyes shimmered with tears. Her brown hair, curled and piled in a loose bun on top of her head for the wedding, was slowly coming undone.

Under Bridget's touch, her sister trembled. "You're not what?"

"Not…" Abby propped herself on one elbow and drew in a deep breath. Something shifted inside her, and when she expelled the breath, her eyes cleared and her shoulders squared. "I'm not like that."

"Not like what?"

"Not…straight."

For one crazy second, Bridget wanted to say, *Of course you're not—your hair is curly*, because she was still wrapped up in her two-by-two, man-and-woman world. Then, like a machine whirring to life, the parts and pieces of the last few years slid into place.

Abby skipping school dances, bowing out of prom. Dating guys no more than once or twice and then saying it didn't work out for vague reasons. Spending her weekend nights with her girlfriends at the beach or practicing for the upcoming softball game, instead of joining everyone else on double dates at the movies.

Abby never mentioning a first kiss. A first crush. A first anything.

"You're gay," Bridget said, and wondered if that was the right thing to say. "I mean, that's cool."

Abby blinked. "Do you mean that?"

Bridget let the information settle over her for a moment. "Yeah. I do. I don't care." Then she stumbled to add, "I mean, I care about you, but I don't care who you fall in love with. That's your life, not mine. All I want is for you to be happy."

"But Ma and Nora and everyone else..." Her eyes shimmered again. "It's an abomination, Ma told me once. A one-way ticket to hell."

"Ma says a lot of things," Bridget said. "But it's you, Abby, her daughter. She won't feel that way about you."

Abby shook her head, and the rest of the curls tumbled free from the bobby pins. "She will. I asked her once, when we were watching this episode of *Gilmore Girls*, what would you think if one of your daughters was gay, and she said, without even pausing for a breath, that she would disown them. Because it was against the church and God and everything she believed in."

"She wouldn't do that." But even as Bridget said the words, she knew they weren't true. Ma had stopped talking to Aunt Mary five years ago. Over what, no one could remember. But no one spoke Aunt Mary's name or mentioned the wall between them. When Ma had a grudge, she held it like it was glued to her heart. But maybe with her daughter, Ma would be different. "It'll all be fine, Abby. Just give it time."

Abby shoved off the bed. "You and your Pollyanna view of the world. Geez, Bridget, get a clue. You think everything is all perfect in little two-by-two lines but it's not. You're so blind. Hell, you rushed into that marriage with Jim and it was—" Abby shook her head. "I gotta go."

She rushed out of the room, with Bridget on her heels. "It was what? A mistake? Isn't that what you said back in the church?"

"I was hot and tired, and I shouldn't have said anything." Abby waved off the words. "Besides, this isn't the time or place. Just let it go. You're already married. It's too fucking late."

"Too late for what?" Bridget grabbed her sister's arm.

Abby shook her head. "Do you really want to know what I was going to tell you this morning? What you re-fused to hear before you put that damned ring on your finger?"

Bridget's stomach flipped. Her throat threatened to close. "Yes." *No.*

"I went to the deli for lunch a week ago, you know the one across town? And I saw Jim leaving with another woman, this tall blonde. He kissed her on the cheek, and I ran after him and confronted him."

"Another…woman?" *Not Jim,* Bridget thought. He'd always been so attentive, so in love with her. She would have known. Would have sensed something, she was sure of it.

"He said it was nothing, but I think he was lying, Bridget. He told me he'd tell you about it, just so you wouldn't worry. But he didn't, did he?" Abby snorted. "You know, he's always been kind of a jerk, but you give him a pass every frigging time."

Bridget shook her head. She'd heard all this before from Abby, the only one of her sisters not to warm to Jim. "You've always said you don't like him. Is it because of Ned? Or Ma? Or are you just…" Bridget leaned in, angry at Abby for spoiling the day, for dampening her joy, "jeal-ous?"

"What would I be jealous about?"

"That you're never going to have this." She waved a hand down her front. "That you're not going to get the big wedding and the dress and all that."

Abby scoffed. "You think I give a shit about a dress? That's not what this is about."

"Maybe not, or maybe you're just trying to ruin my day because you're so unhappy with your life. Your *secret* life."

The barb had cut to the quick, and almost as soon as she said it, Bridget wanted to take the words back.

"You are such a bitch." Abby spun away and headed for the living room.

"A bitch? Me?" Bridget said, her anger back to red-hot now. "Where do you get off telling me who the right man is for me, Abby? You, of all people. You don't even know what you're talking about because you are—"

Abby spun around. "Shut up, Bridget. Just *shut up*."

"I won't shut up. This is my wedding day, Abby. You're the one who should shut the hell up and keep your problems to yourself. At least let me have this one day."

Their shouts had stopped the conversation among the guests, but Bridget didn't care. All she saw was betrayal. Abby, undermining the happiness Bridget had worked so hard to find, and then expecting Bridget to hold Abby's secret tight.

"You only see what you want to," Abby said. "You've always been like that, Bridget. You live in this bubble, and you think that man is so perfect. He's not. And marrying him was the stupidest thing you could have done. You think you're going to have some fairy-tale life. You're not. He's—"

Ma stepped in, trying to referee. But the fight continued until the wedding cake had ended up on the wall, the guests standing around in shocked silence. In the end, Jim had taken Bridget's hand and pulled her out of the house without a word, leaving their reception, and her family, behind them.

They hurt you, babe, he'd whispered as he helped her into the car. *It's just you and me now. And we'll be happy, I promise.*

But had they been? Or had she just convinced herself she was happy because it was easier than fixing all that had gone wrong? Easier than admitting maybe, just maybe, her sister had been right, and easier than facing that little doubt that had lingered even after Jim had explained that woman had been a work friend and Abby had exaggerated the entire thing. And now Nora was echoing Abby's words.

No. Her husband was gone. Tarnishing his memory wouldn't do anyone any good at all.

In Bridget's sunny kitchen, Nora finished eating, got to her feet, and covered the empty Tupperware container. She put a hand on Bridget's shoulder. "I know you're worried about working with me and Ma again. But it's been three years, Bridge. A lot has changed."

Enough that they could start over? She glanced at the baking powder on the counter. Could it be as easy as adding a missing ingredient?

Bridget leaned into Nora's touch. Even though Bridget

was the oldest, it had always been Nora who had stood strong in any storm, quiet and calm, the one who never panicked, which washed tranquility over the other girls. At their father's funeral, Nora had gone up to Magpie, the most devastated of the four girls, and held her hand, tight and sure. Then she'd reached for Bridget's hand and drawn her into their circle. All three of them had gathered Abby up, and the four O'Bannon girls had stood on the mauve carpet in the funeral home by a giant ring of red roses and pooled their strength.

Tears burned in Bridget's eyes now. She needed this. Needed her sisters. Needed that circle again. "If it's okay with you," she said, feeling the words out one at a time, settling the commitment in her heart, "I'll come back to the shop. I'll start tomorrow and stay for as long as you need me."

"I would love that. Seriously." Nora's eyes shimmered, and her smile wobbled.

"Even if all I can bake are dead footballs?"

Nora pivoted away, grabbed the cake pan, and then tossed the ruined cake and the metal dish into the trash. She stepped back, wiped her hands together, and gave Bridget a grin. "What dead footballs?"

TEN

J essie sat in the chair by the window, the sun bouncing off
her blond hair. "I don't think I can do this anymore, Abs."

Abby's heart stilled. She paused in the middle of
adding cream to her coffee. It was a Saturday morning, a
lazy day they usually spent walking around the city, grabbing a sandwich to share, and finding a shady spot in the
gardens to sit and watch the world go by. Sometimes Jessie
would read to her from one of the books she had assigned
to her Lit students at Brown; sometimes Abby would tell
her about how you knew when dough was ready to be
worked into bread. But this morning, Jessie had woken up
and gone to the window, reading to herself while the world
rushed by on the busy street three floors below.

"What, you can't sit by the window anymore?" The
joke fell flat in the quiet morning air.

Jessie shook her head, put the book she'd been reading
on the ledge, and crossed to the kitchen. She was a few
inches taller than Abby, lean and long in all the places

Abby was short and stocky. Jessie leaned her elbows on the counter, the rest of her body stretching like a cat behind her. "I can't keep pretending we aren't a couple to the outside world. I mean, you don't even see your family. What does it matter?"

They'd had this argument a dozen times over the months since Abby had asked Jessie to marry her. The glow of engagement had given way to a simmering tension that had ratcheted up with each step they took toward the wedding. In the early days of her life with Jessie, there had been peace and laughter. But those days had become less and less frequent, and the tension hung over every moment, a threatening storm. "We live together. I don't think that's pretending anything."

"Have you told your family yet?"

Abby glanced at the diamond on Jessie's left hand, a twin to the one on Abby's hand. The diamond was flanked by rubies, Abby's birthstone, a ring that merged two of them into one. The wedding bands they'd ordered were alternating diamonds and rubies, set in platinum. Right now, the bands were sitting in the safe at the jewelry store, waiting for a decision. Even though they had a date and a deposit made on a honeymoon in Key West, Jessie had refused to make any further plans.

Abby turned to put the creamer back in the fridge. "I will."

"Abby, we've been together for four years. We're getting married in two months. You have to tell them sometime."

"They won't understand," Abby said.

"You mean they won't approve. Because we're both women."

Abby couldn't begin to explain to Jessie how her family, staunchly Catholic, lived in a black-and-white world. Her mother, especially, had said more than once that being gay was a choice, and people with any sense would choose to settle down as God had intended for them to do. Ma held tight to that church view, which used the Bible and the Pope to cast a veil over the world, blurring all the things they didn't want to acknowledge. Like abortions and pedophiles. And the fact that love came in many different forms, not just one prescribed by a guy wearing a black shirt and a white collar.

"Your family didn't exactly jump up and down," Abby said.

"My father was an asshole, and he admitted it later. He even apologized straight to your face." Jessie ran a hand through her hair. It settled around her shoulders like a golden river. "My family took a while to come around when I came out to them and, yeah, it was painful as hell. But we got through it." Jessie laced her fingers through Abby's. "Together."

Abby wanted to believe that it was just a matter of giving her family time to absorb the news. But she knew better. She had heard the judgmental comments, as harsh as sandpaper on silk, seen the way her mother shunned Georgi, the vibrant but brash gay man who owned the flower shop next to the bakery, as if he were a leper.

"We don't need my family," Abby said.

That's what she had been telling herself for more than three years. Until that fight with Bridget at her wedding, and Abby had left, hurt that Bridget, of all her sisters, had cut her off. Okay, so Bridget's wedding day wasn't the best timing for telling her that she was making a mistake, but Abby had waited, hoping that she was wrong about Jim, that he would come clean to Bridget before they said "I do." He'd promised Abby he would, but when she'd seen Bridget's oblivious joy that morning, Abby realized Jim hadn't kept his word. And in trying to stop Bridget from making a mistake, Abby had lost her best friend.

If she'd had a single ally, Abby would have tried harder to make her way back to her family. But she had no one. No one but Jessie.

And now the same family that she had disowned was the very roadblock keeping her from the one person who loved her. She thought of the bakery, the memories still so vivid, she could smell the yeast, the vanilla, the chocolate.

An ache started deep in her gut, moving up to fist around her heart. She closed her eyes for a second and willed the ache away. She didn't need them.

Jessie didn't say anything for a long moment. When she spoke again, her eyes shone with unshed tears, and the spark had drained from her usual smile. She tugged her hand out of Abby's. "Is it because you are ashamed of me?"

Abby put her mug on the counter and swung around to take Jessie in her arms. From their first date, it had felt right to hold her. Okay, so she hadn't introduced Jessie to her family, but Jessie didn't understand, couldn't see, how the rest of the O'Bannons would reject this smart, bright, beautiful woman Abby loved so much.

It was protection, not shame, that kept Abby from bringing her fiancée home to meet the family. "I could never be ashamed of you. I love you."

Jessie sighed and stepped out of Abby's arms. "Then tell them." As Jessie left the room, a cloud moved in front of the sun and cast the kitchen in shadow.

ELEVEN

S he sat in the car outside the bakery for a long time, debating.

Almost as soon as Nora left, the mac and cheese devoured, Bridget had started having second thoughts. She'd cleaned up her baking mess and decided to tackle the entire kitchen, mostly to avoid getting sucked into the Netflix vortex again. She'd started at the top, dusting the molding, the cabinets, then opening them up to clean inside, removing and replacing every single dish. While she wiped and dusted and organized, she ran the pros and cons through her head over and over again.

In the end, the mailman made the final decision. He slid another stack of bills through the slot in her front door. They hit the wood floor with a soft thud, and Bridget knew she could only live in this cotton candy world of avoidance for so long. This morning she'd gotten up, pulled on jeans and comfortable shoes, and headed to work at the bakery she'd left what seemed like a century ago.

Except, she reminded herself from her spot in the parking lot, she could only work there again if she actually went *inside.*

The bright pink and white sign hung above her street-side parking space, swinging gently in the breeze. Two women emerged from Charmed by Dessert, carrying white paper bags and laughing together.

Bridget's mind reached back to a bright, warm day in late June, the kind of day when the air was heavy with the scent of the ocean and lazy mornings. School had let out the day before, and Abby and Bridget had hurried out of the house to run to the corner store. Back then, O'Donnell's Sundries was housed on the first floor of a converted house a block away. Painted bright orange with a Kelly-green door, the store could be seen from space, Mr. O'Donnell liked to say. Against one wall, he had dozens of baskets hung from hooks, all at child height. The two girls had come in with two weeks' allowance clutched in their fists, grabbed one paper bag, and stuffed it full of penny candies: Jolly Ranchers, Mary Janes, Atomic Fireballs, Sixlets, a rainbow of sugar wrapped in bright packages.

"You girls be sure to brush your teeth extra good tonight." Mr. O'Donnell peered over the counter at them. Bridget was just tall enough to see over the counter, but Abby was still three inches and one year away from that height. "And be sure to leave a candy or two for the Children of Lir."

"Children of Lir?" Abby mumbled, her mouth already working around a fireball.

"Aye. Don't you two know that story?" Mr. O'Donnell shook his head and waved a gnarled hand. "Ah, they waste your time in school with all that adding and subtracting. You need to know your heritage too."

Bridget had thought she knew enough of that, between Gramma's whisperings about fairies and their mother dragging them to Mass three times a week, but she knew better than to correct an adult. She tore off the top of the Sixlets and popped them one at a time into her mouth.

"Are they big as me?" Abby said, but with the fireball, the words sounded more like *are day bees-ee?*

He chuckled. "They're wee ones. Lir was the god of the sea. When his wife died, he married again, but the new wife didn't like his children and wanted to be alone with Lir, so she turned them into swans. For nine hundred years, the children waited for the curse to be lifted. Our great Saint Patrick came and released them. It's said that the children still wander the earth, disguised as birds. So I leave a bit of a treat for them."

Abby's eyes were wide, her mouth chipmunked by the fireball. "I'll leave two. In case they have a sister." *I wee two, n-kay av sidder.*

"Me too," Bridget said, though Bridget was two years older and didn't really believe in children who became swans. As the two of them walked out of the store, their heads together, they divvied up four pieces for the mythical child spirits. For years after that, they'd tucked candies and little toys around the yard, and when they disappeared—most likely taken by a bird or squirrel—Abby was always sure it was the Children of Lir. Bridget never corrected her.

In the modern day of reality and widowed women, Bridget shook off the memory and got out of the car. She wasn't going to pay the bills by staying in the parking lot or by waiting for some crazy person to leave a million dollars in the backyard. To be honest, if there had been life insurance, Bridget would have used it to buy herself time. Time to think. Time to grieve. Time to make decisions.

She walked into the shop, greeted by the familiar bell, and found a young girl behind the counter, probably the not-super-responsible Dani. "Can I help you?" the girl asked.

"Is Nora here?"

The girl nodded toward the back, her ponytail swinging in a wide arc. "Making a cake."

"Thanks. I'm going to head on back, okay? I'm her sister."

The girl shrugged, nonplussed, and went back to scanning a magazine. Bridget skirted the counter and pushed on the swinging door that led to the kitchen. A three-tier wedding cake dominated the stainless steel work surface, so tall and wide it almost hid Nora from view.

Delicate pink flowers ringed each of the white frosted tiers, interspersed with swooping green stems and leaves that curled around the cake. Faux tree trunks disguised the columns holding each of the tiers afloat, the work so delicate and precise that Bridget had to look twice to know the trees and flowers were made completely out of frosting.

"You are such a genius at decorating," Bridget said.

Nora stepped back and wiped a bead of sweat off her forehead with the back of her hand. "I don't know about that."

"I've always admired what you could do with a little bit of frosting." Bridget grabbed one of the aprons from the hook by the door and slid it over her head. The cotton fabric settled over her with a familiar touch. Bridget tied the strings into a bow at her back and then swept her hair into a ponytail. She washed her hands at the sink and then took the stack of orders and flipped through the thick pile of sheets pinned under the clipboard. "Wow. You weren't kidding. You are crazy busy here."

"Tell me about it. Wedding season, graduation season, and it seems like everyone in the city of Boston is having a baby shower." Nora let out a breath. "I'm so glad you decided to come back."

Bridget nodded, not yet sure she was going to be glad she came back. "What do you want me to do first?"

Nora gestured toward the mixer. "I need three vanilla sponge sheet cakes. And two chocolate sponge. Once we get those in the oven, we need to start on replenishing the cupcakes and cookies out front."

"You saw the cake at my house. Are you sure you want to trust me with this?"

Nora grinned. "Check the pantry. I made sure you wouldn't forget anything."

Bridget ducked inside the walk-in pantry at the back of the shop. Before there was a bakery here, the room had been a parlor. The windows had been turned into walls and the chandelier removed to make room for fluorescent lights, but the thick white cove molding still rimmed the ceiling and added an odd touch of elegance to the rows of metal shelving.

On the right, above the five-gallon tubs of flour and sugar, sat oversized containers of other dry goods. And taped to the front of the baking powder, a giant handwritten sign that said, bridget: use me.

Bridget laughed. Maybe working here again was going to be great after all.

She changed her mind when her mother came in an hour later, huffing past Bridget and beelining straight for Nora. "The O'Haras are coming in at three for Ronald's baptism cake," Ma said. "If you haven't finished decorating it, I'll do it."

"Bridget was going to—"

"I'll do it." Ma spun on her heel, brushed past her oldest daughter, and disappeared into the walk-in refrigerator.

"Guess I'm still out of the will," Bridget whispered to Nora.

"And I was so looking forward to splitting Ma's Hummel collection with you." A twinkle lit Nora's gaze.

Bridget leaned in close, just as their mother emerged from the pantry. "I have one word for you: eBay."

That sent Nora into gales of laughter, the sound ringing in the small kitchen, as sweet as the wedding cake frosting. And just like that, it was as if the years apart and all the fights had been erased. Nora gave Bridget a shoulder nudge, Bridget volleyed back with an elbow. They grinned at each other, like a couple of teenagers holding a delicious secret.

"We are here to work, not play," Ma said. "We have a lot of orders to process. That means we should *all* be busy."

She arched a disapproving brow in Bridget's direction. The unspoken question—*Can I count on you? Or are you going to walk away again?*

In answer, Bridget started measuring eggs and sugar into a mixing bowl. She set it over the double boiler, then turned on the gas and began to whisk as the heat rose.

❦❦

Six hours, eight cakes, and countless cookies later, Bridget hung up the apron and said goodbye to Nora. She grabbed her purse and turned to her mother. "Bye, Ma. See you tomorrow."

Her mother harrumphed and went on stirring peanut butter chips into brownie batter.

Six hours and her mother hadn't said a single word directly to Bridget. She shouldn't be surprised. Her mother had once gone three weeks without talking to Bridget—and she'd still lived at home then. The thought of working here in a silent standoff day after day exhausted Bridget. Life, she had learned, was too damned short for any of that shit.

Bridget leaned over and gave her mother a kiss on the cheek. "You can't stay mad at me forever, Ma."

Her mother nodded, and a glimmer of a tear shone in her pale green eyes. It wasn't a word, but it was progress. Good enough for her first day. She hadn't burned anything or ruined anything. Progress.

Bridget slid into her car, but before she put the key in the ignition, her gaze dropped to the change dish at the front of the center console. Among the quarters and dimes sat a knobbed whelk shell, a spiral of pale coral and white, tapering from the wide home of the long-departed whelk to a narrow point.

She curled her hand around the shell, her palm indenting with the knobbed end. She'd found it two years ago, walking a sandy stretch of Wollaston Beach on a crisp October afternoon. Fall had been moving in, shuttling summer to the side with hasty winds and cloudy mornings. The fried clam restaurant had shuttered its windows for the season, and only one lone hot dog vendor remained, his back hunched against the cold, body pressed against the small cart for warmth.

Jim had taken the new job in Boston the month before, promising that it would mean more time home, more money in the bank, less travel. In those thirty days, she'd seen her husband for six. He'd been in DC, then Chicago, then San Francisco. And on the few nights he was in the same state as Bridget, he'd slept at the office, overwhelmed, he'd said, by corporate tax filings and overdue balance sheets.

She'd woken up alone that morning and splayed her hand across the cool sheet beside her. No Jim. He'd called a few hours later, but no amount of apologizing could make up for the fact that he had spent the night of their anniversary at work. For Bridget, it had been a moment of choice, one of those bridges she needed to cross. South to walk away from the hurt and disappointment or north to trudge forward with the life she was leading

She'd called in sick to work, bundled into a thick sweatshirt, and walked the beach. Just as she turned back to the car, she'd spied the whelk shell, one bit of perfection among dozens of broken shells. She'd tucked it into the change dish, maybe because it was pretty, maybe because it made her think of waking up the morning of her wedding, before the scene with Abby, before everything that followed, when she'd thought everything between them was perfect and unbreakable. In the end, it turned out they were just like all the other shells, damaged.

When she finally got home that evening, Bridget walked in to find Jim, surrounded by flickering candles and hundreds of red roses. She thought of the perfection of that shell, nestled among so many fragmented ones, and had gone to Jim without a word. Nothing was ever that perfect, and it was only in accepting the chips and fractures that people found true happiness. They'd made love, right there on the carpet, while the candles burned down and the roses wilted.

But then there were the financial secrets Jim had kept and the distance that had grown between them over the years. Maybe she'd still been looking for that perfect shell, instead of accepting the imperfect ones.

Or maybe there'd never been anything perfect about her marriage, and Jim's death was opening that reality wider. No. She refused to believe that. Jim had done his best—and like those other shells, he had been far from perfect.

As she put the whelk back into the dish, she noticed a business card. Garrett Andrews. The lawyer. The one who had told her it was okay to let something living depend on her again.

Before she could think about it, Bridget dialed the number. When Garrett answered, the words caught in her throat for a second. She wasn't sure what she was doing or why she was calling, only that she felt this gnawing need to talk to someone who understood the war in her heart. "This is Bridget, from the bird store? I mean, I know it's been a couple months since we met, but hopefully you remember me." She took a deep breath and exhaled it with the next sentences. "I wondered if you had time for a cup of coffee. Turns out I have a hummingbird problem."

TWELVE

Abby decided she had to be a masochist. Why else would she have parked in the back lot at Charmed by Dessert and now stood before the rear entrance? The scuffed door led directly into the kitchen—the same kitchen she had vowed never to visit again.

Are you ashamed of me?

Jessie's voice echoed in Abby's heart. The vulnerable hitch at the end of the question, the tears threatening in her eyes. Jessie had asked the question again in bed last night. When Abby had reassured her that, hell yes, she was proud to be with her, Jessie had just nodded and rolled away.

In the invisible wall between them in that queen-sized bed, Abby knew she was losing Jessie. The longer she let this go, the farther Jessie drifted away. Soon she'd drift too far to bring her back.

This morning, when Abby had said goodbye before she left for work (at the mall cooking store job she hated but was glad paid the bills), she had leaned over to kiss Jessie.

There'd been a moment of hesitation, a shimmer in Jessie's brown eyes, and Abby knew, without her fiancée saying a word, that every single day the hurt between them was multiplying.

Abby's hand hesitated on the cold metal handle. The familiar small sign was mounted in the center of the door, a little worse for wear after several harsh New England winters. rear entrance for charmed by dessert. please come to the front for sweet treats. Was she really ready to do this? Ready to face her family and the consequences of finally telling them the truth?

Are you ashamed of me?

Before Abby could pull on the handle, the door opened, and her mother emerged, a bag of trash over her shoulder like Santa. Her steps stuttered and her eyes widened. "Abigail. What are you doing, sneaking in the back like a criminal?"

Like a criminal? Three years apart and that was how her mother greeted her? Accusatory and pissed? What had she expected? Some movie-worthy reunion filled with tears and tight hugs? If there was one thing Colleen O'Bannon wasn't, it was emotional. She believed in decorum above everything else, whether it was a blister on your foot as you trudged to church, a pet hamster that died on the first day of school, or a daughter who had been distant for three long years.

"I'm not sneaking in like a criminal. I thought it was easier to come in the back instead of the front because… because I wanted to talk to you," Abby said.

Ma nodded and lowered the trash bag to the ground. She parked her hands on her hips. "So talk."

Abby shook her head and let out a long breath. All her life, she'd felt like an adversary of her mother. She often wondered how her life would be different if Ma had died instead of Dad.

With her father, they'd communicated in games of catch in the backyard while the sun began to set, in long walks around the neighborhood, and lazy Sunday afternoons watching the Pats or the Red Sox. Her father had been a man of few words, but he'd been kind and patient, even though he lived in a house teeming with females. Her mother, though, had been the stoic, colder one, the parent Abby had never felt close to. The years apart had only expanded that divide, and Abby's heart squeezed. "I guess I shouldn't have expected a ticker tape parade. Never mind. This was a mistake."

She had started to turn away when her mother called out. "Wait."

That one word made Abby's heart leap with hope. Even after all these years, even though she knew better, she still hoped. She pivoted back. "Yeah?"

"Open the lid to the Dumpster so I can toss the bag in there."

Abby stared at her mother for a solid thirty seconds. She had driven all the way over here, intent on finally telling her mother about Jessie, and instead of being glad to see her daughter again or having any kind of real conversation, she wanted Abby to do trash duty? "I haven't seen you in three years, Ma, except for a drive-by at Jim's funeral. And the first thing you say to me is *open the Dumpster?*"

"For one, that is not the first thing I said to you. For another, I can't think with this trash sitting beside me." Her mother's face pinched, deepening the wrinkles around her mouth, the shadows under her eyes. If Colleen O'Bannon felt exhaustion or remorse or, heck, the beginnings of a cold, she would never show it. Her features were as stony as the concrete under their feet. "In case you forgot, this is a very busy bakery. I can't stand around all day, chattering like a couple of crows on a telephone line."

"No, you can't." Abby shook her head. "I'll let you get back to the thing you love more than your own children."

Then she flipped the lid of the Dumpster and got in her car. When she glanced in her rearview mirror, her mother was already back inside.

THIRTEEN

Bridget sat on a hard wooden chair at the Java Hut, her right leg tapping a staccato against the underside of the table. She folded her hands, then unfolded them and put them on her lap, and then folded them again.

What the hell was she doing here?

She should be home, eating her ten thousandth serving of casserole. Or tending the primroses. Or dealing with the bills. Anything other than getting coffee with another man.

Except Jim was gone and Garrett was...well, she wasn't sure what he was. Yet another thing to add to the list of things she procrastinated about.

She reached for her purse in the opposite chair and started to rise when the oak and glass door to the coffee shop opened and Garrett walked in. He had on a dark blue pinstripe suit with a pale yellow shirt and an ocean color swirled tie that reminded her of van Gogh's *Starry Night*. The top button was undone, the tie wrenched a bit to the side. On another man, that might have made him look tired or harried, but on Garrett, the loosened shirt and tie seemed…roguish.

Good Lord. Now she was thinking in romance novel terms.

When his gaze caught hers, he smiled. A little frisson went through her, but Bridget pushed that aside. Item number seven hundred fifty-three she couldn't deal with right now.

"Hey, how are you?" he asked.

"Fine." Bridget shook her head and cursed. "God, I hate when people say that. My family does it so often, the words should be embroidered in a sampler on the wall. I'm fine. I'm good. When most of us are anything but."

He chuckled. "Okay, then if you're not good or fine, then what are you?"

"A platypus?" A quick bubble of marginally manic laughter slipped out before she sobered. She needed to get out more if the proverbial *how are you?* had her treading on the edge of hysteria. "Honestly, I don't know if I'm up or down or sideways."

"It's okay. You don't have to." He waved at the enormous chalked menu hanging on the wall. "Let's start with a simpler question. Decaf or regular?"

"You think that's a simple question? Obviously you don't know me." She paused, then decided, what the hell, Garrett might as well know what he was in for, agreeing to a cup of coffee with her. With any luck, she'd drive him off, and she could turn this boat around before it went down a river she wasn't sure she wanted to traverse. "I'm compli-cated when it comes to coffee. Half-caf, three creams, one and a half sugars. Not too hot, but if it is too hot, get a side of ice. And on Fridays, I get a drizzle of caramel sauce."

She expected him to mutter something about her be-ing high maintenance or make some snarky comment, but instead, he arched a brow and gave her a look that said *Okay, I get that.* "Why is caramel only on Fridays?"

"It keeps it special that way. I like having something to look forward to at the end of the week." Put that way, her life sounded pitiful. She looked forward to adding caramel syrup to her coffee? Maybe she did need to get out more. She waved in the direction of the barista behind the counter. "If you just say 'Bridget's regular,' they'll know what you mean. Or I can just order it myself. I mean, it is complicated and—"

"It's fine," he said, "and I mean that. So relax, Bridget. It's just coffee."

She realized that she'd been perched on the edge of her seat, her chest tight with anxiety. Had she said too much, been too silly?

Garrett's calming words erased that anxious space, and she sank into the chair. "It is just coffee. Although, here the coffee is pretty exceptional."

He glanced around the room, taking in the dark wood paneling, the chess set on the back table, the sofas in the nook to their right. "So, do you come here often?"

She cocked her head and studied him. "Are you trying to pick me up or ask me a legitimate question?"

"Whichever works best." Garrett's green eyes twinkled, and that half-smile toyed with the edges of his lips.

She barely knew him and already she could tell the difference between his smiles—the friendly one, the flirty one, the gentle one. She couldn't decide if that was good or bad, only that she wasn't ready to figure it out.

"The, uh, legitimate question," Bridget said, dragging her focus away from him and back onto why she was here. "I'm not...I'm not ready for the other."

"Then let's start simply. With some complicated coffee. Then you can tell me how the hummingbirds like the new feeder." He waved off her attempt to pay, crossed to the counter, and ordered the coffees. A minute later, Garrett returned and placed a large coral stoneware mug and saucer before her. "They said this is your favorite cup."

She had drunk coffee from this mug five times a week for almost three years. Always the same chipped edge on the mug, the slight bubble in the saucer. Holding the mug seemed like meeting an old friend. Especially since it had been many weeks since she'd been in the coffee shop. "I like that they're scarred," she said, and then shrugged. "Like...me."

"Like all of us." He slid into the opposite seat. His coffee sat in a disposable cup, rich, strong and plain. Clearly, he was not a complicated coffee kind of guy. Bridget didn't know why, but she liked that.

He also hadn't said a single disparaging word about her coffee order. In the five years total she had been with Jim, he had never remembered how she took her coffee. Whenever she tried to tell him, he'd waved it off, telling her it was like remembering directions for a space shuttle launch. So she'd ordered coffee regular whenever she was with him and tried to ignore the bitter taste of too-little cream and sugar.

A wave of guilt hit her. Was she comparing her late husband—barely cold in the grave, as Ma would say—to another man?

Garrett raised his cup in her direction. "To new friends."

Were they friends? Did she want to be friends? She tapped her mug against his cup and then took a sip. The notes of caramel, mixed with the sweet heaviness of the cream and the crisp bold coffee, washed over her with familiarity. "I know my coffee order is crazy, and it's probably nuts to want to drink out of the same mug every single time, but this…this one thing I know, in a world that doesn't make much sense right now."

"When my wife died," Garrett said, his gaze dropping to his own cup, "I thought the easiest thing to do was to throw my regular routines out the window. I stopped going to the newsstand where we first met and picked up my paper at a vendor in the train station instead. I stopped shopping at the Shaw's down the road from our house and drove five miles to a Stop and Shop. I stopped eating spaghetti on Friday nights because we always had pasta then, especially during Lent. I avoided our favorite restaurants, the streets we used to walk at night, even the dealership where we bought her car two years earlier. And you know what? It didn't make it any better. I think, in fact, it made it harder. People need routine. Especially when we lose someone we love, we need to cling to things we can count on."

He had an easy voice that slid over her like warm rain. She liked listening to him talk, his words measured and calm and true. "What did you do? I mean, do you still not go to those places?"

"When I realized I felt lost, I started going back. Took baby steps. The supermarket first, then I got an oil change at the dealership. Ordered takeout spaghetti one Friday because I can't cook. The last place I added back in was the newsstand. I still go there every morning to get my paper, and you know, it's kind of nice. Sort of like a visit with Maria—that was my wife—every day." He blew on the surface of his coffee and took a tentative sip.

"You must have loved her very much."

"I did." His face softened, his eyes deepening. "I met her when I was in college, at that newsstand. We were both in this required current affairs class, and we were trying to buy the last *Globe* the guy had. Like most college kids, I had procrastinated, and so had she. It was around ten o'clock at night, and the moon was high, and when I saw her, I thought an angel had just walked by." He shook his head, and a flush showed in his cheeks. "I know that's dorky and mushy, but it was true."

He hadn't asked her about her husband, hadn't moseyed into her personal life. She wondered if Jim had ever talked about her like that, with that light in his eyes and

117

that little smile in his voice. Had he ever called her an angel? Ever gotten dorky and mushy about her?

There'd been a time when she'd felt that way about him. When everything Jim did and said seemed like the most important thing in the world. How he could sweep her off her feet with a compliment or some crazy grand gesture. Somewhere along the way, those feelings had begun to fade, like fabric that had been in the sun too long. If she looked closely, she could still see the pattern that had drawn her to him, but the vibrancy and shine had dulled in the years they'd been married. She'd thought a baby would fix that and then realized, before the primroses even took root, that their problems went far deeper.

"So who got to buy the paper?" Bridget asked.

"She did. But she offered to share, so we went to a diner down the street for a coffee while we looked over the news section. Eight hours later, the sun was coming up again, and we realized we had talked the whole night away. We never stopped talking, either, not until..." His voice trailed off and his gaze dropped to his coffee. "Anyway, I'm not here to talk about that. You said you had a hummingbird problem?"

"I'm not sure it's a problem exactly. And I probably shouldn't have asked you to come all the way to Dorchester. I could have texted the question."

"You could have. But I'm glad you didn't." He laid his hand on the table, inching it close to hers but not touching her. "I've been wondering how you were."

The words flattered her, making heat rise in her

cheeks. A cold wash of guilt brought her back to reality. This wasn't a date; it was coffee and an excuse to talk to someone who understood her a little bit. All under the guise of feeding wildlife. "I'm...uh, worried about my hummingbird. I put out the feeder weeks ago, and he hasn't been by yet."

"It takes them a while to warm up, to trust." Garrett's gaze met hers and held. "They see what they want, and it looks beautiful and amazing, but they've been hurt before and they're leery of getting too close too quick."

Bridget became ten times more aware of his hand, just a breath away. "Are we still talking about hummingbirds?"

"I think that's true for anything with a heartbeat." He took another sip of coffee, and the moment broke, retreating onto safer, neutral ground. "Do you want some food? Because I'm starving and I could eat just about anything. I grabbed a sandwich after work, but it wasn't much. I saw they have some cookies in the case there. Want me to get us a couple?"

"They do have cookies." She lowered her voice and leaned across the table. "I've had them and they're good, but not...great."

"Are there better cookies somewhere?"

"There are." She drew in a deep breath and decided to take a page from Magpie's playbook—jump off a cliff and see where she landed. "Let's get out of here and I'll introduce you to Boston's best chocolate chip cookie."

"That's a tall order. You sure you can fill it?"

"I've been doing it almost all my life." She drained

her coffee, waved goodbye to the café staff, and then led the way outside. Night had fallen while they'd been inside, dropping a dark blanket over the neighborhood. In the distance, the lights of Boston sparkled like a diamond choker, but here, on this cozy Dorchester street, the world seemed small and intimate.

Garrett took her hand as they walked, and Bridget didn't pull away. The touch of another human, warm and unassuming, formed a temporary patch for the chasm in her life. Like his conversation, Garrett's hand in hers was easy, comfortable. Welcome.

"I used to love this street when I was a kid," he said.

"Me too." That was another thing that was nice—their shared knowledge of this neighborhood, of the crazy close world in Dorchester, a suburb much like a family reunion, filled with a few crazy aunts and uncles, decades of common memories, and familiar pockets you could ease yourself into when things got too overwhelming. "I love this street because of the way the trees reach across, as if they're old friends meeting again."

He turned to her and smiled. "Exactly. In the winter, when the trees are covered with snow, it's like driving through a tunnel. I used to pretend my mom was taking me to Santa's village."

She laughed. "And when did you stop pretending that?"

He grinned. "Is there ever a time when we should stop believing in magical things?"

The moon seemed to dim, and the stars disappeared

behind hazy clouds. This wasn't her husband's hand and this wasn't her husband's voice. And the future she had dreamed of, with a baby and the primroses and family dinners, was never going to happen.

"Yes, there is a time," she said quietly, and pulled her hand out of his.

He stopped and stepped in front of her. "I know this whole thing sucks right now. I know it seems like every day is going to be gray and dark and impossible to get past, but you will get through it. You'll find your life again. You'll find yourself again."

"I don't know if I want to," she said. It was the first honest thing she'd said in a while, and voicing those doubts lifted a weight off her shoulders. With her mother and her sisters, she had exhausted herself pretending to be okay. But with Garrett, she didn't feel that same pressure. She could be a mess; she could be a platypus—it didn't matter. What she didn't have to be was a woman pretending to be juggling all the balls of her life.

The words began to tumble out, the truth she kept pushing down bubbling to the surface. "I thought I knew where everything was going, where *we* were going, but it turns out I was wrong. We weren't on the same path at all."

"I don't want to pry, and I won't." He looked down at her, an understanding smile on his face. For a moment, she wanted to lean into his chest, put her cheek against the silky *Starry Night* tie, and lay her burdens on another's shoulders. "Even though you're not going to find a rainbow and a lucky leprechaun on the other side, your days will get brighter and better with time."

"Ah, then you haven't known many Irish grand-mothers," she said, affecting her best brogue. It lightened the mood and distracted her from the mile-high list of things she was avoiding. "If you ask my Gramma, there's a leprechaun under every rainbow, waiting to make your wishes come true."

He grinned. "Then you *do* believe in the power of magic."

"I believe in the power of cookies. And cake." She gestured across the street, half grateful and half disappointed their walk had come to an end. "Welcome to the best damned bakery in the greater Boston area."

A streetlight hung over the shop, its yellow puddle of light bouncing off the white paint and giving the small building an ethereal veil. This was the time Bridget used to like best—being at the bakery on the ends of the day, when the rest of the world was waking up or settling in and she was inside, coaxing batter and dough to life.

"Charmed by Dessert? That's a great name." He glanced at her, brows furrowed in confusion. "But it looks closed, and I don't think either one of us wants to stand out here until tomorrow morning."

"We don't have to." She pulled a key out of her pocket and led him across the dark and empty street. None of the other businesses were open, and the few houses scattered down the street—stubborn holdouts against corporate America—were shuttered and quiet.

"You work here?" Garrett asked.

"I used to, and as of today, I do again. My family owns this bakery. My mom and my sister work here." She opened the door, and they stepped inside, while Gramma's bell tinkled happily over their heads. Bridget flicked on a couple of lights and then slid behind the glass counter. "So, Mr. Andrews, what will it be? Although it is past the end of the day and quantities are low, we still have a few of Boston's best chocolate chip cookies and some of our amazing nutty chocolate brownies and…looks like one slice of heavenly chocolate cake."

"That's a no-brainer. Boston's best chocolate chip cookies. Sounds like something that should be put in the city tour guide."

"It was, once." She cupped a pair of cookies with a square of parchment paper and laid the treat on the counter. Garrett slid onto one of the red vinyl bar stools across from her.

He reached for a cookie and then pulled back. "Wait. Aren't you going to join me?"

"Oh, I rarely eat anything here. If I did, I'd weigh twelve thousand pounds." Just tasting the recipes alone probably added a thousand calories a week. "When I was a kid and had the metabolism of a freight train, I'd eat anything I could get my hands on. But those days are long past."

He held up a cookie and brushed it across her lip. Her gaze locked with his, and the cool air of the bakery heated. An awareness of him kindled in the space between them, drawing her closer. She inhaled the sweet scent of chocolate, the light fragrance of vanilla. "Don't you know what they say?" he said, his voice low and rich. "Cookies eaten after dark have no calories."

That made her laugh. "Are you sure you're a lawyer? Because to me, it sounds like you work for *Cosmopolitan* magazine."

"Share with me, Bridget." He patted the bar stool beside him, the invitation for more than the cookie, for more than this moment. "Keep a lonely widower company."

Temptation whispered through the request, tugged at her. She hesitated, then slipped around to the other side and onto the stool. It creaked a little when she spun to the right, toward Garrett. The dim light darkened his hair, sharpened the edges of his jaw, made him seem almost...rakish. "This is breaking all my rules, you know."

And not just the one about not eating the bakery's treats.

"Breaking the rules once in a while is good for you." He handed her a cookie and took a bite of his own.

She waited to eat hers, watching Garrett's reaction. She'd done that ever since she started working at Charmed by Dessert—watched the customer react to that first bite. If they smiled, it was better than any five-star review.

She knew the instant the flavors hit his palate. Garrett closed his eyes, and then that smile of pleasure started, inching across his face one degree at a time. He swallowed and then opened his eyes and looked at her. "You weren't kidding. Those are even better than the cookies my mom made when I was a kid, and she was a hell of a baker."

Bridget picked off a piece of her cookie and held it up in the soft light. A handful of ingredients, mixed and molded into something for people to enjoy. But to Bridget, this wasn't just a cookie—it was a challenge she'd conquered. "I worked on this recipe for two years. Chocolate chip cookies are such a basic, simple thing, but I wanted mine to be more than that. I tried crispier, chewier, bigger chips, smaller chips, butter versus margarine. A hundred different combinations before I finally ended up with these. Not too crispy, not too chewy. Even distribution of chips and nuts, and a nice base dough that isn't too sweet and has only a hint of vanilla."

He arched a brow. "I had no idea so much went into a cookie. It sounds like a science."

"It's more like a gut feeling. I bake something, taste it, adjust it, bake another batch. I'm not always right. I've had a few bombs—just ask me about the butterscotch brownie debacle of 2010—but most of the time, I can sort of *feel* what's going to make the recipe right." She shook her head and let out a little laugh. "That sounds crazy."

"No. It sounds like your passion." He leaned closer to her, his eyes dark and intent. She caught the masculine scent of his cologne, something that lured her in, then kicked off a surprising warmth deep inside her. "You are one hell of an interesting woman, Bridget O'Bannon."

That gut that told her when to add more vanilla and when to sprinkle in some cinnamon told her Garrett was going to kiss her. All she had to do was stay right where she was.

And complicate her life further.

So she backed up, sliding off the stool and wrapping the uneaten cookies in parchment paper. "It's late. We should get going."

"Yes, we should." He took his cookie and slid it into his pocket. When she locked up the shop after they went out, the scent of disappointment hung heavy in the night air.

FOURTEEN

S leep was a mean, fickle bitch.

At night, Bridget tossed and turned, dozing in fits and starts, then waking up and reaching for Jim. Finding only air and cool sheets. For a moment, she could convince herself he was on a business trip, and then the truth would hit her, so hard and cold that she shivered.

She'd barely slept in weeks, months now, and she was beginning to feel the insomnia weighing on her, quadrupled by the knowledge that she was avoiding reality. A little after three, she got up, paced the kitchen, brewed some tea, and sat down at the counter with the pile of unopened mail.

So many bills. The electric company, the water company, the landscapers, the roofing company that had repaired a leak last winter...they went on and on. The business of living came attached to constant payment. She flipped through the envelopes but didn't open a single one. Instead, she stacked them on the corner of the bar and dropped the dishtowel back over the pile. Out of sight, out of mind.

She opened up Jim's laptop—the firm had delivered it by courier immediately after his death along with a box of things from his desk—but the second Windows let out the start-up chime, Bridget shut the lid. Tomorrow, she vowed. Tomorrow.

Far easier to get dressed and drive to the bakery. She could wrap her mind around tarts and cakes for a while and forget. That was really all Bridget wanted to do—forget that her husband had died, forget that she had to deal with this stuff sooner rather than later, forget that the one sister who had been her best friend hadn't so much as called to see how she was. Just...forget.

As she pulled up to the building, she thought of Garrett with a crazy mix of excitement and guilt. Two weeks ago, they had been inside the shop, and she'd both hoped he would and wouldn't kiss her. Maybe it was loneliness, maybe it was attraction—Bridget didn't know and trying to grasp the truth was like trying to catch a feral cat by the tail. He'd texted her a couple times, thanking her for the cookies and conversation. Asking to see her again. She hadn't answered about seeing him again. Like that could-have-been kiss, she pushed it all to the back of her mind, into that crowded room of Things She Didn't Deal With. Pretty soon, she was going to have to convert that thing into a skyscraper.

The front of the shop was still dark, but a soft glow shone under the swinging door that led to the kitchen.

Bridget pushed on the door, and it yielded inward with a slight sigh.

When she saw Bridget, Nora jerked her head up and swiped at her face. She grabbed the rolling pin beside her and pressed it onto a circle of dough. The rolling pin shivered as Nora pressed, lifted, pivoted, pressed, lifted, in furious circles. "You're here early." Nora's voice sounded thick.

"So are you." Bridget came around to Nora's opposite side. "You okay?"

"Yeah, yeah, just overwhelmed with work." Nora offered up a smile. It lasted only a second before fading. "You came back to work here at just the right time."

Bridget slid on an apron. Nora kept working the piecrust, hard and fast, like she was punishing it for something. "Nora—"

"Why don't you start on the cookies? Mrs. Twomey comes in on Tuesday mornings and buys three dozen chocolate chip for her quilting group, so be sure to make extra."

"Okay."

Nora didn't want to talk. Bridget understood that.

So she measured, mixed, and baked, glancing at Nora from time to time. While Bridget churned out cookies, pie after pie went in and out of the oven—caramel apple, French silk, coconut crème. Nora stacked the preorders in boxes and set the rest in the glass case in the front of the shop.

Bridget sensed that Nora needed some time and space, to kick around whatever was weighing on her shoulders.

A hundred times, Bridget opened her mouth to ask but stopped herself. Hell, she was already doing a damned good job of running from her own problems. Adding in someone else's worries would only add to the pile she kept tossing under the dishtowel.

While the cookies baked, Bridget put on a second pot of coffee and then started pulling ingredients from the pantry. Her mind whispered to her hands, the recipe creating itself one item at a time. Flour, sugar, cocoa powder, and then eggs and milk. She set a pan of water on the stove and assembled the base while the water worked itself into a boil. The dry ingredients first, watching them sprinkle through the sifter like snow. Then the wet, mixing them just until the eggs and milk had blurred into the chocolatey batter. As she stirred in the boiling water, the heat woke the cocoa powder from its dry slumber, scenting the air with chocolate.

The world around Bridget disappeared. The kitchen narrowed to just this batter, just these baking pans. She buttered and floured a quartet of round cake pans and then divided the batter, watching the cocoa river settle into its new home.

The cakes baked and cooled while Bridget finished the cookie orders and started on some muffins. A little after seven, a delivery truck came to the back door and dropped off stacked plastic baskets of warm, golden loaves. The breads had been Abby's department, and every time Bridget saw a loaf of sourdough or a glistening knot of challah, she thought of her sister.

"After Abby left, we started buying the bread from another bakery, even though it costs a lot more," Nora said, her voice soft and sad as she slid the breads into place in the front case. "Ma said we were just too busy to make it ourselves without her, but I think she missed Abby and couldn't bear to replace her."

Bridget thought of the space at the table, reserved for a father who had been dead for decades. "I don't know about that. It's like she's been excised from the family."

"Not as much as you think," Nora said. "Ma might not always handle things the most delicately, but she's pretty hurt by Abby leaving."

Bridget scoffed. "Then maybe she should have been more understanding when Abby was here."

"Understanding? About what?"

Don't tell anyone. Promise me.

The timer buzzed, and Bridget took the excuse to duck back into the kitchen to take cookies out of the oven and then start on the frosting for the cake. The weight of her promise seemed heavier today. Maybe it was being back in the bakery, with that sense of a piece missing every time she turned around. Abby should be beside them, laughing and creating. All these years, Bridget had protected her sister's secret, but now she wasn't sure why.

Nora turned on the radio, tuning to an oldies station— *when had the music of the '90s become oldies?*—the notes and lyrics filling the silence of the kitchen. The radio was a forbidden item during the normal workday because their mother thought it made the bakery sound cheap, but whenever they'd had a chance, the girls had powered up some tunes to help alleviate the daily tedium. Toni Braxton yielded to a familiar Latin beat. A memory wove between the girls with the notes.

Bridget grinned at Nora. Nora threw back her head and laughed. The song pulsed, tempting them to move. "Still remember how to do it?"

Nora laughed again. "I don't know."

"Come on, let's try." And there, in the middle of the flour and sugar and warm ovens, the two sisters stood hip to hip while "La Macarena" played in the background. By the time the second verse started, laughter rang in the kitchen, and the two of them gave up on any semblance of the dance. Their hands moved in sync, shoulders, waist, hips, hop, do it again.

"Oh my God. How long has it been since we did that?" Nora asked when the song came to an end and a commercial for Bernie & Phyl's Furniture played, with the same familiar shtick between the elderly owners, their Boston accents thick as they touted the decades' old slogan of quality, comfort, and price.

"Too long." Bridget drew Nora into a hug, and for the first time in a long while, she could feel the bond she'd had with her sister begin to knit back together. The threads were still loose, tenuous, but there.

"We should probably get back to work." Nora's eyes shimmered, and she gave Bridget a watery smile. "Because I think we make much better bakers than we do dancers."

"I don't know. For a while there, we thought we could be the next New Kids on the Block."

Nora chuckled. "Yeah, too bad those Wahlbergs beat the O'Bannons to fame and fortune."

"Well, if we ever get the old group back together again..."

Nora sobered, and the moment of lightness faded. "If we ever do."

Bridget loaded dishes into the dishwasher and set it to run. "Do you talk to her at all?"

Neither of them had to say Abby's name. She was always there, at the back of their minds, a ghost haunting their conversations. "I text once in a while. Sometimes she texts back. Sometimes she doesn't."

"I keep expecting to see her, whipping up a dozen loaves of sourdough or a new flavor of bagel."

Nora nodded. The radio shifted into a news report, and Nora turned to fill tart shells with lemon cream. "Do you know why she left? Was it just over the fight at the wedding?"

"There's a lot more to it, Nora. A lot more." Bridget started the mixer, adding in softened lumps of butter, cream cheese, peanut butter. She slowed the revolutions and added sifted confectioners' sugar, alternating it with tablespoons of heavy cream until the buttercream frosting swirled in the bowl, thick and rich.

As Whitney Houston sang a ballad in the background, Bridget stacked the round chocolate cakes, sandwiching them with the peanut butter frosting. The final coating of buttercream skimmed across the cake, smoothing as she spun the cake stand and ran a long flat knife along the sides. She stored the cake in the freezer while she whipped up a quick chocolate ganache. Then after the cream and chocolate sauce cooled, she retrieved the cold cake and drizzled the ganache over the peanut butter frosting. Dark chocolate rivulets ran down the sides of the cake and puddled on the stand. Bridget mounded a handful of crushed peanut butter candies on top and then stepped back.

"Wow. That's *definitely* not a football." Nora let out a low whistle. "That looks so good. Can we have it for lunch?"

Bridget laughed. "If it doesn't sell first."

"If we store it back here, no one will know it exists, except for us." Nora scooped up a dollop of leftover peanut butter buttercream. "Oh my God. That must be what heaven tastes like."

Nora's praise washed over Bridget. In the three years since she'd left the bakery, Bridget hadn't baked anything more complicated than a batch of brownies. Jim hadn't liked sweets much, and it seemed senseless to bake for herself.

But more than that, in those years apart, being in the kitchen and baking the things she used to make at Charmed by Dessert hurt her heart. Every cup of flour and cracked egg reminded her of her sisters, of the fight they'd had at the wedding, the silent distance between them.

"You didn't lose your touch after all," Nora said.

Bridget had worried about returning to the bakery. Worried that it wouldn't be the same, that she wouldn't feel welcome or comfortable. But then she'd settled in, her hands in the flour, her mind in the recipes, and as the cake came together, she'd begun to feel like she'd . . .

Come home.

"I guess I just needed to be back here," she said.

Nora held Bridget's gaze for a moment, the two of them with twin green eyes and lopsided smiles. Nora's smile crooked. "Yeah, Bridge, you did. And I needed you back just as much."

The kitchen door swung open, ending the moment. Ma walked in, shedding her coat and purse as she did. It was as if the air in the room had been changed, cooled. Ma stopped, gave the cake in Bridget's hands an assessing glance. It was like standing in front of the principal, being lectured for a dress code violation.

After a moment, Ma nodded. "Glad to see you haven't completely forgotten how to bake."

"What do you mean? This was all Duncan Hines, Ma." Bridget tossed Nora a grin and then brought the cake out front and settled it in the display case before returning to help her sister with the tarts.

Ma bustled around the kitchen, tweaking the flute of a piecrust, giving the cookies in the oven a quick check, restacking a tower of brownies on a display plate. She parked her hands on her hips and took a slow spin around the room. "You haven't started on the order for the Chandler birthday party yet."

Nora blew a wisp of hair out of her face. "That party isn't until Saturday. We have time."

"Better to be prepared than caught unaware." Ma flipped through the order sheets. "And there's the rehearsal dinner cake for the Talbots, the order for the church for Sunday services—"

"Ma, how about a, 'great job, girls. You got in early and we're ready to go a half hour before we open'?" Bridget said.

Nora put a hand on Bridget's arm. "It's fine."

It wasn't, but Bridget let the argument go, just as she had a thousand times before. They could have baked enough to feed the entire population of India and their mother still would have found something to complain about.

"I guess *I'll* start on that cake for the Chandlers," Ma said. She paused beside Bridget and put a hand on her daughter's cheek. "Goodness, you look like you haven't slept in a month. A little concealer will do wonders for your eyes. I have some in my purse. Why don't I get it for you?"

"I'm fine, Ma."

"Well, it's your face, and I suppose you are working in the back all day. But if it were me...I'm just saying..." Ma arched a brow and pursed her lips.

That sense of failing, of not being enough, simmered inside Bridget. Her cell phone rang, the vibration making it dance across the stainless steel counter. Bridget scooped up the excuse to avoid another Mom Makeover and headed outside to the alley behind the shop. "Hello?"

"Mrs. Masterson?" a woman asked, her voice soft and smooth, like jazz music. "This is Chase Bank. We have been trying to reach your husband for two days but he hasn't returned our calls, so we contacted you."

Jim's cell phone was sitting beside the pile of bills at home, the battery drained, the screen black. She had no doubt a few of the blinking red lights on the answering machine would be attached to this woman's voice.

"He..." Bridget drew in a breath and expelled it with the words, "passed away."

"Oh. *Oh.* Uh, I'm sorry. I'm so sorry." The woman on the other end stuttered through some more condolences and cleared her throat. "Well, we were calling because your account is overdrawn, and the monthly mortgage payment with Chase is scheduled to be withdrawn today—"

"Wait. Overdrawn?" Impossible. They'd never bounced a check. Or...

At least that's what she believed. Jim could have bounced checks every other day and Bridget wouldn't have known. She had gone along, blindly and blithely, trusting the man who'd put a ring on her finger.

The same husband who had sworn they had adequate life insurance. The same one who promised to work harder at their marriage. The same one who had walked out and—

Died. Breaking all his promises in a single moment.

She didn't want to believe that he had done any of this on purpose. That the man who had whispered *I love you* in their bed at night would have left his wife with an empty bank account and no backup in case the worst happened. But he had, and she couldn't quite bring that fuzzy, faded image she had of her marriage together with the piles of bills and the call from the bank.

"If you could add funds before four o'clock today," the woman went on, relentless, determined, "the payment will be covered."

"How overdrawn am I?" And how had that happened? Jim's last check had been direct-deposited. How could it be gone already?

"Two hundred and seventy-two dollars. Your overdraft protection covered the first five hundred, but the rest is in the negative. Add in the mortgage payment, and you'll need to deposit"—a pause—"two thousand one hundred seventeen dollars and ninety-three cents."

Two grand? Just to get caught up? Bridget thanked the woman, mumbled something about being by later—assuming some genie showed up to grant her wish of a few grand in cash—and hung up the phone.

When Bridget was seven, she'd gotten swept into a rip tide at Wollaston Beach. Two strangers had run in and rescued her, but even now, more than twenty years later, she could feel the suffocating weight of the water. How the waves shoved her into the sandy bottom, stole her breath, closed around her.

All of this, the bills, the bank, the life insurance, was another rip tide pulling her farther and farther out to sea. There were no strangers coming to rescue her. No husband to save the day.

Oh God. What was she going to do? How was she going to pay the bills?

Bridget's knees buckled. Her chest tightened. She slid down the concrete wall, wrapped her arms around her knees, and laid her head on top. She tried to draw in deep breaths, but the fist in her chest only tightened.

The back door opened, and her mother stepped outside. "For goodness' sake, Bridget, get up. It's only nine in the morning. You can't possibly be too tired already."

She didn't need this. Not now. "That isn't it at all, Ma. Just leave me alone." She got to her feet and started to reach past her mother to open the door when Colleen put a hand on her arm.

"What is it then?"

Bridget sighed. "Do you really want to know? Or do you want to tell me about the bags under my eyes or how I should have ironed my jeans or chosen a different sweater or eaten oatmeal instead of Rice Krispies today? Because honestly, I can't handle that. I can't handle anything right now."

"You can handle far more than you know. You're an O'Bannon." Her mother's stern face punctuated the sentence. She crossed her arms over her chest, staring up at her daughter. "Now, tell me what is going on."

Bridget stood there a moment, silent, stubborn. But the waves kept crushing her and her lungs were screaming for air, and she couldn't find her way back to the surface. She opened her mouth, drawing in a breath, and before she could stop them, the words started pouring out of her.

"We were in financial trouble, and Jim never told me. He handled all the bills and told me we were fine." She held up her cell. "I just got off the phone with the bank. My account is overdrawn, and the mortgage payment comes out in the morning. I don't have enough to pay it, and honestly I haven't looked at a single bill, so I don't know how much I need or where I'm going to get it. All I know is I don't have enough."

"But the life insurance—"

"Was canceled six months ago."

Her mother nodded, absorbing the information. No emotion flickered on her face, only the stoic practicality that had gotten her through the last sixty years of her life. "Here is what you are going to do. You will take an advance on your paycheck from here and drive over to the bank on your lunch hour and cover the bills. Then, when you get home, you will open those envelopes and see what you are dealing with. This is no time to keep your head buried in the sand, Bridget."

"I can't—"

"You can, and you will. I'll draw up the check myself. Now, get back inside and finish making the cake for the Chandlers."

"And just like that, everything's fixed?" Bridget shook her head.

"Of course not." Her mother's green eyes softened, and her gaze blurred. It was as close to emotional as Colleen got. "Some things can never be fixed. All we can do is bandage them up and move on."

"Is that what you're doing with Abby?"

The question hung in the air while traffic went by outside and a garbage truck sounded a steady *beep-beep*. Around them, life moved forward at the frantic pace of a city that rarely paused.

Before her mother turned on her heel and went back inside, she said, "Like I said, not everything can be fixed."

FIFTEEN

There were days when Colleen wished she had taken up smoking. Then she would have had an excuse to go outside, escape the bakery, and grab a few moments alone, away from the tension that hung in the air. Instead, she hefted a trash bag that was only half full and announced to Nora that she was taking it out back.

As she lifted the lid to the Dumpster, she thought of Abby. Just a few weeks ago, her fourth daughter had stood here, longing and apology in her voice, and Colleen had done what she always did—

Drove her away again.

Colleen threw in the bag, closed the lid again. All her life, she'd thought she was a good mother. Prided herself, actually, on raising four girls single-handedly while running a business. But two of her daughters had stopped talking to her for years, one had married a man who, well, none of them had ever completely warmed to.

Now, instead of enjoying these years with her daughters, the way Erma Waterstone did, going on those silly vacations to every corner of the world with her girls, Colleen felt like the connections between her and her daughters were fraying more by the day.

And she had no idea what to do about that, except what she'd always done. Keep her head down and keep on working. As she turned to go back inside, Nora emerged from the bakery.

"Hey, Ma. What are you doing out here?"

"Taking out the trash." She brushed her hands together. She could see concern in Nora's eyes, the worry that maybe her mother's frequent trips out back were about something other than empty trash cans. "Well, I should get back to work."

"I forgot to tell you that when the bread delivery came, they mentioned they were low on croissants but promised to get us extra tomorrow."

"Good. Those sell well." She brushed past Nora.

"Not as well as Abby's used to."

Colleen hesitated, her hand on the door handle. "No, not as well."

"Why don't you call her? I doubt she likes that job at the mall, and she was the best bread baker I've ever met. It'd be nice to have her working here again."

Colleen's hand tightened on the metal handle. "Abigail made her choices."

"So, is that it? One of us disappoints you or takes some time away from the family and they're dead to you?" Nora closed the distance between them. "Bridget walked away, too, but now she's back. How can you forgive one of us and not the other?"

"It's not about forgiveness. Abigail...she wasn't happy here."

"Yeah, she was, Ma." Nora's gaze narrowed. A moment later, light dawned in her eyes. "You think she doesn't want to be here, and you're afraid to ask her. Because she might say no."

Colleen knew Abby would say no. Too much time had passed, too many hurts.

And the worst one of all? Colleen throwing her own daughter out of the house after the scene at Bridget's wedding and telling her she wasn't welcome there again. That she was no longer a daughter of Colleen's.

Abby's visit here the other day had been an olive branch, but Colleen knew the damage had been done. And knew how her daughter really felt about her.

Dad was the one who loved me, Ma. Not you. Why didn't you love me like he did? I don't need you. I don't need someone who treats me like an outsider in my own goddamned family.

Then Colleen had said those awful things, and Abby had left. The door between them shut firm.

"We have just the right amount of help right now." Colleen tugged open the door. "Remind the bread company to send us extra rolls. I promised Mrs. Williams we would have them for her family dinner this weekend."

Then she went back inside and back to work.

The cake sold before lunch to a woman hosting an office party that afternoon. Nora looked like she might cry as the boxed dessert left the building. While her sister was at lunch, Bridget whipped up two more, storing one in the freezer with a giant note that said nora: eat me.

Later, Bridget stood in the tiny office at the back of the bakery while her mother hand-wrote a check, adding "Advance on Wages" to the memo line. The whole experience took fifteen years off her life and reduced her to a mumbling, resentful yet grateful high schooler. She hated herself for needing the money, hated being put in the position of depending on her mother to save her ass.

"You really should consider clipping coupons," Ma said. "And going to thrift stores. Why, when you girls were little, I was always at the Goodwill. I bought groceries in bulk and cooked ahead for a month…"

The interest rate on a loan from her mother was unlimited advice on how to run her life. So Bridget listened and nodded and promised to buy the Sunday paper for the coupons. Then she grabbed the check and zipped out to make the deposit.

When she got back, she buried herself in work for the rest of the day. Far better to bake than think about how she was thirty years old and still taking a handout from her mother.

Garrett texted twice more, but Bridget didn't reply. They were friendly, nonflirty texts, and while it was nice to have a man interested, this whole new world of widowhood left her unsure how to proceed. So she kept on avoiding and procrastinating. At this rate, she was going to be a gold medalist in those sports.

She and Nora worked side by side the rest of the day, their familiar rhythm of weaving in and out of each other as they created cakes, cookies, pies, tarts, a well-choreographed dance. Their mother stayed mostly out front, working the register and taking the phone orders. During an afternoon lull, Bridget sat down with a cup of coffee and her phone.

Magpie had texted a couple times, from whatever remote location she was at today. **Heard you're back at the old grindstone. How many times did Ma redo your work?**

There was an old bet between the girls—whoever had been ordered to do the most redos at work that day from their perfectionist mother had to do the last batch of dirty dishes. Magpie, being the youngest, lost that bet the most often, until she went off to college, got a degree in journalism, and started traveling the world as a freelancer.

Only twice, Bridget replied. **I think that's some kind of record.**

Hold on while I call Guinness. A pause, then: **How's GrumpyFace Nora?**

Okay. A little distant. Seems to have something on her mind.

Bridget glanced over at her sister, who was turned toward the wall with her phone, immersed in a low-volume argument with someone. From the snatches of conversation Bridget heard, it sounded like Nora was arguing with Ben, her husband, about picking up the kids.

Eat something decadent today, Magpie texted back. And do something unexpected. Life is better when you don't always play by the rules. Ciao!

The last made Bridget think of Garrett, of the moment in the bakery. She scrolled back through his texts, debated replying, and then the oven timer dinged and she put her phone away instead. The rest of the day passed in a blur of dishes and desserts, until the last order went out the door and the three of them sighed with relief.

As she was locking up the bakery at the end of the day, Ma turned to Bridget. Her face was stern, her eyes hard with admonishment. "Go home and look at those bills, Bridget. Procrastinating only makes things worse. When your father died—"

"You were right back at work. I know, Ma."

"I had children depending on me. I couldn't afford to keep my eyes closed to reality. In those days, if people had life insurance, it wasn't much. Your dad had a policy for a few hundred dollars. I had a mortgage and rent and you girls, and if you think I wasn't worried or scared, you're wrong."

"You never showed it." None of them had ever seen their mother cry or break down or admit she was overwhelmed. Colleen O'Bannon wore unflappable like it was a perfume.

Bridget thought of all the nights the sisters had huddled together in Bridget's bed, alone and scared and whispering memories of their father. They questioned the priest's promises that Dad was watching over them and that one day they'd see him again. To four girls under ten, heaven seemed like an impossible, unreachable place.

"You girls were young," her mother said. "What would have happened if I broke down?"

"We would have known you cared," Bridget said. *That we weren't alone. That it was okay to fall apart once in a while. That we didn't always have to put on the "I'm just fine" face and keep chugging forward.* "That Dad dying broke your heart as much as it did ours."

Her mother pursed her lips. "Grieving is best done in private."

Bridget sighed. Her mother was an impenetrable wall. Why did she even bother trying to carve out a chink? Bridget grabbed the last leftover chocolate peanut butter cake and closed it in a box. "I gotta go."

"Look at those bills," her mother called behind her. "You'll be glad you did."

Bridget got in her car, started the engine, and turned left, toward home. Toward bills and voice mails and questions. That rip tide was still pulling at Bridget, trying to drag her away from the safety of shore. Her throat tightened, and every breath seemed harder to draw.

What she needed, more than a drink, more than a check, was that steady voice of calm and reason that had eased her nerves before her first day of school and the time she fell off her bike and when a hurricane blew through Massachusetts. Her father, holding her tight and whispering in her ear.

You are strong, Bridget. And when you don't feel strong, rely on your sisters.

The bills could wait.

A half mile down the road, Bridget came to a stoplight, and instead of staying in the middle lane to go straight, she darted into the left lane, making a squealing U-turn and earning a honking ragefest from the drivers behind her.

She drove through Dorchester, past the brick buildings that cemented Codman Square, and down Norfolk to the edge of Mattapan. Just two miles from the center of Dorchester, the town had separated itself from its neighbor in the nineteenth century. The ads for jerk chicken and sushi and chili dogs spoke for the ethnic melting pot that made up quirky, unique Mattapan. The town was as colorful as its inhabitants, bright yellow restaurants nestled beside orange apartment buildings and blue gas stations.

Bridget turned onto a small side street and wrangled her way into a parallel parking space. On the corner sat a three-story brick building, a converted mill with palladium windows and a silent towering smokestack.

She debated for a long time, keys in hand, then finally grabbed the box, got out of the car and ducked into the building, past a woman walking out with a Pomeranian dressed in a purple raincoat. The stairwell smelled faintly of Indian food and burnt popcorn. As she emerged on the third floor, she heard the muffled sounds of an argument.

Bridget tightened her grip on her keys, even though she was alone in the hall. At the door for 3-B, she pressed the doorbell and waited. The low sound of the TV went mute, followed by the soft patter of footsteps on the wooden floor, the snicking of a trio of locks unlatched, and then the door opened.

Abby stood on the other side wearing a pair of dark blue fleece sweatpants, a BU sweatshirt, and a pair of Mickey Mouse socks. Her hair was shorter now, colored a black so dark that it shimmered in the light. Abby's eyes widened, and her jaw dropped. "Bridge."

"Hey, Abby." That was all Bridget had. She'd come here with no plan, no agenda. And as the voices down the hall rose in volume, becoming shouts, Bridget began to wonder why she'd come here at all.

"Sorry. The Joliettes are fighting again," Abby said. "It'll be over faster than it started, and then they'll be having crazy, loud makeup sex."

"Oh." Bridget wasn't sure what to say to that.

The discomfort stretched between them, with neither saying a word. The Joliettes went on arguing, but all Bridget could catch were snatches of the conversation. *You never tell me . . . I can't talk to you . . . why is the chicken burned?* The quintessential American love story—after the vows were exchanged.

"You . . . uh, want to come in?" Abby said finally.

"I just came by for a second. To see how you're doing."

"You drove through Boston, during rush hour, to stop by for a second?"

Bridget shrugged. "I didn't have anything else to do."

Abby laughed. "Well, at least you haven't changed. As brutally honest as ever."

Three years of harsh words, still clutched in a tight fist between them. She could turn around and leave, go back the way she came. Her shoes, flat, easy Keds broken in by years of wear, half turned toward the stairwell.

She shifted the box in her hands. "I...I brought cake."

"From the bakery?" Abby licked her lips and drew in a breath. The scent of chocolate and peanut butter danced on the air, a note above the Indian food cooking down the hall. "I haven't had cake from there in...forever."

"I know." Bridget held the white cardboard box between them like a peace offering. And maybe it was—dessert to smooth this rubble-filled path.

"May I?" When Bridget nodded, Abby leaned forward, untied the red string, and peeled back the white lid. She rose on her toes and peered into the box. "Oh my God, that looks amazing. Did you bake it?"

"Yeah." Bridget let out a long sigh. Yes, she'd returned to the bakery, even though she'd vowed a hundred times never to go back to work there. *They'll hurt you, babe,* Jim had said.

But in the end, Jim had been the one to hurt her. By dying too soon and spending too much. "Turns out Jim didn't have any life insurance, and I...don't have any money, so I went back to work. I even had to borrow from Ma."

Abby grimaced. "Oh man. Did that make you feel like you were seventeen again?"

"Yep. Complete with the lectures." Bridget rolled her eyes. "God, I half expected her to give me a curfew."

Abby laughed. The commonality of dealing with Ma narrowed the gap between them by a millimeter. Then Abby sobered and took a step back. "Well, thank you. For the cake, and for coming by."

The door was going to shut. Bridget's Keds still pointed toward the exit, to the land of Avoidance and Procrastination she'd been in for so long. When had she become this woman afraid of confrontation? Who walked away and acquiesced?

She'd done it for so long now that she couldn't seem to find another way. It seemed easier to sidestep the issues than to tackle them, a skill she'd perfected in her marriage. Keep going forward, stuffing the feelings and fears into some dark place, because leaving them in the light meant dealing with them. Only when her mother infuriated her did some of the old Bridget arise—the woman who had been strong and confident and opinionated. But now she stood in Abby's hall, forcing herself to stand in place instead of bolting for the exit.

Abby bit her upper lip, and her green eyes glistened. Was she feeling the same as Bridget? Unsure if she should take the risk to reach out? Afraid of being hurt? Rejected?

"Bridge..." Abby's voice trailed off, and a pained look filled her face. In that moment, Bridget could see the younger sister who had crawled into her bed on a stormy night, clutching her favorite blanket. Abby had curled up on Bridget's pillow and listened to Bridget make up stories about pirates and princesses and mermaids until the storm passed and the skies calmed.

Hadn't enough time gone by? Was she really going to hold this grudge for almost half a decade, like her mother had with Aunt Mary? Or let the storm play out until they finally got to the other side of calm?

"You came but you didn't stay," Bridget blurted out, the hurt rolling through her syllables. "I thought of all days, you'd...you'd be there for me."

Abby dipped her head, and a black wing of hair swung in front of her eyes. "Yeah. About that...I'm sorry. I should have been. It was just...with everyone there, I chickened out and I didn't want to cause a scene at the funeral. So I left, and I meant to come by and see you and talk to you, but I was afraid..."

"Afraid I wouldn't open the door."

Abby nodded. Bridget nodded too. She knew that fear. It was what had kept her from going to apartment 3-B for three years.

"It doesn't matter anymore, Abs, and frankly, I couldn't care less who said what or why or when." Three years apart, and she realized she truly didn't care why she and Abby had stopped talking. She didn't care about Abby's lifestyle—hell, she'd never cared about that. What Abby had said at the wedding still stung, but Jim was gone, and maybe none of that mattered.

Either way, they were a family. Families fought, families hurt each other, but families also made up, and it was high time Bridget did that with Abby.

She took a step closer to her sister. "If I've learned any-thing these last few months, Abby, it's that life is short, and

I don't give a shit about some argument we had. I just..."
Bridget drew in a breath and thought of those nights after
Dad died when she and Abby had whispered across the
small divide between their beds, of that nervous opening
night of the school play when Abby had told Bridget a silly
joke, of all the times Abby had been there, and all the
times Abby hadn't and Bridget had wished she was. "I miss
my sister."

"Oh, Bridge, I miss you too." Abby's eyes flooded but
still held that wary edge, like a stray afraid of being abandoned again. "But you know, you have two spare sisters.
You don't need me."

"I need all three of you. But especially you. We were so
close, Abs. Best friends. I...I don't know what to do without you in my life. I need you to be there to yell at me or
hug me, or tell me to stop watching so much Netflix."

Abby parked her fists on her hips and feigned a glare.
"Stop watching so much Netflix."

Bridget laughed, and her feet shifted toward the door,
toward her sister. "Remember when Charlie Phillips broke
up with me? You came home and found me sitting on the
floor of our room, eating directly out of a tub of—"

"Breyer's Rocky Road," Abby said.

"I'd eaten probably half of it, sobbing all over my
spoon. You got down, took the spoon away, and—"

"Told you to stop hogging all the ice cream because
chances were one of us was gonna have a bad day and need
it." Abby shook her head, a smile on her lips. "I forgot all
about that until you mentioned it."

Bridget shrugged and gave Abby a crooked smile. "Sometimes we just need a sister to show up at the right time."

Abby's smile trembled. "Yeah, sometimes we do."

The Joliettes had stopped screaming. Silence for a moment, then the slam of a door. Abby glanced across the hall and motioned behind her. "Uh...unless you want to hear Mr. Joliette telling Mrs. Joliette what he wants to do to her in graphic Italian, you should come in. Jessie's here, and I'd like you to meet her."

This wasn't just Abby opening the door and letting Bridget into her apartment; it was her letting her sister into her life, into the world she had kept secret from everyone else. The significance wasn't lost on Bridget. "I'd like that."

Abby led Bridget into the apartment, glancing back every few seconds as if to make sure she was still following. The third-floor apartment had two-story ceilings, hardwood floors, and two palladium windows that started at the molding and stretched up ten feet. There was a window seat across from the white granite kitchen and a bright spray of red tulips on the counter. The entire space was light and bright, minimalist yet welcoming.

A blonde sat on one of the bar stools, her long hair swung across her face like a curtain while she read the paper. She looked up at Bridget's entrance and smiled. She had a wide smile, with a slight gap between her front teeth. Her gaze flicked to Abby's, and the look in her eyes softened, the smile brightened, before she turned her attention back and put out a hand. "You must be Bridget."

"And you must be Jessie." Bridget extended her right hand, balancing the box in the other. The two other women exchanged another glance, and in that second, Bridget saw one thing—

Love.

It was the way their shoulders relaxed, their smiles eased, their eyes held. Something private and deep charged the air between them, and for a moment, Bridget was jealous. Had anyone ever looked at her like that?

She brushed off the thought. Her marriage to Jim may not have been lovey-dovey, and certainly hadn't been perfect, but it had been happy for a time.

A whisper started in the back of her mind. *If he loved you and was so happy, then why didn't you know about the life insurance? The bank balance? If you loved each other and were so happy, why were you thinking of—*

No. Jim was dead. Thinking about those things led nowhere good.

"So, what do you do for work, Jessie?" The most inane question ever, but it silenced those whispers.

"I'm a literature professor at Brown," she said. "Specifically literature of the eighteenth century."

Bridget thought of the last book she'd read. Somehow, admitting she'd gotten swept up in the latest Stephen King novel didn't sound so impressive. "Sounds like a great job. I work part-time for the *Globe*. I have a column on baking that runs every Sunday."

"I've seen it." Jessie nodded toward Abby. "Abby's shown me. She's quite proud of you."

"Really?"

Abby shrugged. "Yeah."

That surprised Bridget. She'd often wondered if, in those years when Abby had cut them off, she'd also cut off her family in her heart and mind. She turned to her sister. "And I hear you're doing great things at Williams-Sonoma."

"It's sales. Not rocket science."

"You added a Cooking with Abby workshop every weekend. I saw it listed in the paper. I thought of going, but…"

"You should have," Abby said.

"Yeah," Bridget said softly. "I should have."

A moment of silence extended between them, built on a tenuous, fragile moment. Jessie glanced at Bridget and Abby and then got to her feet. "Well, I don't know about you guys, but I'm dying to try some of this cake. It looks amazing."

"If Bridget baked it, I guarantee it's going to be the best cake you've ever eaten." Abby pulled a knife out of one of the drawers and grabbed three dessert plates. She sliced up the cake, and the three of them sat around the bar and dug in.

Bridget watched her sister eat that first bite. Anticipating. Hoping.

Abby's eyes closed, and she let out a soft moan. "Oh my God, this is so good," she said. "You have no idea how much I miss working there and being your taste tester."

Jessie took her own first bite, and the reaction mirrored

Abby's. Her brows arched in surprise. "Wow. You weren't kidding about it being the best cake I've ever eaten. I could literally eat just this for the rest of my life."

Abby laughed. "Try working at the bakery. It was so tempting to just stuff our faces every day."

Bridget speared a bite of cake with her fork. It wasn't perfect—she'd lost a little of her touch and would need to tweak the moistness of the batter—but it was damned good, if she did say so herself. "Why don't you come back? Ma's buying the bread from somewhere else, and I know she's not making much, if any, profit off of it."

"Bridge, it's not as easy as just walking back in, and you know it. I threw your wedding cake across the room and told Ma off in front of the entire family. Not to mention, I called you a bitch and told you that you were marrying a cheating asshole. I think I burned that bridge." Abby shook her head. "No, I *nuked* it."

Jessie glanced at Abby. Some unspoken communication whispered between them. Jessie nodded and picked up her plate. "I'm going to eat this out on the balcony. It's such a gorgeous day."

When Jessie had gone outside, Bridget pushed her plate away. She'd lost the desire for the cake. "She's nice."

A slow smile curved across Abby's face, and her gaze strayed to Jessie, sitting in one of the wrought-iron chairs, her knees drawn up to her chest. "She's incredible. She dragged me back from the edge when I was . . . in a really bad spot."

"I'm glad." Bridget steepled her hands and studied

the gold flecks in the white granite. They sparkled and danced in the glow from the overhead lights, almost like they were winking at her. "You and I really fucked things up, didn't we?"

"No, I did. I never should have gone off like that."

"I never should have threatened to tell everyone about you. I got so mad when you said that about Jim, and I just...lost it."

That whispering voice in her head wondered if Abby had been right. If Jim had loosened the reins on the budget and checkbook, Bridget would have seen this financial sinkhole coming. She could have prepared. Spent less. Saved more.

Don't believe them, Jim had said a thousand times. *They're just jealous of what we have. How you and I can be an island unto ourselves.*

Now Bridget was stranded on that island, and the only lifeboat she could take was attached to her mother. In her head, she cursed Jim for not telling her, for leaving her in the dark. But the truth was, she'd been in the dark about Jim and her marriage for a long time before he died.

"I think you're brave, Abby," Bridget said. "You're living your life, true to who you are. Sometimes I wonder if I truly did that. Ever."

"But I am chicken, Bridget," Abby said. "I haven't told anyone in the family about Jessie. In fact, we're supposed to get married in a couple months. Now she's put it all on hold until I tell my family about her."

"You're getting *married?*"

159

Abby held up her left hand. A square-cut diamond surrounded by tiny rubies sparkled back. "Yup."

Bridget leaned over and drew Abby into a hug. Her sister smelled of orange blossoms and almonds, the same shampoo she had used for as long as Bridget could remember. It made her think of that last time, when Abby had been crying and Bridget had hugged her, and how much she had missed that scent over the years. "I'm so happy for you."

"Are you really?"

Bridget drew back. Abby's green eyes swam, and Bridget's heart broke for all the hurts they had piled onto each other, all the words they hadn't said, all the years they had missed. "I saw how you looked at her when I came in. And how she looked at you." A tiny bit of envy ran through her, and for the hundredth time in the months since Jim died, she wondered if she'd convinced herself of a reality that had never quite existed. She'd been too busy looking at the primroses to notice the weeds right in front of her. "You know, I thought I knew everything when I got married. I thought I could tell other people about love and forever and finding the right person. But not once in my married life did Jim ever look at me like that, and I don't think I ever looked at him that way either."

Abby, who had always been the tough one—the one who fell down, skinned her knee, and got back up without shedding a tear—seemed to melt a little every time she glanced at her fiancée. "I love her, Bridge. I really do. I can't imagine my life without her."

Bridget tried to reach back, to remember when she had felt that way about Jim. When living without him had been unthinkable. Already, that moment when she'd said *I do* seemed a hundred years ago, the memory just out of reach, floating away like a balloon caught in the breeze. "Then you should marry her."

"I can't. She won't marry me. Not until I introduce her to Ma. Jessie thinks"—Abby's gaze strayed to the patio again—"that I'm ashamed of her. But I'm not. I'm ashamed…of them."

Of the family. Of how they would react. How all that old school Catholic upbringing had created a bias against anyone who stepped outside the prescribed lines of the church. Bridget had heard it more than once. "They're the ones losing out, Abby."

Abby's smile wavered. "I don't think they know that."

"You can't keep this secret forever." All those secrets had done was divide the sisters. With Abby exiled and Magpie off to who-knew-where, the bakery echoed and the family dinners had lost a lot of their luster.

"Ah, but keeping secrets is what we do best in this family, Bridge," Abby said. Her gaze went to the window, to some place far beyond the sunny view. "Just ask Ma."

The hairs on the back of Bridget's neck rose. She thought of the whispers of aunts at holiday dinners, conversations that had cut off whenever any of the girls entered the room. All her life, there'd been this feeling…a sense, really, that there was a chapter missing in the O'Bannon family book, like the "missing" chapters of the

Bible that only Catholics read because at some point Martin Luther had decided they shouldn't be part of the story. "What do you mean? Do you know something I don't?"

Abby shook her head, slid off the bar stool, and loaded the plates into the sink. "There are things in this family that no one ever talks about," she said. "Things that would change everything if people knew. Things that aren't mine to share."

SIXTEEN

The supermarket was bright and loud and happy for a Sunday morning. Twin toddlers dashed past Bridget, trailed by a weary mother with bloodshot eyes and a stained T-shirt. Their mother caught them, one in each arm, and then hoisted the boys into the basket of the cart. As she did, she gave Bridget a smile, the kind that said, *Kids, you know what I mean?* as if everyone at the Stop and Shop was in this motherhood club.

Yeah, Bridget didn't know and now probably never would. She watched the mom head over to the citrus fruits and wondered if everything would be different today if she'd had a baby. Would Jim have been home more? Traveling less? Would the stress of their marriage have eased?

She already knew those answers, had known them before Jim died. She'd watched the primroses grow and realized she'd been holding on to a fantasy that was never going to happen. Jim didn't want kids.

They'll just tie us down, babe. Keep us hostage to soccer

schedules and school field trips. I'd rather be out, with you, enjoying life.

Except he hadn't done that with her. There'd always been another trip to take, another late night at the office, another excuse. And Bridget had begun to realize that she'd linked her life to a man who wanted to travel a totally different road.

Bridget watched a couple walk through the store, their hands sharing the cart's handle, fingers nestled side by side. They laughed and kissed and picked out grapes and strawberries. Six months ago, she and Jim had been in this very same market, doing the very same thing. Had they been that happy too?

For a moment, she could almost feel Jim beside her, his broad shoulders touching hers from time to time, his blue eyes connecting with hers. In that second, she missed her husband with an ache that went bone-deep. She missed his voice, his touch, his corny jokes. Okay, so things weren't perfect, but maybe there would have been a chance to fix it, if he had lived. Or maybe she was just telling herself that because the bad memories were fading.

Maybe it was just seeing Abby and Jessie Friday night that had made her all melancholy. Another night without sleep, another night in an empty bed. Another morning waking up and realizing this was her life now, like it or not.

"I see you're skipping church too." Nora swung her cart up beside Bridget's and gave her a grin. "Ma would have a shit fit if she saw us here instead of at Mass."

"I was afraid if I went to church Father McBride would

talk me into volunteering at some orphanage in Guatemala."

Nora laughed. "Hey, that might be more exciting than our lives. In fact, if I could run off to Guatemala for a week or two, I think I would."

Bridget looked behind her sister. "Where are the kids? Home with Ben?"

Nora fiddled with her purse, settling it in the seat of the cart. "Ben's...out of town. I'm paying my babysitter a small fortune to get a half hour to myself. And where do I spend it? Here." She rolled her eyes. "I really need to get a life. Why are you here?"

Bridget didn't remind Nora that at least she still had a husband and her kids. That was more of a life than Bridget had right now. "I needed something other than lasagna to eat."

Guilt flickered over Nora's face. "Bridge, I could have made you—"

She put up a hand. "Stop. I don't want any of you making me anything anymore. I need to start doing this stuff for myself. Moving forward. Living again, or some facsimile of it."

"Okay, okay." Nora shrugged. "Sorry. I have that tendency to try to take care of everyone. It's got to be the masochistic mom in me."

Bridget surveyed the produce department. The idea of filling her cart, or deciding what she wanted to eat for the next week, seemed like a wily snake she couldn't get a grasp on. Start small, she told herself, and the bigger stuff would follow. She stared at the towering pile of bunched bananas.

She reached for a set of four and pulled her hand back. Drifted her fingers over a small bunch of three, then another set of five, then a quartet of ones nearly ready to yellow.

"They're bananas, not puppies, Bridge. Just pick some."

"I don't want to buy too many. If I buy four and then end up throwing one away, Jim will be mad. He hates waste and..."

"What? The world will explode? It's a banana." Nora plucked up a bunch and dropped it into her cart. Then she paused and covered Bridget's hand with her own. "Jim is gone, sweetie. You can buy however many bananas you want."

Nora's words climbed over the Muzak on the store sound system, wrapping around the whir in Bridget's mind before finally settling in. Jim *was* gone. There was no one to ask her about the groceries when she got home. No one to give her that look when one lone banana turned too dark to eat. "I can buy however many bananas I want."

Nora laughed. "You say that like you've never done it before. Come on, let's go hit the chocolate aisle."

Her sister started to turn away. Bridget laid a hand on Nora's arm. "I can buy ten or twenty or two, and no one is going to care," she said. "No one is going to say anything if I waste a banana."

"Who would do that?" Understanding dawned in Nora's green eyes. "Wait, are you saying Jim would give you shit for buying too many bananas?"

The mother with the twins glared at Nora for cursing and pushed her cart away fast.

Put that way, it sounded bad. A wave of guilt crashed over Bridget. Jim had been a good man, maybe a little too frugal in some areas, but a good man nonetheless. She never should have said anything. "Well, wasting food is wrong and—"

"And it's a fucking banana, Bridge." Nora tossed a glance at the retreating mom, as if saying, *Take that, lady.* Then she reached over and grabbed two thick bunches of bananas and put them in Bridget's cart. "Buy ten, buy thirty. Buy all the damned bananas you want."

Bridget watched the bananas multiply in her cart. Then, like a dam bursting, she laughed, and reached for one bunch, another. They filled the basket, an explosion of yellow. "What am I going to tell the checkout girl?"

"That you're supporting three chimpanzees at home." Nora's gaze softened. "Bridge, I know he just died a few months ago, but don't you think it's time you started looking at things realistically?"

She bristled. All her life, her mother had been telling her what to think, what to do, what to say. Now her sisters were doing it too. "You're not the expert on my marriage, Nora. So please don't try to tell me how to look at things. My husband is dead, and to be honest, sometimes I wish he was still here to tell me not to buy so many damned bananas."

She put every last bunch back on the shelf and turned away.

167

A woman in a bright pink dress sat on Bridget's front step Sunday afternoon, shading herself with a wide umbrella ringed with floating yellow ducklings. A quartet of leopard-print suitcases flanked her, and a small Chihuahua with a black studded collar lay at her feet, its belly turned toward the bright spring sun.

Bridget stepped out of the car, carrying the single bag of groceries she'd ended up with—sans bananas—and crossed the front lawn. She could feel a wide smile breaking across her face, a little leap of joy in her step. "Aunt Mary? What are you doing here?"

"Visiting my favorite niece in her time of need." As if she were Mary Poppins instead of Mary O'Bannon, Aunt Mary got to her feet, clicking the umbrella closed and tucking it under one arm. The Chihuahua scrambled to his paws and waited, tail wagging. "I am sorry I couldn't be here sooner, but Pedro and I were off on an adventure and just now got the news. I'm so sorry, dear."

Mary O'Bannon was Ma's older sister, separated by more than sixteen years, and had always marched to her own beat, as Ma put it. She didn't fit the stereotype of the good Catholic girl, quiet and demure in church, lady-like with boys, and spending her senior years baking for church bake sales and knitting afghans for wounded veterans. Aunt Mary was wild and unpredictable and adventurous. She'd never settled down with anything or anyone, except her dog, who went on every adventure. Magpie was a lot like her and, of the four O'Bannon girls, the closest to Aunt Mary.

Bridget glanced at the suitcases. "And you are staying…"

"Why, here, of course." Aunt Mary's face brightened, as if the answer had been obvious all along. "I know how hard it is to lose someone you love and how every little thing seems to be a hundred times harder. I'm here to pick up the slack."

It had only been a few weeks since her mother and sisters had stopped hovering over her. Bridget wasn't so sure she wanted someone else around every day. "I'm doing fine, Aunt Mary, really."

Her aunt leaned in close, squinting until the wrinkles around her green eyes became deep grooves. "No. You're not." She leaned back and gave Bridget a smile. "Now, let's get these bags inside and open a bottle of wine."

"It's only two o'clock in the afternoon."

"Time is but an illusion, someone smarter than me once said. And wine is the solution, someone else said."

Bridget laughed. It sounded like something her grandmother would have said. "That makes no sense."

"It doesn't have to." Aunt Mary looped her arm through Bridget's. "That's the best part about life. Not everything has to add up neatly. Now, where's the guest room?"

❧❧❧

Being outside seemed to center Bridget again. The sun was warm and bright, the wine cool and crisp. She closed her eyes so she wouldn't have to look at the uncut grass or at the hummingbird feeder, hanging alone and unvisited on the window.

After she'd come home from seeing Abby on Friday night, Bridget had vowed to look at the bills. Instead, she'd gone to bed early, watching the last season of *Dexter* until the wee hours of the morning. She put in a full day at the bakery on Saturday and then rinsed and repeated the same Netflix-enabled avoidance last night.

All weekend, her mind kept returning to what Abby had said. *There are things in this family that no one ever talks about. Things that would change everything, if people knew.*

Bridget had pressed Abby, but her sister had shaken her head and changed the subject. That night, Bridget, Jessie, and Abby had gone out to dinner at an Italian place close to their apartment. The more Bridget got to know Jessie, the more she liked her. If Bridget had had any doubts about the choices Abby had made, they were erased when she saw her with Jessie.

She'd tried to bring up the topic of secrets again just before she left, but Abby wouldn't talk about it. "I never should have said anything," Abby said. "Just let it go, Bridge. It's no big deal, really."

Bridget thought of those whispers, of the hurried glances of aunts and uncles over the years. There'd always been this undercurrent of *something* lurking at the edges of the adult conversations but Bridget had been too young to figure it out. Then she'd gotten married and poured herself into her life with Jim, pushing everything to do with her family to the side.

Now, though, her Spidey senses were tingling. Whatever Abby knew seemed to be bigger than she let on. At work on Saturday, Bridget had debated asking Nora, but the bakery had been busy, with Ma flying back and forth making deliveries, and by the time the day ended, Bridget had convinced herself that Abby was talking in generalities.

Except... what if she wasn't?

Bridget tipped her head up to the sun. Whatever Abby had meant or not meant could get in line with all the other things Bridget was letting wait. "Okay, so maybe this was a great idea. I can't remember the last time I sat outside and just enjoyed the day."

"All the greatest ideas start with wine," Aunt Mary said. She had her feet propped on the deck railing, her dog snoozing in the shadow under her legs.

"I'm glad you came to visit. I bet Nora and Ma will be glad to see you. Abby too."

"Has that situation resolved?" Aunt Mary asked.

"You mean, has Ma started talking to her again? Nope. I went and saw Abby Friday night. She's really, really happy." Bridget ended the sentence before she could add *with her girlfriend.*

"That's nice to hear. I miss her. I will have to call her while I'm here and see if we can do lunch." Aunt Mary took another sip of wine and let out a long breath. "Bridget, I have to apologize. I wasn't quite honest with you earlier."

"What, no wise person said wine solves everything?"

There was no answering chuckle from her aunt, no

witty rejoinder. Bridget opened her eyes and turned toward Mary. She started to make another joke but stopped when she saw the worry etched in Mary's face. A tremor ran through Bridget's chest, and she whispered a quick *Please say everything is okay* prayer. She'd lost more than she wanted to in the last few months and couldn't bear one more monumental change. "What is it?"

"I'm sick, sweetheart." Aunt Mary's hand covered Bridget's. For the first time, she noticed the thinness in her features, the fragility of her fingers. "My heart's about worn out. These last few weeks..." She sighed. "I wasn't on an adventure. I was in the hospital. Heart attack, which happened when I was in New York, about to fly to Australia. I ended up in the hospital, where they opened me up and repaired a blockage or two."

"Oh, Aunt Mary—"

"Now, I don't want any sympathy or chicken soup," she said, putting up a hand to ward off Bridget's words. "I just want to visit with my family and spend some time recuperating. The doctor says I've got to take it easy, get back up to speed gradually, and to eat a little better. Then I'll be good to go for a while more, like a car that just got a tune-up. Course, my engine's got a couple hundred thousand miles on it, but it's not ready for the junkyard yet."

Bridget realized when they'd opened the wine, Aunt Mary had taken a glass but had barely sipped from the goblet. Her aunt's face was paler than usual, her breath and her words hitching a bit. How could she not have noticed earlier? "I'm so sorry. I didn't know."

"No one does. I didn't tell a soul. I didn't want to be a burden. But then I realized this is one thing I can't do on my own. And I have some...business to take care of while I'm here. So that's why I'm hoping I can stay with you."

"Of course you can. As long as you need."

"Good." Aunt Mary leaned back in her chair and turned her face to the sun. "It'll do you good to have something to focus on, or rather, someone. I suspect you've been lying in bed for way too many days, wondering how on earth you're going to move forward. I did that myself once. Spent a solid month doing nothing but crying."

She'd always thought of Aunt Mary as invincible, the kind of woman who lived life by her own rules, never needing anyone or attaching too long to any one person. To think of her, depressed and sobbing, added a new dimension to a woman who could have been a modern-day commercial for Rosie the Riveter. "You did? Why?"

"The usual. Boy meets girl, girl falls for boy, and boy breaks her heart. I was fifteen and thought the sun rose and set on Billy Donnelly's smile. I met him at a church camp that my mom sent me to. He was tall and dark-haired and as handsome as sin."

Bridget leaned forward. "Ooh, Aunt Mary. A summer fling?"

"I thought it was going to be more. I really thought he loved me. But after the camp ended and we all went back to our lives, I only saw Billy three more times. And the third time was with another girl on his arm. Four months later, he and his family moved to California."

"Have you looked him up? He's probably on social media."

Aunt Mary smoothed away a wrinkle in her skirt. "Some things are better left in the past."

Even five decades later, Bridget could see that Aunt Mary still had a soft spot for Billy Donnelly in her heart. Maybe while she was staying here, Bridget could teach her aunt about Facebook. If nothing else but to see if Billy had maintained his good looks—or hopefully gotten fat and bald and lonely.

"And you never married or settled down," Bridget added.

"Nope. One love of my life was enough." Aunt Mary turned to Bridget. "Speaking of losing the love of your life, which I am so, so sorry about…how are you handling things, my dear?"

"I'm not." Bridget sighed. "I'm pretty much avoiding anything that seems like a decision. My mother thinks I should be donating Jim's clothes to Goodwill and moving on. Like with some mission trip to Haiti or something. I keep trying to tell her I'm not ready for anything yet. I'm still…processing this."

Procrastinating was the real word Bridget should have used. But *processing* sounded better. More active.

"Your mother…" Aunt Mary shook her head. "She only sees and hears what she wants to."

Bridget snorted. "Ain't that the truth. She thinks we should all grieve the way she did—by not doing it at all and pretending everything is fine."

"Your mother grieved when Michael died. But she did it privately. She was so lost..." Aunt Mary's voice trailed off. She cleared her throat. "Anyway, she is a good woman, Bridget. Who loves you all like a mother lion. Don't ever doubt that."

Aunt Mary hadn't been here when Ma had been on Bridget's case every five seconds about the shadows under her eyes or what clothes she chose to wear or whether she took too many helpings of mashed potatoes. Maybe she did love her daughters, but she also loved to criticize them, and that was something Bridget could do without right now. "Let me go get you something to eat. Then we can talk some more."

"I'd like that," Aunt Mary said. "I have so much I want to tell you. To tell all you girls."

As Bridget went inside, she wondered what her aunt had meant by *business to attend to* and things she wanted to tell them. For a second, she thought of Abby's reference to a secret, then brushed off the thought. She'd watched way too many crime shows in the last few weeks because she was starting to think there was some kind of family-wide cover-up.

Bridget fixed Aunt Mary a grilled cheese sandwich and added some grapes on the side. By the time she finished, Aunt Mary had fallen asleep in the chair with her dog on her lap, his tiny head tucked between his paws.

A houseguest and a pet. Exactly the last thing Bridget needed right now.

SEVENTEEN

Colleen O'Bannon tightened her grip on her purse and strode out of church, her low, sensible heels clacking on the marble foyer and the brick stoop. Father McBride stood just outside the massive oak and stained glass doors, extending a hand to every parishioner leaving evening Mass.

Every time she stepped through the doors of Our Lady, Colleen found peace. When her girls had been little, church had been the only time all four of them were quiet. Going to Mass several times a week gave Colleen an escape from the demands of four girls under ten, a bakery that required more than full-time effort, and a house that always seemed to need fixing. She'd come here, and she'd find a few hours to avoid the bottle of wine under her sink. She'd walk through these doors, look into the stained glass eyes of Mother Mary, and feel a peace settle over her. Her husband, God rest his soul, had died and left her alone, but at least here Colleen had always felt like she had someone looking out for her.

She stepped up to the priest she'd known for forty years. When Father McBride first arrived at Our Lady, he had been a dark-haired, enthusiastic, hurried young man ready to make a change in the world. Over the last few decades, he had settled into his role, into Dorchester, into the lives of the parishioners. He'd almost become an extra family member in Colleen's eyes. At Christmas, she brought him his favorite pecan pie, and when he looked a little drawn and tired, she'd leave a batch of brownies in his office. He was a good man, with a kind heart, a soothing voice, and a ready smile. And he had been there, with his calm wisdom, to give her the strength to pull herself together.

"Father, thank you for another wonderful service," Colleen said.

He took her hand and then covered their clasped palms. The warmth of his hands was welcome. "I'm so glad you enjoyed it," Father McBride said. "It's always a pleasure to see you, Colleen."

The words made her feel as pleased as a child who had gotten an A from her teacher. "Thank you, Father."

He released her hands. A small line formed on her left, but Father McBride ignored it. "And how are your daughters? Bridget?"

"They're fine. We're all fine. Thank you for asking." Colleen nodded and smiled. She'd spoken the word *fine* so many times in her life that it should be engraved on her palm. But what should she really say? The truth?

One daughter was struggling after her husband's death.

Another was lost, as distant as a European country. The third was always there, but in the last few months, her heart and mind seemed to be somewhere else. And her last daughter? She was always somewhere other than here. None of them were drug addicts or in jail or hobos on the street, so she considered that *fine*.

Colleen drew her coat closer and fastened the top button. It was summer, but Colleen had noticed as she aged that she never seemed to feel warm. The never-ending New England winters were brutal, and summer never seemed to be hot enough to make up for the cold.

"That's wonderful." Father McBride waved at someone inside, then turned back to her. "Colleen, could you wait a moment? There's someone I'd like you to meet."

She wanted to say no, but the good Catholic schoolgirl breeding in her said yes. A part of Colleen wanted to just go home and relax, but she knew, as soon as she opened her door, she'd find something to occupy the hours until bed. Between the bakery and church and the house, Colleen was ten times busier than any other sixty-two-year-old she knew, but no matter how hard she tried, she was never busy enough.

The remaining parishioners flooded out of the church, breaking like the Red Sea around Colleen and the priest. Down the center strode a tall man with a creased fedora and a tweed jacket. He had on a pressed white shirt but no tie, and his brown shoes—which didn't match his black belt—could use a good polish. He pushed his glasses up on his nose and thrust out a hand. She'd seen him many times at church but never met him before. "Colleen O'Bannon, I've heard wonderful things about you from Father McBride."

She made a token effort at the handshake, but only because the priest was watching. "I've heard nothing about you."

The man chuckled. "Ah, that's because I keep a low profile. Roger O'Sullivan."

Father McBride put a hand on Roger's back and gave him a warm smile. "Roger here runs a transitional housing facility on Blue Hill Avenue. He's helped a number of people make the leap from living on the streets to living in homes of their own. One of the true champions for Dorchester." Someone called Father McBride's name, and the priest pivoted toward a woman standing on the steps of the side entrance. "Goodness, that's Dorothy, wanting my help to set up the chairs for the AA meeting. I'll let you two get acquainted and let Roger tell you all about his brilliant idea."

After Father McBride was gone, Roger dipped his head. "Father makes it all sound grander than it is. I'm not doing this single-handedly. I work with a wonderful, dedicated team. They're the magic behind the scenes. I just take all the glory."

"Well, that's not very Christian of you." Colleen had places to be, things to do, a warm home to get back to. She had no desire to stand in the cold and listen to this man spout off about himself. "If you listened at all today, you'd have heard Father McBride say we are to do the Lord's work and be humble about it. Now, if you'll excuse me, I should be on my way."

"Wait. I think you got the wrong impression, Miss O'Bannon."

She scowled. "It's Mrs."

"Oh, well, I apologize." Confusion filled Roger's brown eyes. "Father McBride mentioned once that you were widowed."

"I am, God rest my husband's soul." She crossed herself and issued a silent prayer to the man above. "But that doesn't mean I run around acting free as a loon on a lake, dating every man in the city."

"Of course, of course. I understand."

Roger's murmured words were like dozens of other similar trite phrases she had heard over the years. Those people who hadn't lost a spouse didn't understand. Couldn't possibly see how the loneliness invaded every inch of her skin and how she'd learned to steel her heart so it could never ever be broken again.

She looked for Father McBride, but he had gone inside. Only a few people lingered, milling around outside the church, their conversations carrying on the breeze. "I apologize, Mr...."

"O'Sullivan."

"But I must go, Mr. O'Sullivan." She kept her tone firm, sure, ending the conversation with an emphatic period. "Have a nice evening."

She turned away but then he touched her arm, a mere flicker of his hand. She glanced up at him, surprised. His eyes softened, warming from coffee to mocha. "If you'll give me just a second, I wanted to ask you a question."

Colleen gripped the strap of her purse and squared her shoulders. She should be leaving. Shouldn't listen to this stranger a minute longer. But he seemed nice. Earnest even. And if Father McBride thought they should talk, perhaps it wouldn't hurt to hear the man out. "So ask."

He chuckled. "You get straight to the point."

"I see no logical reason to stand outside on a chilly evening and waste my time with someone I don't even know." Two women brushed by. Colleen gave them a little wave.

"Ah, but if you gave me a chance, you would know me, and I hope you will give me that chance." Roger smiled at her. "How about we go across the street and get a cup of coffee?"

"I am not in the habit of 'going across the street' with people I don't even know."

"It's late. You said you're chilly. I could use a bite to eat, and I suspect you could too." He put up a finger, cutting off her next objection. "And before you say that we'll be alone or too hidden, the windows are big and bright, and if I were to accost you, the whole city would see it."

"*Are* you planning to accost me?"

"I think if I did, you would have me flat on my back and begging for my life in five seconds flat." Roger's eyes twinkled, and that smile of his kept lingering on his face. "The way I hear it, Colleen O'Bannon, you are one tough cookie."

Every second she stood here made it harder to stand firm in her resolve. It had to be the chill in the air. Or the end of a long week at the bakery. "Well, I have no idea who is talking about me like that."

"Just a message on the back of the north wind."

Colleen let out a hiccup of a laugh. How ironic that Roger had referenced a novel she knew as well as her own name. "I read that book to my girls when they were little. Abigail was scared of storms until I told her it was just the North Wind, coming to invite her to play. She sat by the window so many nights, waiting to fly through the air, like in the story." She caught herself and drew up as tall as she could against a man a solid foot taller than her. "I'm rambling. I'm sorry, Mr. O'Sullivan."

"It was a great story. Don't apologize. My daughter loved that book too. I read it a lot to her. I still do sometimes. Just...well, just because." A shadow dropped over his face, but then he brightened and waved toward the diner, and she realized the church parking lot had emptied while they'd been talking. "Let's get you warmed up. I hear the diner has the best apple pie in the state."

"They do not." She raised her chin. "I do."

"Ah, Mrs. O'Bannon, I daresay we could both take a lesson in humility." He crooked his arm. "Come, let's go see just how subpar that pie really is."

Colleen refused the offer of his arm and marched forward. She was chilled, and she could use a bite to eat. And it was only polite to hear the man out. But he didn't have to treat it like a date. "I am perfectly capable of crossing the street on my own. I've been doing it for sixty-two years."

"And I've been doing it for sixty-five." The light changed, giving them a chance to cross. "I've lived in this city all my life. Only not always in a house."

She glanced up at him. "You were homeless?"

He nodded. "From the ages of thirteen to seventeen. It's an experience I never forgot. Which is why I do what I do. Accolades aside." He pushed on the door to the diner and released a whoosh of warm air.

The diner sported typical fifties-style décor—yellow countertop, red chairs and booths, bright white tile floors. A dozen women from church filled three tables pushed together at the back of the small building. They looked up when Colleen entered and gave her a little nod. A few men sat at the long counter while two cops commandeered a corner booth. Waitresses in short pink dresses and white aprons bustled from table to table, calling out orders over their shoulders to the kitchen.

Roger waited while Colleen slid into one of the booths, and then he slipped onto the opposite vinyl bench. He signaled to one of the waitresses and a moment later, a bubbly brunette showed up with two mugs and a steaming pot of coffee.

"How are the kids, Juliet?" he asked the waitress.

"Just fine. Beth is so damned excited to start that new job at the bowling alley, and Jeremy is driving me crazy, asking about when you're going to take him to another baseball game."

"I'm glad he enjoyed it. Next time I get tickets, I'll give you a call."

"Thank you. It's nice to see him..." Her smile wavered. "Just nice to see him with someone who's a good influence."

"He's a good kid, Juliet. You've done a great job with him, and with Beth and Scott."

"I'm trying." She flushed and dropped her gaze. She flipped over the mugs, filled them. "There's coffee. I'll be back with extra cream, Roger."

"Well," Colleen began, settling a paper napkin across her lap after the waitress had disappeared into the kitchen, "she seems to know you quite well."

"Juliet is one of our success stories. Single mom of two, recovering heroin addict, left penniless by an asshole of an ex—pardon my French, Mrs. O'Bannon—and came to us as a last resort."

Colleen glanced again at the perky waitress, bouncing around the space behind the counter, shouting out orders, collecting checks, greeting customers. "*She* was a drug addict? And homeless?"

"Not every addict goes around unwashed and speaking gibberish."

"I...I didn't mean that. I just meant—"

His hand covered hers. Colleen's words caught in her throat. It was the second time he'd touched her, and this time, his touch lingered. "I know what you meant. It's okay."

She withdrew her hand and wrapped it around her coffee mug instead. "You said you wanted to talk to me about something."

Juliet dropped off the extra cream. Roger thanked her and went on. "You own a bakery, Father McBride tells me. A very successful one."

Colleen drew herself up. The bakery, a business conversation. Her comfort zone. "Three generations strong. Started by my mother, and now my daughters work there."

"That's awesome. So few businesses make it past the first generation." He poured a sugar into his coffee and reached for the creamers. He held the bowl out to her, but Colleen shook her head. He started talking again as he opened the tiny creamers, one, two, three, four, five, and dumped them into his coffee. "I know we just met, but I'd like to ask you for two favors."

She stiffened. "Okay…"

"It's not as bad as it sounds." He chuckled and took a sip of his lightened coffee. "You probably have some leftover baked goods at the end of the day. If you aren't already donating them somewhere, I would appreciate it if you would consider donating them to Sophie's Home. That's the center I run. I can pick them up at the end of the day, and in exchange, I could provide some free intern labor."

"Oh, we don't need any help. And we already donate most of the leftovers to the mission house," she said, and then reconsidered. He seemed like a nice enough man, and clearly his facility was doing good work. It would only be right to support him. "But I can put some aside for you.

If... if you really don't mind coming by to pick them up from time to time."

"It would be my pleasure." He smiled. "I realize you are probably well staffed but the help I'm offering is more of a selfish thing. Many of the women and teenagers who come to Sophie's Home have no career skills. Some don't even have a high school diploma. We've found that the number one way to help them get off the streets—and see hope at the end of the tunnel—is to equip them with job skills. I've already worked out partnerships with a local coffee shop, this diner, a nursery, and the bowling alley that Juliet's daughter works at. Your bakery would be a wonderful fit."

"I'm not sure—"

"Just think about it." He signaled to Juliet. "Now, no more business. Let's just enjoy some pie and conversation."

Juliet dished up two pieces of pie and brought them to the table. "Here's your pie. Enjoy!"

Colleen took a bite. The crust of the apple pie was good—moist, yet flaky, not overly sweet. The filling had a tad more cinnamon than she used, but overall, it was a good pie. "Not bad."

Roger grinned. "I told you that it would be good. I'll have to swing by your bakery sometime soon and do a comparison."

The thought of him swinging by caused a little flutter in her chest. A flutter Colleen hadn't felt in decades. She dropped her attention back to the pie.

"Did you grow up around here?"

Roger's question caught her by surprise. "Why...why do you ask?"

"This is the conversation part of the evening." He grinned. "We talked business; now we can talk personal."

"Oh. Oh...well, I'm not sure we should. I mean, it's really just about the bakery."

"Wouldn't you like to know who is stopping by your shop on a regular basis? You may find out I'm a terrible person, maybe some kind of misogynistic paranoid schizophrenic."

"Are you a misogynistic paranoid schizophrenic?"

"You'll just have to converse with me to find out." Then he grinned and popped a bit of pie in his mouth.

What would it hurt to talk to him a bit more? It was chilly outside and the coffee was warm and the lights were bright, and she wasn't quite ready to go home to her empty house yet. "Yes, I grew up in Dorchester. I started working at the bakery when I was twelve and started running it when I was twenty, because my mom was battling her first round with cancer. I met my late husband on that very street"— she waved toward the street in front of Our Lady Church— "when he was handing out flyers for a music festival downtown. I took a flyer, he asked to go with me, and before I knew it, we were living on Park Street with four little girls." That was the most she had ever talked about her life, her family. Her husband, for that matter. "What about you?"

"I grew up everywhere." He wrapped his hands around his coffee mug. "Army brat. I've lived all over the country and in a few other countries as well. I met my wife—"

"You're married?" The interjection took Colleen by surprise. Why did she care? And why was she interrupting him?

"Divorced. Ten years now. We met in Japan, when I was living over there with my parents. Got married too young, tried to start a life in a country she didn't know, and it went south pretty quick after our daughter was born. She had some relatives in the Boston area so we moved here, and after the divorce, I stayed. Vowed to do something with myself after I spent way too many years in a management job that seemed pointless. So, thus was born Sophie's Home."

The word *divorced* sent a strange hum through Colleen. She shouldn't care if this man—a stranger, really—was involved with anyone or not. She certainly wasn't looking for a date or a spouse. "I think it's good you decided to do something to make a difference."

"I'm trying," he said, and then his gaze went to somewhere far in the distance. "It's never enough though, it seems."

"Never busy enough," Colleen added softly.

Roger's eyes met hers. He had this direct way of looking at her that made her cheeks heat and her hands tremble. "We sound like two kindred spirits."

Colleen cleared her throat and took a long sip of coffee, to fill the tension between them. And to get herself back on track. "You said you had two favors to ask."

"Ah, yes. The first was business. The second is personal." He waited until her gaze met his again. This time, there was a hint of amusement in his eyes. "I'd like to ask you out."

"Me? Why?"

"Because you are stubborn and smart and successful, and quite beautiful when you smile."

Her lips curved, and then she drew herself back and swallowed the smile. She had the strangest urge to giggle, to flirt—did she even remember how?—and to say yes to him. Then her mind threw on the brakes and dragged her back to reality. She'd lost her one love, and she didn't need nor want another. "I don't think that's appropriate, Mr. O'Sullivan. We are talking business—"

"We're talking about you donating some bread to my shelter. That's hardly plotting a corporate takeover. Besides, we're not getting any younger. Why not say yes?"

Colleen gathered her purse to her side and slid out of the booth. "I will give your offer—and I'm speaking strictly of the offer to provide interns at my shop—consideration, Mr. O'Sullivan. Have a good evening." Emphatic period at the end.

Then she left, her mostly uneaten pie still on the table.

EIGHTEEN

The letter opener glared back at Bridget, the overhead kitchen light dancing off the blade. The world was quiet, everyone with any sense asleep in their beds. Even though she had to be at the bakery in a few hours, Bridget had rolled out of bed, paced the floors for a while, and then finally gone down to the kitchen. She sat there, drank an entire glass of chardonnay, poured a second, took a deep breath, and started slitting the flaps. It was time. Actually, it was past time.

One after another, the bills piled up—gas, electric, trash, mortgage, credit cards....

At the bottom of the pile, the bank statement. She took a long gulp of the wine and opened the envelope. She'd been hoping for a mistake, one of those Monopoly Chance cards that said *Bank error in your favor: collect two thousand dollars*.

But there was no bright orange card, no accounting error. Her heart fell and her lungs tightened. She could feel that rip tide closing over her again, heavier, thicker. How was she ever going to get out of this mess?

Her phone buzzed, and the screen lit with a text message from Magpie: **Heading back into town in a couple days. Heard you are still surviving at Charmed, you glutton for punishment. Want to make your favorite sister some black and white cookies? ?**

Bridget chuckled. Those had always been Magpie's favorite. She had loved them when she was little, even though she could barely hold the oversized two-tone frosted sugar cookies. Ma would always bake a few extras for holidays and Magpie's birthday and as a reward for good grades. **Definitely! And hey, I took your advice. Did something unexpected.**

The phone rang, and Bridget jumped. "Hello?"

"You can't just text something like that and not expect me to call you." In the background, Bridget could hear a band and voices. "What'd you do?"

"Went to see Abby."

"You did? That's great!" Magpie mumbled something about being right back. A moment later, the background noise dropped away. "Sorry, I was in a club. But I'm outside now. Tell me all about it. How is she? Did you meet Jessie?"

"Wait, you know about Jessie?"

"Yup. I saw pictures of her about a year ago, I think, when I just showed up on Abby's doorstep. I mean, Abby didn't tell me about them being involved but I could tell from the pictures. They looked so happy, you know?"

"And you never said anything?"

"About what? About the fact that she's involved with a woman? Hell, I don't care. All I care about is that you all are happy. She could marry a schnauzer and I'll stand beside her and hold her bouquet."

Bridget laughed. "Magpie, you are one of a kind."

"That's what they keep telling me. Probably a good thing too."

They talked a little while longer, and then Magpie said she had to go. "Our taxi's here. But I'll be home Wednesday. See you then?"

"For sure."

"Good. You sound better, Bridge. Much better." Magpie shouted she'd be right there and then came back to the phone. "And if you want one more piece of advice, let me share what the shaman I interviewed today told me."

Bridget waited, sure this was going to be something deep and profound and involving chakras or something.

"Don't worry about the shit you encounter. Life will flush it away."

Bridget laughed. "That's advice?"

"Best advice I heard today. Love you, Bridge. See you soon!" Then she hung up, leaving Bridget alone in her kitchen again. With the shit she'd encountered, courtesy of her letter opener.

None of it was going to get any better if she kept procrastinating or processing, depending on what kind of spin she wanted to put on it, so, fortified with that second glass of chardonnay, she crossed to the rolltop desk in the corner of the dining room, pulled open the file drawer where

Jim kept a meticulous set of records, and found the last six months of bank statements.

In a second, it was clear why she was so far behind. For months, they'd been skating along the edge of not having enough money. There'd been the Audi Jim had bought and insisted they could afford. The new lawn mower he'd bought on sale. The set of skis that had never seen snow. The carbon golf clubs she'd bought him for Christmas. Expenses that had eaten up the rest of what disposable income they'd had. As she scanned the bank statement, she saw that the deposit she'd put down for the funeral home had been the tipping point.

But she also saw one other thing—a number of sizeable cash withdrawals, all of them coming at the same time every month. Where had that money gone? She didn't remember Jim carrying around hundreds of dollars in cash. What had he spent it on?

In a way, it didn't matter. Because now she was broke. She owed McLaughlin & Sons another fifteen thousand dollars and, it seemed, a whole lot of money to pretty much every single company in Boston. Even if she worked full-time at the bakery and kept her column with the paper, she wouldn't make enough to cover it all.

Despite Magpie's voice of reason, Bridget was pretty sure there was no magic toilet coming to flush this all away.

Anger flared in her chest. How could Jim have done this to her? Kept her in the dark about their financial situation? And where had the money gone? Gambling? A mistress?

But more, how could she have kept her head buried in the sand for so many years, leaving her unprepared and on the edge of financial ruin?

"You're up late."

Bridget turned. "Hey, Aunt Mary. Did I wake you? I'm sorry if I did."

"No, no, dear. I hardly sleep as it is." Aunt Mary got a glass of water, sat down beside her niece, and glanced at the mounds of bills covering the countertop. The Chihuahua looked up at his mistress, let out a yawn, and curled up on the floor. Pedro didn't seem to do much more than nap and eat. "Looks like a shitstorm hit you," Aunt Mary said.

"Pretty much." Bridget leafed through the mail, but it was all more of the same. Overdue, past due, red letters and numbers and demands for money she didn't have.

Aunt Mary sat at the bar in a deep purple robe tied loosely over a pale pink cotton nightgown. Her face was bare, which made her look younger, and paler.

Like Magpie, Aunt Mary had only worked in the bakery a little before going off on her own life. Five years ago, she'd come to Ma's house—Bridget had been there that night for dinner—and after the meal, Aunt Mary and Ma had done the dishes together in the kitchen. They'd gone in laughing, talking like sisters do, but at some point between adding the Dawn and getting out the dishtowel, they'd had a fight. Aunt Mary had left with barely a word for her nieces, and Ma had refused to talk about it. As far as Bridget knew, the sisters hadn't talked in all that time. She wondered if that was part of the business Aunt Mary wanted to settle during her stay. Either way, she looked worried and drawn, and Bridget vowed to do as much for her aunt as she could.

"Have you looked at the retirement?" Aunt Mary said. "If Jim had money there and you're his beneficiary, you could cash in part or all of it."

"I never thought of that. Let me look. I think I saw the statement..." She riffled through the piles around her but came up empty. In the desk, she found an annual statement from a few years ago. But at least it had the account number and customer service information. Two years ago, there was a hundred thousand dollars in the account. Surely there was more by now. "I'll call them in the morning. Thanks, Aunt Mary."

"You're welcome." Pedro was at her feet, his tail wagging, his nose turned up to her. "Pedro needs to go out. Do you mind?"

"Not at all." Bridget called the dog to her and stepped out onto the back porch. The yard was silent and dark, the primroses too small to be seen. The dog darted off, did what he needed to do, and came rushing back in. Bridget left the door open behind her and leaned against the jamb. "Can I ask you something, Aunt Mary?"

"Sure."

"Why did you and Ma stop talking?" The question just popped out, fueled by all the wine, the dark night, the worries somersaulting around in her mind. Ever since the day she went to Abby's, Bridget realized she had fallen into the same patterns her mother had followed—putting up a wall and cutting off the people in her life. For so long, she'd believed that it was the best decision, but with Jim gone, it had created a yawning cavern in Bridget's life. One she never wanted to create again.

"Ah, that's a story too long for the telling." Aunt Mary got to her feet and called the dog to her. "I should probably get back to bed." She started to shuffle out of the kitchen.

"Abby says there are secrets in this family. Do you know anything about them?"

Aunt Mary froze and reached to brace herself on the corner of the wall. She didn't turn around, and when she spoke, her voice was soft, pained. "Good night, Bridget. Get some sleep. Everything looks better in the morning."

❧❧❧

A cloud of flour poofed up from the belly of the eighty-quart mixer. Bridget closed the safety cage over the stainless steel bowl, which dropped the massive paddle into place, and then flipped the switch to low. The cake batter began to come together, going from a jumbled mix to a butter yellow ribbon.

She detached the bowl, wheeled it over to the counter, and then scooped the batter into the cake pans and slid them into the oven. While they baked, she started a batch of macarons, whipping the egg whites until they became stiff clouds. She folded in sifted sugar, almond flour, and confectioners' sugar, easing her touch with each step. Macarons required a delicate hand. A little too much mixing and they morphed from fluffy teats into hard lumps.

She loved this kind of recipe. Her mind would sink into the steps, and everything else would drop away. One of her friends had talked about meditation and how concentrating on breathing calmed all the noises in her head. Bridget didn't sit cross-legged and *ohhmmm*—she baked.

When she was done, she piped thick circles onto silicon mats. The repetitive action—pipe, lift, pipe, lift—kept her mind from focusing on the wall clock as the time ticked past the wee hours of the morning and closer to normal working hours. She'd gone back to bed after looking at the bills, slept for a couple fitful hours, and then headed down to the bakery to get to work. Her head pounded from the wine, but she popped a couple Tylenol and immersed herself in batter. The cakes finished baking, the cookies took their place in the oven, and Bridget moved on to whipping up vanilla buttercream, tinting some pink, some blue, some pale yellow.

A little after eight-thirty, her mother came in and peered at the trio of piping bags. "The blue ones don't sell as well. Make more yellow instead."

Cut past any kind of pleasantries and get right to the criticism. "Good morning, Ma. How are you?"

"I'll be fine when we quit wasting money here. We can't afford to make cookies people aren't going to buy."

Bridget sighed. It was early in the day, and the last thing she wanted was an argument over piping colors. "Ma, I've worked twenty-one spring seasons here. All three colors sell equally well. If we have extra blue ones, I promise I'll eat them myself."

Her mother pursed her lips. "We will see what is left over at the end of the day."

"So…" Bridget finished with the blue frosting and switched to the pink. "Aunt Mary is in town."

Her mother froze, her apron half tied. "How do you know that?"

"She was sitting on my doorstep when I got home yesterday."

"Oh. Well. That's…good." Ma finished tying her apron and ducked into the walk-in freezer, returning with several trays of unfrosted cupcakes. She readied a piping bag of vanilla buttercream and started topping the cupcakes with thick swirls of frosting. "Nora will be in late today. She had to take the kids to school."

"Aren't you curious about how she is?"

"I think Nora's been working too many hours lately. She needs some time off. She looks a little ragged. Don't you agree?"

"I was asking about Aunt Mary. Aren't you at least a little curious?"

"And Magpie will be home in two days. I was thinking of having a family dinner on Wednesday night. Or Friday night. We could have fish—"

"Ma. I'm talking about Aunt Mary, and you are talking about everything else."

Her mother frosted the cupcakes in fast and furious movements, back and forth, up and down the line. By the second row, the little frosting peaks that normally decorated every cupcake at Charmed by Dessert were falling to the right, spilling onto the tray.

"Ma, you're—" Bridget saw a tear slide down her mother's cheek and land on the counter. "Are you okay?"

"I'm fine." But her voice was choked and thick.

"Here, let me have that." Bridget laid a gentle hand on her mother's and pried the piping bag out of her hands. She slid the tray of ruined cupcakes to the side. She leaned against the counter, arms over her chest, in the pose her mother usually took. "Why are you crying?"

"I'm not."

Bridget sighed. "Good Lord, Ma, for someone who goes to church every other day, you sure do lie a lot."

Her mother's gaze sharpened. "I do not lie."

"Uh-huh. And you're not crying?"

"I...I have something in my eye."

"This isn't about Aunt Mary? Are you upset because she didn't call you? Or see you first?"

"This is about getting the work done today. We are far too busy to stand around, making idle conversation." She pulled the next tray of cupcakes over and went back to work, this time taking more time to make sure every frosting cloud was perfect. She kept moving, as if nothing had happened, as if those tears had been a mirage. "We have a rush order for one of those sponge cakes with the strawberry layers. If you could get started on that soon..."

Her mother went on, listing every order they had on tap for the day, talking about everything but the real issues.

Her tears dried up; her movements became more efficient—

In short, she got back to work. As usual.

Her mother was an immovable wall sometimes. If she didn't want to talk about something, she didn't. If she didn't want to change her mind, she didn't. So Bridget gave up trying and concentrated on her job. Without Nora there to break the tension, the kitchen seemed to close in on Bridget. She glanced at the clock about twelve thousand times, willing the hour to reach nine so her sister would be here. And so Bridget could call the retirement account management company and find out if she had a way out of this mess.

Her mother pulled a cooled sheet cake out of the freezer and put it on the counter for Bridget to add the strawberry filling. Instead of turning away, she lingered, with that pointed look that said a lecture was on its way. "Bridget, I'm concerned about your finances."

"Join the club," Bridget muttered.

"And I think if you made more judicious decisions—"

"Make more judicious decisions? I didn't make hardly any decisions." What was Nora doing? Walking to work backward? Why wasn't she here to save Bridget from yet another lecture? "Ma, Jim was the one in charge of our money. He just made some stupid spending choices, like his car and that trip to Aruba. Everyone does that kind of thing."

"Not everyone. Men who have families are usually smarter than that." Her mother moved behind her to retrieve the white whipped cream frosting that would be sandwiched between the strawberries and the sponge cake. "Why did you trust him?"

Bridget wheeled around. "Why did I trust him? What did you lecture us on for our whole lives? Your husband is the head of your household. The wife is there as a support mate, not as a chief. Let him lead, and you follow."

"I didn't mean following him down a rabbit hole of debt and bad decisions."

"How would you really know anyway? Dad died, and you never got married again. You never even dated again." Bridget laid a thick swath of whipped cream over the strawberries, then stacked on the next layer of cake. She started sprinkling on another set of macerated strawberries, her movements quick and jerky. "Before you start criticizing me, Ma, have the guts to step outside your own comfort zone."

Her mother gasped and took a step back. "What is with you lately? You've never talked back like this before."

"I'm a grown woman. And I am sick and tired of people telling me what to do. I don't know what I want to do, but I do know, whatever choice I make going forward, it's going to be mine, not something forced on me."

"I'm not forcing anything on you."

"No. You're not. You're just making it damned hard to do anything else." *And making me question everything I thought I knew.* She cursed her mother for that, for tarnishing the image she had of her marriage, her husband. All of them had done that, as if Jim's death gave her sisters and her mother permission to say things they would have normally kept to themselves. And to remind Bridget of the very concerns she had tried to stop thinking about.

"I took care of you after Jim passed away. I gave you back your job here," her mother said, ticking off her fingers as she listed the ways she'd helped Bridget. "I gave you a loan. And this is the way you repay me? By treating me like some unwelcome rodent at your dinner party?"

Bridget rolled her eyes. "Ma, don't get dramatic. Just let me make my own choices. If I want to spend my money on supporting elephants in South Africa, I can. And if I want to make ten pounds of blue frosting, let me."

"You aren't paying the bills here."

"No, but I own one-fifth of this bakery. That should give me some say in how things are done."

Her mother shook her head and turned away, back to a platter of sugar cookies.

"What?"

Twelve cookies were topped with white frosting swirls before her mother answered. "You want a say in how things are done? Try staying here instead of abandoning your family when we needed you most."

Bridget opened her mouth to reply. Then realized she had no answer for that. No way to heal that wound. Her mother was right—she had abandoned them all. She'd walked away and never looked back, not realizing the price she would pay later. How doing so would fracture the bond she had with the rest of her sisters. "At the time, it seemed like the best choice."

"For who?" her mother asked. "You? Or your husband?"

The phone rang, and Bridget jumped. She answered the call, taking the order for a cake rush job. By the time she was done, her mother had finished the cookies and was busy filling the cases at the front of the shop. For now, the topic was tabled. Bridget should have felt relief but instead this gnawing sense of dread churned in her stomach.

At 9:15, Nora came in, and Ma brushed by her to tend to a walk-in customer. Nora dropped her purse on the table in the corner and hung her coat on the hook, exchanging it for an apron. "What'd I miss?"

"Aunt Mary is in town. Ma doesn't want to talk about it. Instead, as a diversionary tactic I think, Ma tried to tell me how to be more fiscally responsible, including a lecture on blue frosting, and I pulled the 'I own one-fifth' card."

"Geez. All that before nine-fifteen in the morning?"

Bridget shrugged. "What can I say? I'm efficient."

Nora grabbed the clipboard and flipped through the day's orders and then began assembling ingredients. "Back the truck up. Aunt Mary is in town? Since when?"

Bridget told her about her aunt being there the day before and how she'd asked to stay at Bridget's house. "I've missed her, so it's been nice catching up."

"Aunt Mary has a house of her own in Revere, not that she's ever there. Why is she staying with you?"

Bridget glanced at the swinging door that led to the front of the shop. She could hear her mother out there, moving chairs and setting up the few tables. "I don't know if she wants me to tell anyone."

"Which is all the more reason to tell me." Nora leaned in closer to Bridget. "Besides, you know I'm a vault. I never told Ma about how you used to sneak out at night to go see what's-his-name."

"Charlie Phillips. Cutest boy in the eleventh grade." Nora had caught Bridget one night, and she'd made her sister pinkie swear that she wouldn't tell their mother. "Aunt Mary had a heart attack, and she needs time to recuperate."

Nora put a hand to her mouth. "Is she okay?"

"I think so. She looks a little worn down, but I think she'll be okay. If you want to visit, I'm sure she'd love to see you. In fact"—Bridget glanced again at that closed door—"I think I'll offer to have family dinner on Wednesday night."

"Oh, you have balls of steel, sis. Really?"

"Hey, I've already told off my mother in front of a priest. I need to top that somehow." Bridget grinned and realized what this would mean. Her entire family in one room—something that hadn't happened since her wedding. And look how well that ended. "Do you mind if I duck out and make a quick phone call?"

"Hiring bouncers for Wednesday night?"

"Something like that. I should be right back." Bridget headed out back with her cell phone. She pulled a folded paper out of her pocket and hesitated. What if the answer she got wasn't the one she wanted?

Jim had always handled all the calls to the bank when they messed up a deposit or the credit card companies when he'd lost his wallet once. He'd been the one to deal with the cable company and the repairmen. *It's just easier, babe, and then you don't have to stress.*

At some point, she'd let him take over, let him be the voice for the two of them. And now, standing here in the sun, she was shaking so badly that the numbers on the paper blurred before her. When had she become afraid of dealing with these things?

She closed her eyes, inhaled, and opened her eyes again. Her hand steadied, and she dialed the number, then waited what seemed like ten hours to connect to a peppy customer service rep named Davita.

"I'm calling because my husband passed away, and I want to cash in his retirement," Bridget told her. "There should be more than a hundred thousand in there."

"Oh, I'm so sorry for your loss, Mrs. Masterson. So very sorry. Let me pull up his account." A couple minutes of keys clacking, and then Davita came back on the line. This time, her voice had flattened from peppy to apologetic. "Uh...his balance is, well, it's forty thousand dollars."

"Forty...forty thousand? That's it?" The last time they'd talked about his retirement—last Christmas? The one before?—Jim had said he was maxing out his contributions and should hit two hundred thousand by the end of the year. Where had that money gone?

"From what I can see of the account history, he made a sizeable loan against his 401k a couple years ago—"

The deck they'd put on the back. The new landscaping and the windows they'd replaced. All purchases Jim said were covered by savings. She'd never questioned, never looked, just gone on like an idiot, blindly trusting. But sixty thousand dollars? The repairs hadn't added up to that much.

"And his contribution level has decreased since then," Davita went on. "When you factor in the loan repayment, the amount in his retirement account hasn't moved up much. I'm sorry, Mrs. Masterson. Is there anything else I can help you with?"

Bridget sank down against the wall until she reached the concrete. Her chest tightened, her breath caught, and a part of her wanted to ball up in a corner and cry. Instead, she pulled herself together enough to start the cashing-in process—something that would take about a month, Davita said, from start to finish. She hung up the phone, pressed it to her head and—

Prayed.

NINETEEN

On Wednesday, Bridget loaded what felt like the seven hundredth cake of the day into the oven and then bent to the side, stretching the aches out of her back. She'd skipped lunch, forgone breaks, and instead kept working because measuring sugar and baking soda kept her from thinking.

Ma had boxed up all the leftover pastries from the day before and left to make a delivery, without saying anything about where she was going. Nora zipped out to bring a forgotten trombone to her eldest at school, leaving Bridget alone at the bakery. When the bell over the door tinkled, Bridget sighed. She abandoned a half-rolled piecrust, pushed on the swinging door that led to the front, and pasted on a smile as she did. "Welcome to—"

Garrett stood there, holding a small ceramic pot. The bright red geranium in the center popped against the dark blue of his suit and the white and blue stripes of his oxford shirt. This time, he was in work mode, his tie straight, all knotted and severe and professional. He smiled, and her heart skipped a beat. "I hear the chocolate chip cookies here are the best in the state."

"In the state? No, in the nation." A nervous flutter went through her, and she cursed herself for not taking off the flour-covered apron or checking her hair before she'd come out front. Then cursed herself again for caring what Garrett thought of her appearance. "Did you come here to buy some?"

"Nope. I came here to see you. I've texted, and you haven't answered me."

"I've been...busy." *Busy avoiding you and all the questions meeting you has opened up.*

He stepped forward and set the geranium on the counter. "For you. Actually, for your hummingbird."

Such a small gesture, but so thoughtful. He'd chosen a hardy annual, in the right shade to attract the hummingbird. And even better, the plant was almost entirely self-sufficient. "Thank you. I still haven't seen him." Of course, she'd been gone most days at the bakery, so maybe the hummingbird was visiting while she was working. She'd faithfully changed the nectar and washed the feeder every few days, but it never seemed like the level had budged.

"Well, maybe if you put this outside, it'll draw him near." Garrett put his hands in his pockets and glanced around the bakery. "It looks a little different in the daytime."

Less intimate. Less...close. "Lights make all the difference."

"That and a full case of desserts." Garrett leaned forward and peered into the glass case. "Wow. You guys make pretty much everything, don't you? Did you bake all of this yourself?"

"No. My mother and my sister work here too. And we have some part-time help when things get really busy." She put the geranium on the back counter, reached in the display case, and grabbed two chocolate chip cookies, sliding them into a white paper bag. She held them out to Garrett. "Here you go. No charge."

"Ah, Bridget, you wouldn't be trying to get rid of me already, would you?" He took a step forward but didn't take the cookies. "The plant, you know, was mostly an excuse to stop by and ask you to lunch."

She froze. A part of her was happy—flattered—that he was asking her out. But the other part of her was saying her husband had only been gone for a few months and it was too soon to date again. "I...I'm the only one working right now. I can't leave."

Then, as if conjured up by the words, Nora breezed back into the shop. "I'm back, Bridge, if you want to take your lunch now."

Garrett grinned. "Seems I came at the right time."

Nora glanced at Bridget, then at Garrett, and back again. She mouthed, *Did he ask you out?*

Bridget gave her sister a half-nod. Technically, it was just lunch, and maybe only to talk about birds, so she wasn't sure it was an actual date. Uh-huh, and maybe she could keep telling herself the geranium was just a neighborly gesture.

Nora tipped her head in the direction of the door. Bridget hesitated. Nora rolled her eyes and stepped forward, putting out her hand. "I'm sorry. I don't think we've met. I'm Nora, one of Bridget's sisters."

"Garrett Andrews, a...friend. And fellow hummingbird lover."

Nora arched a brow in Bridget's direction. "Hummingbirds?"

"Long story. I'll explain later." Outside, she saw her mother's car turn into the back parking lot. She could stand here and explain the presence of a man bringing her flowers when her mother arrived, or get out of here and get a sandwich. She ripped off her apron and handed it to Nora and grabbed her purse from under the counter. "I'm going to lunch."

"I'll hold down the fort. Have fun." Nora leaned over to Bridget's ear. "And I mean that."

⁂

Ten minutes later, she and Garrett were seated in a little Cuban café a couple blocks from the bakery. The restaurant was cozy and small, with colorful murals of life on Cuban streets filling the walls. They'd ordered a colada to split—dividing the rich Cuban coffee between their cups. Garrett had thought to ask for extra cream and sugar for her and kept his mostly plain. Bridget had opted for a shredded roast pork sandwich while Garrett ordered the traditional Cuban sandwich.

They were seated at a round table with a tile top, so tiny their knees touched under the table from time to time. Every inch of Bridget was aware—very aware—of Garrett. Of his cologne. Of the mesmerizing structure of his muscular hands. Of the slight shadow of stubble along his jaw.

"How did your mom like the bird feeders?" she asked after the waiter had left. Concentrate on conversation instead of how her leg brushed against his.

"I got a gold star—both of them were exactly what she wanted. I hung them in the yard, outside the window where she can see them when she's in her chair." Garrett took a sip of coffee. "My mom is in a wheelchair, so the view outside her room is pretty important."

"I'm so sorry. But what a thoughtful thing to do." *Thoughtful*—that was the word she'd use to describe Garrett. He'd remembered the way she took her coffee, the tenderness of giving his mother a gift that would allow her to appreciate the view from her limited world.

"It's okay. She's been like that for a few years. She had a stroke and never fully recovered. She gets out more now than she did before, and that helps her spirits a lot. Gotta love the BAT buses."

"They're great. I know lots of my mom's friends who use them." She'd seen the little white and red buses that darted around the city, bringing people to doctor's appointments and shopping malls.

Garrett's salt and pepper hair was a little long, and one lock kept swooping onto his forehead, in a Clark Kent kind of way. She watched him sip his coffee, and thinking about his hands on her instead made parts of her warm. She cleared her throat and jerked her gaze back to his face. "So, what kind of lawyer are you, anyway? The Tom Cruise-interrogating-Jack Nicholson kind?"

He chuckled and shook his head. "Sorry to disappoint you, but I'm just a boring corporate attorney. None of that exciting courtroom *you can't handle the truth* type stuff. Most of my job is pretty routine. Not nearly as much fun as your job, I'm sure."

"Ha. Mine's pretty routine too. We make the same things every day for the display case." The routine had become so familiar that, even after three years away, Bridget had slipped right back into it. Except for a few tweaks—like the addition of the scones—everything at Charmed by Dessert was the same as when she'd left. "The only time we get to be creative is with the orders. Some people will order a cake, and just say I trust you, and then we can have a little fun. And once in a while, I'll create something new for the bakery, just to change things up." She explained how Nora did the decorating, her mother managed most of the day-to-day, and Bridget was in charge of the majority of the baking. She didn't mention her other sisters because that was way too much complication for a simple lunch conversation.

The waiter brought their sandwiches. Bridget dove into hers—she'd been up since three and she was ravenous now—but Garrett just held his sandwich and didn't eat it yet. "I really admire someone who can do that," he said. "Just create something out of thin air."

Heat stole into her cheeks at the compliment. "It's not all that complicated. I mean, if you know the rules of baking and the basics of the recipes, it's not that tough to create something new. It's all about"—she paused, searching for the right word—"balance."

"Ah, a truth for baking and for life."

"So true." She took another bite of her sandwich. It was good—the bread toasted just right, the pork tender and slightly sweet. The meat was paired with lime-glazed red onions and a dash of cilantro. The French fries had been hand-cut, with that perfect mix of a crusty outside and soft inside.

"So tell me … how do you balance your life these days, Bridget?" Garrett asked.

She scoffed. "I don't. I go to work. I go to sleep. Rinse, repeat."

He chuckled. "Sounds like me. I work, I sleep. I have a few properties I own and rent out, and that, in a nutshell, is my excitement for a weekday."

"You aren't dating anyone?" Damn it. Why had she asked that? Maybe she could pretend it was a side effect of choking on her coffee or something. She shoved another bite of sandwich into her mouth before she said anything else stupid.

"Not yet." He gave her a smile. "There's this stubborn woman I know who puts more thought into the perfect chocolate chip cookie than most people put into planning a vacation around the world. I'd love to see her more often, but she's really making me work for it."

For a second, Bridget was going to say, *You should try harder. I'm sure she's interested*, then realized he was talking about her. She didn't know whether to be flattered or scared off. She liked Garrett—liked his smile, liked his eyes, liked talking to him. Did she want to date him?

Wasn't that kind of what she was doing? The coffee, the late night in the bakery, and now lunch? He'd brought her flowers today, paid for the food both times they went out.

Anyone who could add two and two would call that dating. Was that wrong? Was it too soon?

She caught him staring at her, and desire fluttered through her. She shifted in her seat, which only made her leg connect with his. Awareness zipped through her veins, and she had to remind herself to breathe. There was just something about him—the kindness in his face? The way he paid attention? Something that drew her closer, even as her mind was screaming, *Caution!*

"I know you probably aren't ready to date yet," Garrett went on, as if he'd read her mind. "But I'm hoping we can be friends and maybe get some coffee or sandwiches once in a while. I really like you, Bridget."

"I like you too." The wave of guilt that she shouldn't even be thinking about another man—what did that say about her loyalty to Jim?—hit her again, but this time, it wasn't a tidal wave, more of a strong surf. It had been more than three months, not a lot of time but enough to edge her toward the thought of a different life.

"Then let's take this at a turtle pace," Garrett said.

"You need time to go through the stages and changes, and I'll just be here, a friend, nothing more for a while. Okay?"

Exactly the kind of pace she liked lately. She smiled at him and covered his hand with her own. The connection felt warm, comforting, something she could stand on until she found her footing. *For a while*. "Yeah. That sounds like a great idea."

✹✧✧✹

When Bridget got back to work an hour later, Nora grabbed her arm. Ma was working the cash register, ringing up a sale. She nodded toward her eldest daughter.

"Bridget—"

"Not now, Ma," Nora said. "I need to talk to Bridge real quick." She hauled her into the back and pounced the second the swinging door shut behind them. "So...what happened?"

"We had lunch. That's all. We're friends for now. More...maybe down the road." Bridget slid her apron on and knotted it behind her back. "Right now, all I want to concentrate on is work and paying the bills."

And not think about the too-short walk back to the bakery. How Garrett had held her hand, and she'd felt as light-headed as a teenager. Just before they reached Charmed by Dessert, he had pulled her to him, and just when she thought he was going to kiss her, he instead drew her in for a brief hug. "I'll call you."

"Okay," she said, because she didn't have any other words right then. She'd walked into work, riding a cloud.

"Well, he was hot, I'll say that," Nora said. "And a woman can always use a hot guy friend. Especially one who's straight." She grinned and slipped into place beside Bridget, the two of them falling into a seamless unspoken partnership of assembling a three-tier cake and applying a crumb coat of thin, nearly transparent buttercream. "So tell me about him. How'd you meet? What's the hummingbird thing?"

Bridget explained about making the trip to the bird store and the hummingbird feeder she'd bought. How Garrett had showed her which one to get. "I know it sounds crazy, but ever since I saw that bird the day of the funeral, I feel like that hummingbird is...I don't know, a message of some kind. Or messenger. But he hasn't been back in a while."

"Maybe he had other messages to deliver." Nora stepped back, assessing the cake.

"A one-bird pony express?"

"Exactly." Nora cleaned the cake knife and started on the finish layer of buttercream, swiping it onto the cake rounds in smooth, practiced strokes, while Bridget piped tiny pink roses along the bottom layer. "Well, I'm glad you went to lunch with that guy. He seemed really nice. And he bought you a plant."

"For the hummingbird, not me." Bridget reconsidered her answer. Maybe saying the plant was for the hummingbird was a cover for buying one for her. The gesture made heat fill her cheeks. Except she had loved the way he'd paid attention, how he'd watched her when she talked, held her hand as they walked. "Okay, maybe that was nice."

Ma came into the kitchen with an order sheet in her

hands. "We have a rush job for a retirement cake we need to deliver this afternoon."

Bridget took the sheet and scanned the order. A simple vanilla sheet cake with white buttercream. "No problem. I can have this done in no time. Nora, you good for decorating it?"

Nora rose on her tiptoes and peered over Bridget's shoulder. "Sure. Can you get me a picture of the company logo this afternoon? I'll go by that to do the design."

Bridget mixed up the batter, got the cake in the oven, printed off the information Nora needed, and then took a quick break to check her phone. Abby had responded to her invite for dinner that night with an enthusiastic *I'd love to come.*

Bridget had the guest list. She had the dishes planned. What she didn't have was a way to defuse the potential bomb that would detonate when Ma walked in, assuming Ma agreed to come to dinner. Her mother wasn't one of those people who loved surprises. In Colleen O'Bannon's ideal world, she could see through walls and know what was coming before it hit her. As long as Bridget could remember, her mother had had a predictable schedule—she went to work at four in the morning to get the baking started, came home to wake the girls and get them off to school, then back to work, home again after school, then Mass, then dinner and homework help and bed. Every weekday, exactly the same. On Saturdays, the girls went to work with her, and on Sundays, they all went to church. Rain, sleet, snow—nothing varied.

Same thing went for the rest of her life. Anyone who looked in her closet would see dozens of the same cardigans, skirts, and blouses in a rainbow of neutrals—taupe, navy, white, black. She ate oatmeal for breakfast every day, a salad for lunch, and some kind of meat and potatoes for dinner. She colored her hair on the tenth of the month, saw her allergist on the thirteenth.

Once, the girls had banded together and thrown their mother a surprise birthday party for her fiftieth. She'd walked into the house, saw the group of guests standing there—and walked right back out. It had taken a good fifteen minutes to convince her to come back inside, and only with the promise of never, ever surprising her again.

Bridget headed out front with a tray of cookies to replenish the display case. Her mother was making a handwritten list of supplies to order, her penmanship neat and precise. Maybe it was the bright sun streaming into the shop, but her mother looked more tired than usual, her face more lined. "Ma, you're still coming to dinner at my house tonight, right?"

"Of course."

"Great." Bridget drew in a breath. "I invited all the girls, you know." Okay, so maybe that wasn't being specific and saying Abby and Aunt Mary would be there. But it wasn't *technically* lying and thus not *technically* a surprise.

Her mother nodded, immersed in the task of determining flour and sugar quantities. "I'll make a side dish."

"Sounds good. I'm bringing some black and white cookies for Magpie."

"They're her favorite." Ma still hadn't looked up, nor had she put the pieces together about what *all the girls* meant.

Bridget leaned against the counter and straightened the pile of Charmed by Dessert flyers. "Why haven't you talked to Abby in three years?"

Yeah, just a casual question about the nuclear bomb in the middle of the family.

Her mother kept on listing things on the paper but her posture was rigid, her jaw stony. "She made her choices."

"You're her mother, Ma. You don't just cut off a kid like that." That was the part that Bridget understood least. Except she'd done the same thing. She'd been bitter at Abby for ruining her wedding, angry with her for what she'd said about Jim, and used all that to fuel her grudge. Now, though, after his death, it all seemed so pointless.

"Do you really think I'd do that to one of my children? I love you all." Ma's eyes glistened with a sadness that seemed to reach her soul. "I tried, Bridget. I tried several times to talk to her. I left her messages. I sent her a card. I even went to her apartment, rang the bell. She was inside—I could hear her—but she..." Ma paused and shook her head, and when she spoke again, her words had a raw, jagged edge. "She didn't even open the door. Do you know how much that hurts to have your own child ignore you like that? I tried, Bridget, but she didn't want to try too."

"Maybe she had a reason for not opening the door." Like a live-in fiancée no one knew about.

"And maybe what she said at the wedding was the truth. What she said to me," her mother added quietly.

In those few words was the crux of why Ma wore that armor over her hurt, why she hadn't made amends. When Abby had argued with Bridget in the living room that day, Ma had tried to defuse the moment by nudging Abby toward Ned the orthopedist again. This time, Abby had exploded. *I wish Dad were here, because he would have cared about why I ran out of the room. Not you, Mom. All you want to do is control my life. Control who I date, who I love, who I marry. I'm not a fucking doll you can manipulate.*

The F-bomb was what ignited Ma's temper. It was the one word the girls knew better than to use. Abby had her mouth washed out with a bar of Ivory soap when she was eleven, and that was enough to convince the rest of the girls they never wanted to say *that* word in front of Ma.

Ma's face reddened, and she advanced on Abby, saying things about how it was her house and she wasn't going to allow her daughter to disrespect her, and how dare she ruin Bridget's special day.

Nora grabbed Abby's arm and said they were a family, a team at the bakery, so calm down and let's work this out. She'd whispered something in Abby's ear, but instead of calming, it had only inflamed Abby more. She'd picked up the cake, told Nora to mind her own business, and then flung the cake at the wall. Bridget started to cry and screamed at Abby, calling her selfish.

You want to marry an asshole, Bridget, I can't stop you, Abby had said. *But I'm not going to stand here and pretend I'm happy while you do it.*

That was when Jim had grabbed Bridget's hand and

convinced her they needed to leave. She remembered casting one last look over her shoulder as they ran out the door. The living room floor was covered with chunks of wedding cake and the fallout from a family fight that had brewed for decades. A fight that had never really ended.

If they didn't start to settle some of this, tonight would be a rerun of the wedding. "Ma, I don't think Abby meant half of what she said," Bridget said. "You know how people say things when they get mad."

"Drunkenness and anger 'tis said tell the truth," her mother said, still listing and planning, the moment of emotion wiped away. "There's a reason that saying has been around for hundreds of years."

"Well, you kinda do have a tendency to tell us what to do, Ma." *Kinda* was putting it mildly. But Bridget wasn't up to a full-on battle with her mother, so she couched the words.

Her mother scowled. "I only do it because I care about you girls. If you ever had children, you'd understand." Ma gathered up the order sheets and disappeared into the back of the shop, leaving Bridget alone.

Yet another thing that Colleen controlled, Bridget realized—the end of a conversation.

TWENTY

T he dinner was a disaster before the mashed potatoes
ended up on the floor.

Nora arrived early, along with Magpie. They greeted
Aunt Mary with joyful hugs and nonstop questions and
helped Bridget finish cooking. Aunt Mary sat at the bar
while the three sisters cooked, falling into their old
rhythms, like lifelong dance partners.

Nora peeled and boiled the potatoes, Bridget basted
the roast chicken, and Magpie whipped up a purple cab-
bage and pecan salad. They chatted and laughed, Magpie
sharing stories of people she'd met, Aunt Mary talking
about the new trick she'd taught Pedro, and Nora telling
about her kids and their upcoming band recital.

A little before six, the doorbell rang. Bridget let Abby
in with a hug while the others called out greetings from the
kitchen. "I'm so glad you came, Abby. Nora and Magpie
are here, and so is Aunt Mary."

"Ma?"

"Not yet."

Hesitancy stuttered Abby's stride. "Do you think she'll come?"

"Of course she will." Bridget didn't add that she never had given her mother the complete guest list. She figured it was good payback for springing Father McBride and his mission work on her a few weeks earlier.

Abby smoothed her hair and glanced down at her light blue V-neck sweater and jeans. "Am I dressed okay?"

"Abs, you're here. That's all I care about." Bridget hugged her sister again and kept her arm over Abby's shoulders as they walked down the hall to the kitchen. Abby leaned into her, as if drawing strength from her older sister, just like when she was a little girl.

Magpie burst forward and rushed into Abby for a hug. "You came! I'm so glad."

Aunt Mary joined the hug and then Nora, the five of them bonding in a tight circle. Abby started to cry, Nora teased her, and all of them laughed. Pedro danced at their feet and barked. For the first time that Bridget could remember, her kitchen felt warm and welcoming. Like a home.

Why had she spent all those years alone with just her husband? Why hadn't she had a family dinner long before this? When Jim had been alive, she'd convinced herself that Jim and Bridget Island was a utopia. As she felt her sisters' arms tighten around her, she knew she'd been fooling herself. This...*this* was what she'd been missing.

"Well. I didn't realize there would be such a crowd tonight."

Bridget turned at the sound of her mother's voice. Ma stood in the doorway, holding a casserole dish, looking uncomfortable and angry and shocked all at the same time. The circle dissipated, the girls stepping back with lowered heads, as if they'd been caught raiding the cookie jar.

Bridget took Abby's hand. Her sister's fingers tightened around hers, and for a second, she was seven and Abby was five, and she was telling Abby to trust her as they crossed a busy street. She gave Abby's fingers a squeeze. *Trust me*.

"I told you it was a family dinner, Ma," Bridget said. "This is our family. All the O'Bannon girls, together."

Ma pursed her lips. "You should have told me you expected more people. I would have made more colcannon."

"You made enough to feed an army of O'Bannons." Aunt Mary strode forward and took the casserole dish from Colleen's hands. She gave her sister a smile. "I'm glad you came. It's far past time we talked to each other, Colleen."

"A family dinner is not the place for a conversation like that." Ma turned away, hanging her coat over the back of a chair and her purse off the arm. She crossed to the sink, washed her hands, and checked on the progress of dinner. All actions that put her back to her daughters and sister and the conversations she didn't want to have.

Bridget glanced at Abby and mouthed, *Give it some time*. Abby nodded, but there were tears in her eyes. She grabbed the plates and silverware and disappeared into the dining room.

"You are overcooking those potatoes," Ma said to no one in particular. She grabbed an apron out of the drawer and then picked up the pan and drained the potatoes. When she was done, she raided the fridge for some milk and butter. She drizzled in the milk, then added a hearty slab of butter and started mashing with furious movements. "Don't add too much milk. It makes them runny. You want the potatoes to have some depth to them."

Bridget put a hand on her mother's back. "Ma, did you see Abby was here?"

"Of course I did. But I'm mashing the potatoes right now. I can't stop and talk to everyone."

Nora reached over and took the masher out of her mother's hand. "I'll mash the potatoes. You go say hello to Abby and Aunt Mary."

Without the wall of cooking as a shield, Ma stood in the kitchen wringing her hands on her apron. She glanced at the stove as if some other task would magically appear. Bridget moved in front of the oven door while Magpie sprinkled the pecans on her salad—a conspiracy of sisters.

Abby came back into the kitchen and picked up the stack of napkins at the end of the counter. She hesitated. Shifted her weight from foot to foot. "Hey, Ma."

"Abigail," she said to her middle daughter. The two of them stood there, statues on the tile.

The room in the air was as tense and thick as a snowbank. The timer dinged, popping Bridget into action. She took the chicken out of the oven while Magpie dressed and tossed the salad. Nora went on mashing, all of them watching the other three.

"Oh, for Pete's sake, that is *not* how you greet someone

you haven't seen in a long time, Colleen, nor how you greet your child." Aunt Mary grabbed Abby by one arm, Colleen by the other, then mushed the three of them into a giant hug. "Life is too short to stay mad. Nothing like almost dying to teach you that lesson."

Ma drew back and looked up at her sister. "Almost dying?"

"Had a little heart trouble." Mary patted the left side of her chest. "But thanks to Bridget here, I've had time to take it easy and rest up. And now I get to spend the evening with all my nieces and my sister. A true family night. The only sourpuss here is you, Colleen, so you better put your smile on and quit keeping a grudge in your fist."

Abby arched an amused brow but didn't say anything.

"I'm not doing any of that," Ma said.

Aunt Mary leaned closer to Colleen. She lowered her voice. "You are and you know it. You've always been like that. Madder than a wet hornet at the simplest things. Now, I realize years ago that maybe it was a necessary thing. Easier than dealing with losing a husband when you had a bunch of little girls at home. But I think you've been so angry for so long, you've forgotten how to be happy."

Ma scowled. "I've done no such thing."

"Then prove it." Aunt Mary put her hands on her hips. "Make some small talk with your daughter, with me." Aunt Mary stepped back and waved between Abby and Ma.

The only sound in the room was the scraping of the metal masher against the stainless steel pot. Magpie stopped tossing the salad, and Bridget left the half-carved chicken on the platter. Abby stared at her mother, her face expectant, hopeful, but wary.

"This is foolishness," her mother said. "I've already talked to Abby, and I talked to you. I'm not going to stand here and be forced to talk about the weather or the price of beans in India. I need to wash up for dinner."

Then she spun on her heel and out of the room. Aunt Mary sighed. Even Pedro sighed and lowered himself onto his paws.

"She's never going to change. I don't know why I even try." Abby grabbed her car keys off the counter. "Thanks for the invite, Bridge, but I don't think I can stay."

Aunt Mary put a hand on Abby's. Her kind eyes met her niece's with the understanding of someone who had known Ma all her life. "Your mother is stubborn and a pain in the ass, but she loves you all. She's also made her own fair share of mistakes, though admitting that is something she may never do. Give her a little time to warm up. She's got her porcupine quills up because she's so afraid of being hurt."

"*She's* afraid? How about having a mother who barely acknowledges your existence for three years? *I'm* the hurt one. Not her."

"Give her a minute," Aunt Mary said, and gave Abby's hand a squeeze. "I know her, better than you think, and in case you forget, I was at that wedding too. There were enough hurtful words tossed around to sink the *Titanic*, so it's not surprising you all are facing off like a couple of badgers. Now, let's all go sit at the table and have some delicious dinner. Without a single cross word. Okay?"

"Okay," Abby said. "But if she starts in on me—"

"You will be polite and kind because, no matter what, she is your mother. And she raised all of you single-handedly, which is a very brave and difficult thing to do. You have no idea how hard your mother's life was during those years, or what she went through." Aunt Mary looked at each of the girls in turn. "Now, let's eat. And remember, not a single cross word."

The girls filed into the dining room carrying the carved chicken, the salad, a bowl of mashed potatoes, and the colcannon their mother had brought. Bridget sat at one end of the table with Nora and Abby on one side and Magpie and Aunt Mary on the other. Ma walked into the room and took the only other available seat at the head of the table. She looked around and then back at Bridget. "You didn't set a place for your husband."

Bridget sighed. "Because he's dead, Ma, and I'm not going to spend the next twenty years of my life mourning him, just because it's what you did with Dad."

Nora nudged her under the table and made a keep-the-peace face. "How about we table the dead spouse talk for now and instead say grace?" she asked. "Ma, would you do the honors?"

They all bowed their heads and clasped their hands. And waited. After a solid minute of silence, Bridget looked up. "Ma?"

"I'm sorry. I'm just not up to that." Her voice was thick. Her face was red, and her hands were trembling. "I didn't expect to come here and be interrogated by my sister or disrespected by my daughter. I came for a family dinner."

Magpie snorted. "Ma, this *is* family dinner. Since when did we ever have normal meals where everyone got along?"

Bridget had been hoping for some Hallmark movie moment tonight. Everyone arrived, hugged and cried, and all was well again. She'd forgotten that they were O'Bannons—fiery and complicated and stubborn. And this entire dinner had a very good chance of going south before she even served the chicken.

"Can we at least pretend to get along?" Bridget said. "Please? It's the first time we've all been together in forever. I kinda miss those family dinners. The ones where we laughed and made faces in our mashed potatoes and talked about boys and school and how much broccoli we had to eat in order to have ice cream for dessert."

After a moment, Ma finally spoke, her voice quiet and her gaze on somewhere distant. "We had those kinds of dinners when you girls were little and your father was alive." Ma's face softened. "Michael had this way of coaxing a smile out of a lemon."

"Dad was fun," Abby said, her voice low and sad. "A lot of fun. I miss him so much."

The air in the room stilled. The food began to cool, vapors of heat wafting off the chicken and mashed potatoes, but no one reached for a spoon or a bowl.

An eternity seemed to pass until Abby gestured toward the platter. "Can you pass the chicken, please?"

Ma picked up the dish and passed it to Abby but didn't

let go. "I have been very mad at you for a long time for ruining your sister's wedding, you know. And for walking out on the bakery."

"I know, Ma. And I'm sorry." Abby sighed. "Can we just have one nice family dinner? Let's talk about it later. Okay?"

Another moment passed. Then something in Ma seemed to let go, and the stiff tension in her shoulders eased.

"All right. But we *will* talk later." Ma released the plate. Abby took some chicken, Ma passed the colcannon, and for a moment, everything was normal.

For a moment.

Nora was the first to talk, telling them all about her kids and their end-of-school-year activities. Magpie started talking about a trip she'd taken to Haiti and the rundown schools she'd seen there. Aunt Mary chimed in about a similar situation she'd seen in South Africa, while Ma asked questions about their trips and reminded Nora to bring her grandchildren by more often.

Bridget watched this large group of strong O'Bannon women, all of them determined and stubborn and beautiful, while they dished up their plates and then segued into familiar common ground—food. They debated the use of cream cheese in mashed potatoes, whether basting with orange juice made for a crispier chicken skin, and how the pecans in the salad were especially sweet this year. The scene was as warm as the food in her belly, and she vowed to have more family dinners. Nothing was truly fixed, of course, and she knew the dinner was merely a Band-Aid hiding still raw and open wounds, but it was a start.

Bridget had the bowl of mashed potatoes in her hand when she heard the front door open. For a weird second, she thought it was Jim, home from work. Then she remembered, and it hurt all over again, although the loss was tempering with time, the pain becoming more manageable.

Nora glanced at Bridget. "Did you invite anyone else?"

"Nope. Not unless we have a sister we don't know about." Bridget started to get to her feet, leaving the mashed potatoes on the corner of the table, when Abby's fiancée strode into the dining room. Tall and blond and mad as hell.

"Oh crap," Bridget said.

"Shit," Magpie said.

Abby just sat there, frozen, mouth agape, eyes wide. She glanced at Ma and then at Bridget, as if saying, *Do something.*

Bridget had no idea what to do. Kick Jessie out? Invite her to stay?

"This is where you are? With the family you told me you don't talk to?" Jessie waved her hands as she spoke, stopping from time to time to wipe away a tear.

"It's *complicated*, Jessie." Abby scrambled out of her chair. "What are you doing here and how did you find me?"

"Like an idiot, I followed you. I saw the text from Bridget about the family dinner, and I was hurt. You...you didn't even ask me if I wanted to go." The last word caught on a sob.

Ma looked at Bridget. Bridget looked away. This wasn't her thing to explain. "Uh, I can set another place at the table…," Bridget said. When in doubt, offer food—yet another O'Bannon family motto.

"There's no need to. She's not staying." Abby pulled Jessie to the side of the room and lowered her voice. "You can't force my hand. Just give me some time."

"Time? That's all I've given you, Abby." Jessie shook her head, and a tear rolled down her cheek.

Nora gave Bridget a what-the-hell-is-up look. Aunt Mary sipped at her water and kept silent. Magpie was already out of her seat, rushing over to try to smooth things over, but Abby waved her back.

Before Bridget could stop her, Ma rose and crossed to Jessie. She put out her hand. Always the polite hostess, even when it wasn't her home. "Hello, I'm Bridget's mother. Are you a friend of hers?"

Jessie leaned forward, extending her hand. "No, Mrs. O'Bannon, I'm—"

Abby yanked Jessie back and then stepped in front of her, a human wall between them. "She's my…my… friend, Ma. And I'm sorry, but we're leaving."

Hurt crumpled Jessie's face. She started to speak, but Abby tugged on her hand and yanked Jessie out of the dining room. As she did, her hip bumped the mashed potatoes. The dish tumbled to the carpet, in a horrible replay of the cake at the wedding, landing with a thick, smushy thud. A second later, the door shut, and Abby and Jessie were gone.

"I think I'm going to come to family dinners more often, if it means a food fight," Magpie said. "So…what's for dessert, Bridge?"

TWENTY-ONE

Bridget brought out two more bottles of wine. Magpie and Aunt Mary waved off the alcohol, Nora drained her water glass and replaced it with chardonnay, and Bridget topped off her second glass of the night and set the bottle on the table.

"You know...I wouldn't mind a glass," Ma said.

The girls exchanged raised brows. Aunt Mary gave her sister a questioning glance.

"I can have one glass," Ma said.

"Sure you can, Ma." Bridget grabbed a wineglass out of the hutch, filled it with chardonnay, and handed it to her mother. She sank into the seat Abby had vacated. "I'm sorry about what happened there. I had no idea Jessie was going to show up."

"And who exactly is this Jessie woman? Because she seemed to be...too angry to be just a friend."

Bridget sure as heck wasn't going to share the truth. For one, her sister had asked her not to, and for another, she already had mashed potatoes ground into her carpet. She didn't need any other food hitting the floor—or walls. "That is for Abby to tell you, Ma. Not me."

Her mother took that in with a nod, sat back in her seat, and took a big gulp of wine. Another, a third. Then she placed the empty glass on the table and got to her feet. "Thank you for a lovely dinner, Bridget, but I'm feeling quite tired and think I'll go home now."

"Ma, let me drive you." Magpie scrambled to her feet. "You've had what, one glass of wine in fifty years? You give lightweight a whole new meaning. Bridge will bring your car to work tomorrow."

"I'm perfectly capable—"

"Maybe you are, Ma, but that won't stop us from once in a while telling you what to do. Let Magpie chauffeur you." Bridget gave her mother a hug, but Ma had already withdrawn into that stoic shell she wore so well.

"Colleen, let your daughter drive you," Aunt Mary said. "Actually, before you go, I'd like to talk to you, if I could."

"I'm fine, Mary. Quit lecturing me. The chicken was wonderful." Ma placed a hand on Bridget's cheek. "But I'd baste it with butter next time. The skin was a little...soft."

Bridget rolled her eyes. She could have been as good a chef as Emeril Lagasse and her mother still would have found some kind of fault. "Good night, Ma."

"And you should have rolls next time. No dinner is complete without a little bread too."

"Leave the girl alone, Colleen. She did a wonderful

job." Aunt Mary slid her arm through her sister's. "Magpie, can you bring the car around? Colleen and I are going to chat out front for a moment."

"Sure." Magpie left in a flurry of hugs and kisses and with a container of black and white cookies that Bridget pressed into her hands. "Thanks for dinner! Love you all!"

Ma and Aunt Mary went out front, and as soon as the door shut, Nora and Bridget both bounded onto the sofa and peeked through the blinds. "What do you think they're talking about?" Nora asked.

"I don't know. But the last time they talked alone like that, they ended up arguing and not speaking for five years."

Aunt Mary and Ma stood about a foot apart on the walkway, half in shadow, half lit by the porch light. Aunt Mary moved her arms when she talked, as expressive as a peacock. Ma stayed still, tucked into herself, her responses back seeming measured, cold.

"Can you hear anything?" Nora asked.

"No. And if I open the window, I'm sure they're going to hear that."

Nora glanced at Bridget, and they shared a conspiratorial smile. "It's like we're kids again, huh? Spying on the neighbors and making up stories about them."

"Remember that time Mrs. Nuzio caught us spying on her and the mailman? I thought she was going to beat us with that spatula." Bridget laughed. "She told Ma, and Ma told her that if she didn't want people spying, she shouldn't do things in secret."

"Ma stood right between us and Mrs. Nuzio. For a minute, I thought Ma might deck her." Nora shook her head, and her features softened. "For all her faults, Ma does stand up for us when it matters most, you know."

"Yeah? Tell that to Abby." Bridget moved away from the window and slid onto the caramel leather sofa. Bridget could still see the sad realization on Abby's face when she'd introduced Jessie, as if she'd given up on her family ever accepting the truth.

Nora dropped back onto the sofa, curling one leg underneath her so she could face Bridget. "Was that Abby's girlfriend? I mean, I kinda figured it out from the way Jessie acted and how Abby rushed her out of here."

"Not just her girlfriend," Bridget said. "Fiancée."

"Oh." Nora thought about that a moment. "Well, that's good. I mean, if she's happy enough with Jessie to want to get married, then I'm happy for her."

"You need to tell her that." Nora had accepted Abby with the same nonplussed attitude as the other girls. Now if only Ma could do the same. But maybe, with the support of her sisters, Abby would feel more inclined to be honest. "Abby is convinced that no one in the family will accept her if she comes out."

Although Bridget doubted it would be a secret for long either way. Ma wasn't a stupid woman, and from her questions tonight, her suspicions had been raised. It was only a matter of time before Ma put the pieces together. And once she did, then it would be up to their mother to either accept her daughter or shun her again.

"How long have you known?"

"Since my wedding day."

Nora's eyes widened. "Oh my God. Really? That whole crazy thing with the cake and the fight...that was because Ma kept trying to set her up with Jim's cousin, wasn't it? She kept on saying, 'oh, he's an orthopedist,' as if that automatically made him Mr. Right."

Bridget nodded. "And Abby quit the bakery, and the family, I think because she didn't feel like we accepted her."

"Because Ma has never been very accepting of anyone who is different. Like Georgi the florist. And that guy at church, and those two women who lived on our block." Nora shook her head. "She's cordial, but—"

"Judgmental."

"Yeah. I can see why Abby has avoided that." Nora sipped at her wine. "But why wouldn't she tell me?"

"I don't know, Nora. I really don't. Maybe..."

"What? Say it."

Bridget drew her knees up to her chest. "Maybe she was sure you would be like Ma. You've always been the good one, the one who never broke any rules, who never—"

"Took a stand. Or caused an uproar. Or threw a cake at the wall."

"Well, yeah." Bridget gave her sister a lopsided smile. "But it's okay. That's who you are. The peacemaker."

Nora was silent for a long while. "Ever since Dad died, I didn't want any of us to split up, you know? We're all each other has, and that's what I told Abby at the wedding. I reminded her that she should stop arguing and protect the family."

"Not realizing that she was fighting because she felt like her family wasn't behind her."

"Yeah." Nora sighed. "If I had known, I would have handled that so differently."

"You and me both." Bridget thought of that day in her bedroom, when she was distracted by the wedding dress and the veil and all the details, instead of seeing the true picture. Of her sister Abby, of the man Bridget had chosen to marry. "I had blinders on that day. I had no idea how much Abby was hurting. And to compound all that, I...I never talked to her after that either. Not till last week."

Nora's gaze dropped to her hands. Her voice slid into a softer, sadder range. "You didn't talk to any of us after your wedding. It was like you cut off your right arm to go live with the left."

Hurt echoed in her sister's words, and for the first time, Bridget realized that her sisters had been suffering the same as she had all these years. She'd been so angry at them and so ready to dismiss them from her life.

In the months since the funeral, she'd made amends with Magpie, carved some inroads with Nora, and had begun to do the same with Abby and with her mother. But tension still charged the air between them, still colored every word they exchanged.

The irony of her wanting the family to accept Abby—and Abby's choice in a mate—seemed like God's ha-ha way of making her see this all through a new lens. Bridget had abandoned her family because she didn't feel like they accepted her husband. She finally saw how that hurt spread through the family, like a ripple in a pond.

"I cut everyone off because I wanted to make my marriage work," Bridget said.

Put that way, the excuse sounded thin. How could she explain how swept up she was, in love and eagerness to make that happy, perfect bubble last as long as possible? One week away from her family turned into two, then turned into months, then years, and she kept telling herself it was all for the best. She didn't want them to dim the happiness she'd felt.

Except that the happiness had dimmed all on its own. And the marriage she had worked so hard to preserve had already started to die, long before her husband did.

"You made your marriage work by giving Jim control over who you saw?" Nora threw up her hands. "I'm sorry. I shouldn't be saying that. But...damn it, Bridget, it sucked when you did that. All of a sudden, you were gone. Gone from the bakery, gone from our lives, just...gone."

Bridget reached for her sister's hand. "I'm sorry, Nora. I...thought I was doing the right thing. I was so angry with all of you, and so hurt by what Abby had said. And the longer I stayed away, the easier it got to do that, and the harder it got to come back."

Nora picked at the edge of one of the throw pillows. "Do you regret it? Marrying him?"

Regret. It was a word Bridget had kicked around a lot in her head these last few months. "No. Not entirely. I loved him, and I think he loved me too. But somewhere along the way, I forgot who I was and who I wanted to be. I caved instead of fought."

Nora scoffed. "Welcome to the club. I can't tell you how many arguments I either didn't have or just let Ben win. And when it comes to Ma and the bakery, I try to make as few waves as possible. Life is more peaceful that way."

"Maybe so. But it's also emptier." Bridget looked around her living room, at the furniture that she had agreed to buy even though she'd never really loved it, at the man-sized television that dominated one wall, at the rows and rows of Jim's books that filled the bookcases, while her favorites were relegated to one bottom shelf. These few months alone had begun to wipe away that fog of denial and made her start to see the bills, the bananas, even the furniture, in new ways. "I went into my marriage expecting a Cinderella ending, but the reality never matched my fantasies. Maybe we were just mismatched, or maybe"—Bridget drew a pillow to her chest and whispered the thought that had grown in strength in the days since she'd run down the grass and dropped into the primroses—"I wanted that fantasy so much, I gave up myself to try to get it."

❧❧❧

Magpie's little two-seater idled on the street at the end of Bridget's walk. The sun had set, and the neighborhood was winding down. The occasional laugh of a child, or a mother calling out bedtime, punctuated the air.

Mary stood across from Colleen, her long hair curling around her shoulders and lifting in the slight breeze. They were such opposites—the prim and proper Colleen, and the wild, unpinned Mary. Magpie far more resembled Mary in spirit than Colleen ever had.

"So, have you told the girls yet?" It was the same question Mary had asked five years ago, the same question that had set off Colleen's cold war.

Colleen gripped the strap of her purse tighter. The leather had heft, weight, solidity. But it wasn't enough to protect her from the conversation she didn't want to have—then or now. "Of course not. They have no need to know my personal business."

Mary sighed. "This isn't personal business, Colleen. It's…family history. And I don't want to keep it secret anymore."

"You've been perfectly content to keep this a secret for sixty-two years. Why are you going to start changing things now?"

"Because I'm dying, Colleen." Mary took a step closer, and the lamplight from the porch highlighted her thinner frame, gaunt face, pale skin. "Maybe not today, maybe not tomorrow, but my ticker only has so many hours and minutes left on it, and I don't want to live another day of my life as a liar."

Colleen struggled to hold back the wave of emotion that washed over her. She wasn't a woman given to drama or tears, but the thought of losing Mary forever, even after everything, swamped her. She swallowed hard and drew in a fortifying breath. "You're fine, Mary. Maybe a little wear and tear, but we all have that."

"I'm seventy-eight, Colleen. I'm not getting any younger." Mary grasped Colleen's hand, impressing the words into her palm. "I want to live the rest of my days with truth. As the person I'm supposed to be. The person I was too scared to be six decades ago."

Colleen shook her head. All her life, Colleen had espoused the virtues of living a Christian life. No sex before marriage, no children out of wedlock, no deceit, no coveting. For twenty years, she had stayed true to her husband, believing God meant it when He said that He intended for each of us to have only one partner.

Yet, behind all that, she'd hidden things. The ten years after her husband died that she had spent secretly drinking every night, lonely and lost. The fact that Mary had come to her house, dumped out all the bottles, and stayed with her for two weeks until she could face her days without a drink bookending them. Then the secret Mary had dumped in her lap five years ago, a secret that Colleen had always suspected, really, but never voiced. Keep the peace, keep the façade, and they would all be *just fine.*

How could she face the same daughters she had faithfully brought to Mass, the priest she had known most of her life, and most of all herself? "I can't do that. What will my kids think? Can't we just leave things as they are?"

"You think perpetuating a lie is better than telling the

truth?" Mary said. "Being honest is also a commandment, you know, in case you're not up to date on your Moses."

"So I tell the truth and teach my girls, hey, it's okay to have a child out of wedlock? To pass that child off as your sister for sixty-two years? To drop that little bombshell on her at her fifty-seventh birthday party? That it all turns out okay in the end? Maybe I should tell them I spent their childhoods drinking while I'm at it. Just cement that door between us for good." The same fear she'd felt five years ago when Mary had told her the truth began to close Colleen's throat.

She still remembered standing in the kitchen, up to her elbows in soapy water while Mary dried the dishes. *I have something to tell you,* Mary had said, somewhere between the good casserole dish and Grandma's gravy boat. *Something I should have said a long time ago.*

Colleen kept on washing, plunging the sponge in and out of tall narrow glasses. A sense of dread filled her chest, but she continued to concentrate on the soap bubbles multiplying, then popping, over and over again with each dish.

I should have told you when Mom died, Mary went on, *but I chickened out. And now I just . . . I want you to know. It doesn't have to change anything, but you should know.*

But it had, it had changed everything. Colleen's entire childhood had been a lie, her mother had covered up those lies, and the relationship she had with the woman she thought was her sister was a lie. She'd ended up shouting at Mary, and Mary had stormed out, hurt and angry.

Those feelings still colored Mary's words, charging the air between them.

"First of all, your girls are grown adults now," Mary said. "They are also fallible human beings who know it is okay to screw up once in a while. That even you screw up. And this whole thing about me being your mom is all on me, not you."

"You don't understand. This is going to affect all of us. Not just you."

Mary leaned in, until Colleen could see her own reflection in Mary's eyes. "Wait a minute. Are you ashamed of me? Ashamed of being born out of wedlock? It's not the nineteen hundreds, Colleen."

Magpie rolled down the window of her Miata. "Ma? You almost ready? I gotta be at the airport early tomorrow morning."

"Magpie needs to leave," Colleen said. She tugged her hand out of Mary's. "I have to go."

Because leaving meant she didn't have to deal with the questions in the air. The ones about death and truth and all the things Colleen had faced once in her life and never wanted to face again.

"Then let's set a time to talk. When are you free, Colleen?"

Colleen glanced at Magpie's car and then back at Mary. "I don't know. I have the bakery and then I go to Mass, and I've got some other errands to run."

"In other words, you're still too busy to deal with anything," Mary said. "The same thing you've been saying as long as I've known you. Are you...are you dealing with your problems and stress the same way you used to?"

Colleen looked away. "That was twenty years in the past, Mary. Stop bringing that up. I'm fine now."

"If that's true, I'm glad. You know, your girls think you are this always-perfect person who never makes a mistake. It would be nice for them to know you are human too. Maybe give you all something to bond over."

Why did Mary have to keep nagging at her? Did she think it would change anything? That Colleen would all of a sudden have some epiphany and confess?

"Our family is fine. I'm fine." Now she was lying to herself and to everyone else. But no one understood how those frantic hours, filled with baking and praying and simply moving, kept her mind from wandering down paths she couldn't take. The ones that said she'd been lonely in that big house on Park, that she wondered how her life would have been different if Mary had been honest sixty-two years ago, and the one that said maybe she wasn't as right about everything as she thought she was.

"You, my dear daughter, are an expert at avoidance. So when you are ready to deal with the truth, you know where to find me." Mary gave the leash a tug. Pedro popped to his feet and trotted off beside his mistress and back up toward the house.

Colleen strode down the walkway and got into Magpie's car. As her daughter pulled away from the curb, Colleen glanced in the side mirror. Mary stood on the porch, a silhouette beneath the light from the sconce.

I'm dying, Colleen.

Colleen imagined that silhouette gone, the dark, blank hole that would be in her life when Mary passed away. She closed her eyes and leaned her head against the window and waited until she was home to let the tears fall.

TWENTY-TWO

T he night after the disaster that had been the dinner at Bridget's, Abby stood in the private event room at the back of Lombardi's Italian restaurant. The restaurant manager, a slight man with a hunched back, waited by the door, a contract in his hands. Jessie, as stiff and silent as a toy soldier beside Abby. Still stewing about the night before.

Abby had tried explaining after they left Bridget's house but Jessie refused to talk to her the entire night. She'd left for work before Abby got up, leaving the bed cold and empty. Abby had lain there for a long time alone, her head on Jessie's pillow, inhaling the fruity scent of Jessie's shampoo and wishing she could rewind, do that moment over, and erase the word *friend*.

Abby had texted Jessie after work, asking if she was still planning on coming to this appointment with the event manager, but there'd been no response. That Jessie was here at all Abby took as a good sign. If she could just get a second to explain...

"This is going to be perfect, don't you think?" Abby said. The room was small—only big enough for forty people—and lined with wine bottles. The long oak table recalled the days of knights and kings, with high-backed leather chairs and studding on the feet. "I can't wait to marry you, Jessie."

Jessie's gaze dropped to the floor. In that instant, she seemed to deflate, as if all the fight had left her. "About that..."

Abby wanted to stop Jessie before she spoke another word, to somehow head off what was coming next. Her mind whirred, grasping at words, but none of them could explain why she labeled Jessie as "friend" instead of "fiancée."

"I was wrong last night not to tell them the truth," Abby said, her words a rushing river trying to keep the boat from landing. "I got scared, and I said the first thing that came to mind, and it was wrong. I just knew how my mother would react, and I..." She let out a long breath. "I couldn't do that to you."

"What? You think I couldn't handle a little judgment? Some snide remark? Or some sermon about how I'm going straight to hell? I've heard it all, Abby, and unlike you, I'm not afraid to tell the world to go to fucking hell." Jessie put up her hands and stepped back. "I can't do this anymore. I don't even know why I came today. I can't marry you. And I sure as hell can't rent this room for a wedding we aren't going to have."

Jessie hurried out of Lombardi's. Abby ran after her,

catching Jessie in the parking lot of the restaurant. "Wait. Please. Can we just talk for five seconds?"

A soft rain fell, misting in the air before hitting their skin. Tiny streams ran down the cars and along the pavement. "We should call the flower shop when we get home," Jessie finally said, her voice soft and sad. Her gaze was distant, far from Abby. "And the minister and—"

Abby reached for her, but Jessie's hand was limp. "Jessie, don't do this. Please."

"I'll cancel the appointment at the dress shop," she went on, almost an automaton now. "I think we can still get our deposit back on the trip to Key West."

"Jessie, please. *Don't.* Let me explain."

Jessie swallowed and finally met Abby's gaze. But her eyes were flat, her face a stone. "There is no explanation that will make this better. Outside of our bedroom, you can't be honest about the kind of person you love, never mind who you love. Why would I marry someone who is living a lie?"

Abby leaned against the brick façade and turned her face to the rain. For a second, she wished she still smoked because, if there was ever a time to need a cigarette, it was now. "You don't understand. My family isn't like your family."

"You mean they aren't complicated and infuriating and imperfect? Because all families are like that. The difference is you, Abby. You are too scared to tell them the truth. And to me, that says you're too scared to be committed to me." Jessie slipped off her ring, placed it on the hood of the car, and turned and walked away.

The rain started to come down hard, so hard and fast, that it blurred Jessie into the gray. A second later, she slipped into a cab and was gone. Abby stood in the parking lot for a long, long time while the rain drenched her hair, soaked her shirt, slid down her legs.

TWENTY-THREE

The delivery van was a ruse.

When Bridget saw the Allston address for an office baby shower cake, she'd offered to deliver it on her lunch break. Ma handed over the keys without protest, her face lined and shadowed, as if she hadn't slept well the night before. When Bridget asked her about it, Ma had shrugged the whole thing off as "allergies."

Bridget doubted her mother had an allergy to anything other than talking about the stuff they buried in the O'Bannon family. But she let it go because she was in a good mood and didn't want to spoil it by arguing with her mother or hearing again how she really should consider brightening up her hair color.

Bridget popped into the kitchen to grab the finished pink and blue cake out of the freezer. "Nora, I'm going to run this cake over to the party. After work, I was wondering…would you and Ben like to come over tonight? Bring the kids, if you want."

Such a normal request, but Bridget held her breath. The dinner—despite the mashed potatoes on the floor and the fight with Abby and Jessie—had left her craving more time with her sisters. Aunt Mary had mentioned this morning how much she had enjoyed seeing the girls, and Bridget decided maybe she should try again, but on a smaller scale. Maybe then all the food would stay on the table.

Nora's brows arched with surprise. She paused in piping roses around a birthday cake. "Tonight? I'd love to but Ben...Ben's working."

"No problem. Just bring the kids. We'll make it a girls' night."

"Are you sure, Bridge? I mean, you have a really nice house and these are rambunctious kids—"

Bridget put a hand on Nora's shoulder. "I'm sure. I'll give Abs a call too. Magpie is already off to who knows where, but Aunt Mary will be there."

"That'll be nice, Bridge." Nora smiled. "Really nice."

A minute later, Bridget was in the ancient delivery van they kept in the back of Charmed by Dessert. The white box van had seen better days, and the air-conditioning was as fickle as a teenage girl at her first dance, but it got them from Point A to Point B. Bridget headed up Columbus, then cut across Brookline and into Allston, before hopping onto Soldiers Field Road.

The Charles River wound by on her right, bright and blue and flanked by green. The day was sunny, temps in the mid-80s, and people were pouring out of their offices to enjoy a little summer sunshine.

She found the address for the architectural firm she needed, parked, and had the cake dropped off in record time. Then she sat in the van for two full minutes, nerves churning in her stomach, before she managed to send out a text.

I'm in your neighborhood right now. Do you have time for a quick lunch?

She waited, her heart in her throat, and then a ping. Sure. Meet me in the lobby in five?

She put the van in gear, drove a few more blocks along Soldiers Field, then parked again. The rearview mirror re-assured her that she looked fine—not as pale and worn as she had three months ago. She'd opted to wear jeans and a V-neck dark brown and pink Charmed by Dessert T-shirt today, with a minimal coating of flour. She smoothed her hair, grabbed a bag from the seat beside her, and then walked across the lot and into the lobby of the ten-story brick building.

She wandered over to the elevators and reached out, tracing over the letters of Garrett's name on the engraved directory. She wondered about this man, a man she barely knew but who seemed to sit at the edges of her thoughts. Whenever she looked for the hummingbird, she thought of him. Heck, when she saw any kind of bird, she thought of him. More than once, she'd peeked out front when she heard the shop bell ring, hoping it was him.

They'd texted a lot, short little messages that could have been read as friendship only—the *How was your day?* kind of thing that never got too personal and every once in a while, a *Stop by for lunch if you're ever in the area* message from him. Then last night, maybe because of the wine or maybe because the family fight still rang in her head, Bridget had been up late and sent off a text. She leaned on the wall by the elevator, tugged out her phone, and reread it.

I'm thinking I might become a diplomatic lawyer, she wrote. Mediation between North and South Korea HAS to be easier than dealing with my family. Sigh.

She hadn't even expected an answer, but a second later, there'd been a ping. I know what you mean. Last Thanksgiving, my uncle Elvin got drunk and ended up dropping the turkey on the floor. The dogs had a better meal than we did.

Ha ha. We must have similar families.

Aren't all Dorchester families a little rough around the edges? he wrote. But that's what makes them the best. They're stubborn but strong, loud but loyal, and crazy but comfortable.

You must know my family well ;-)

I know at least one member of your family. Hopefully I get to know her better soon.

You've been talking to my sisters?

Just you, Bridget. Not interested in anyone else. :-)

That had sent a little trill through her heart. She'd read the message over several times, her finger hovering over the reply button. She wondered if Garrett was lying in his bed, too, waiting for those iMessage bubbles to show she was answering. In the end, she sidestepped the conversation entirely, saying she was tired and wishing him good night.

In the morning, she'd woken up and thought about the coffees they'd gotten together, the lunch at the Cuban restaurant, the conversations they'd had. Garrett made her smile, made her laugh, and she wanted more. So here she was, asking a man out for the first time in her life.

The elevator doors opened, Bridget jerked back, and Garrett appeared, as if rereading the text exchange had manifested him. He grinned. "I didn't mean you had to be right at the elevator door when it opened."

"Oh, well, I was just…" She waved at the directory. "Seeing where your office is."

He thumbed behind him. "I can take you on a tour after lunch if you want, but I assure you, it's decorated in Early Lawyer. Brown and Boring as Hell."

Bridget laughed. "Okay, then maybe we can skip that part." She held up the bag in her hand. "I brought dessert. Do you know where we can get lunch?"

"Practically right outside the door." He pressed on the glass door and held it for her. They fell into a natural rhythm once they started walking along the paved esplanade that snaked along the river.

A sculling crew glided down the river in a bright white boat that seemed to stretch for miles. Their every move synced, and the flat blue of the river passed under the boat in a blur. A couple rollerblading hand in hand passed them, nearly colliding with another couple coming in the opposite direction with a baby stroller.

Garrett sent a little wave toward the toddler in the

stroller. The towheaded boy mimicked a waving reply. "Did you and your late husband ever have kids?" he asked.

"I wanted to," Bridget said. "But it never seemed like the right time." Easier to say that than get into the late-night arguments with Jim. And how it became increasingly clear in the last two months before his death that he didn't want kids soon—or ever. That she had begun to accept the fate of her marriage long before his death hastened it along.

"I wanted kids too," Garrett said, "but once my wife was diagnosed, she didn't think it would be right to leave me to raise a child alone. We thought we'd have more time—that she'd beat the cancer and we could live our lives out in rocking chairs but she declined pretty fast after the diagnosis." He sighed. "That was both the worst and the...not best, more...the most blessed part of the whole thing. It was awful to see this healthy, vibrant woman be reduced to a hospital bed and a bunch of machines, but in another way, I'm glad she didn't spend years suffering."

"I'm sorry," Bridget said. "Both for what you went through and for what you lost. It sounds like you loved her a great deal."

"I did. And I used to think that would preclude me from ever finding love again." He loosened his tie and un-buttoned the top button. Somehow, that made him seem more open, a little more vulnerable. "But you know what? I think loving one person makes it easier to love another. Your heart is already open. Sort of like with kids. Parents love all of them, no matter how many they have."

Did her mother love all her girls equally? Did she accept them all the same? "I'd like to think that's possible. My mother never remarried after my dad died twenty years ago. To me, that's kind of sad. I can see waiting a while, but she's a staunch believer in staying true to one man forever. I think that's unrealistic, especially at my age."

"So are you saying you don't want to spend the rest of your life alone?"

"Well, I have no immediate plans for anything in the future but..." She thought about the years that stretched ahead, the dreams she'd once had. If she did it over again, could it be better? Happier? "I'd like to believe there's the possibility of finding the right person someday."

Garrett glanced over at her. "Your late husband wasn't the right one for you?"

"I thought he was. But in the months since he died...I'm not so sure. Honestly, I wasn't so sure about that for a long time before he died." She shook her head. "I feel wrong for even admitting that. I mean, he died. I should be grieving and honoring his memory. But the truth is..."

She watched the sculling crew pass by on their return trip. Their synchronized pulls were poetry in motion, everything working together as one, as it should, because doing so made the journey easier and better for everyone in the boat. At her wedding, the priest had said something about her and Jim setting off in a boat of their own and how there was never a single captain. *You share the duties of piloting the ship,* he said, *and then neither of you carries the burdens for too long alone.*

Jim had been the captain from day one, and every time

she'd tried to lead, he'd made her feel unsure, inadequate. She'd felt alone more times than she could count, even lying in the same bed with him.

"The truth is...I was leaving him. We'd had one too many fights, and I was planning on asking for a divorce after he got back from his trip." She ran a hand over her face. She hadn't thought about her decision since Jim died. The whole memory filled her with guilt, as if her even thinking that she no longer needed him had somehow resulted in the accident. "God, that makes me sound like a horrible person. What kind of wife does that? And then her husband dies?"

Garrett stopped walking and turned toward her. He took both her hands in his and met her gaze. "Number one, marriages fall apart all the time. That doesn't make you a bad wife. Number two, you thinking that or planning that was in no way responsible for what happened to him."

"But we had a big fight that morning, and I can't help but think that he was distracted getting out of the taxi and—"

Bridget spun away from Garrett and faced the water. She wrapped her arms around her waist and held as tight as she could, as if doing so would hold back the guilt, the regret. "I never should have fought with him. I should have tried harder."

"You did the best you could. That accident is no one's fault but the driver who hit your husband." Garrett's hands were on her shoulders, his tall, warm body behind her, shielding her from the afternoon sun. He offered shade and solace, a place for her to open up her heart. "And moving on with your life is not a sin or an affront to what you had. You're alive, Bridget. It won't change anything if you admit that the life you had with him wasn't perfect and that you dreamed of something more. Maybe accepting that will help you move out of this limbo."

She thought of the bills, still unpaid. The house that needed to be sold. The clothes in the closet, razor in the sink, the Audi she couldn't afford in the garage. All the decisions she had hesitated on making, the questions she hadn't answered.

And the solid steadiness of this man, if only she got brave enough to let go of the dock and take a risk on her future.

"I know how hard it is," Garrett said. "I felt so guilty after my wife died, like I should have tried harder to save her. Found more doctors, tried more treatments. It took me a full year before I moved her purse from the counter and put her shoes away. Little by little, I gave myself permission to move forward."

Permission to move forward. Would giving herself that alleviate the guilt that weighed on her shoulders? Curb the procrastination?

They had stopped walking in front of a small restaurant that faced the water. Several wrought-iron bistro tables sat outside, under the shade of an oak tree. The scent of burgers and dogs wafted out of the open service windows, where a line of people in suits and dour dresses began to form.

"Let's have lunch," Garrett said, "and talk about important subjects, like whether chili has to have beans or just ground beef."

She laughed. "Beans, of course. As a nod to Boston. And why are we changing the subject?"

"Because"—he took her hand in his, and the touch felt right, comfortable—"life is too short to dwell on the past."

TWENTY-FOUR

At the end of the workday, Colleen stood outside the white two-story Cape that housed the headquarters for Sophie's Home. She shifted the box in her arms and wondered for the hundredth time why she kept making these deliveries personally. After all, Roger had said he would gladly pick up the leftovers. Still, every other day, she drove over here after work and then hurried off to Mass.

She strode up the stairs and into the building. The wood floor hall was dim, but the rooms flanking it were bright and airy, decorated in whites and yellows with welcoming sofas and colorful curtains and toys for the children. On her right, a mom was sitting on the carpeted floor while her twin toddlers constructed something out of Legos. To her left, a group of women shuffled through a rack of clothes while they debated the best option for an upcoming job interview.

Roger had done good work here—she saw it every time

she walked in. Families drawing together, rebuilding their lives, finding homes. She admired him for that, which was why she was here, supporting him. That was all it was— common admiration for someone doing good work.

And one more thing to occupy her time and her mind. After dinner at Bridget's, the drama with Abby and the mashed potatoes, and then the conversation with Mary, that was all Colleen wanted—an empty mind. Then she could avoid thinking about the fractures and fissures in her family, and the secrets better left in the dark.

Roger emerged from his office, and a smile broke across his face. "Mrs. O'Bannon, so nice to see you again. What treats have you brought us today?"

"We had a last-minute cancellation for an order, so I have six dozen cupcakes." She lifted the lid of the top box. "They were for a bridal shower, so they're all decorated in pink and yellow. I hope that's okay." She didn't add that she had made extra, just to bring some over here today. There were so many women housed in Roger's facility that she reasoned they would appreciate the pastel-colored desserts.

"Frosting is great, no matter what color it is." He took the box from her and looked down. "And what's in the second box?"

"An apple pie. I told you I had the best apple pie around."

He grinned. "Do I get to taste it and decide for myself?"

Ever since he'd raved about that diner pie, she'd vowed to bring him one of hers. The bakery had been so busy the last few weeks that she'd barely had time to fill the regular orders, never mind extras for the case. Plus, she didn't want him thinking she'd gone out of her way to bake the pie. That would seem forward, and if there was one thing Colleen didn't want to seem, it was forward. "One bite and you will see it's no contest at all, Mr. O'Sullivan."

"Oh, please, call me Roger. We know each other now. I see you practically every day." He waved toward his office. "Why don't you come on in and share this pie with me?"

Every time she'd stopped by, her deliveries had been quick. In, out, back in the car, and off to Mass. Never had he invited her to stay. "Oh, I should—"

"Have some of this pie. If it's as delicious as you claim, then you shouldn't be able to resist."

"It's not a claim, Mr.—" She stopped herself. "Roger— it's the truth."

"Then you should be here to hear me admit that." He stepped into the room and pulled out a chair. "Please, Mrs. O'Bannon, sit."

"Well…" She glanced down the hall toward the door. Back at him. "Just for a moment."

He grabbed a pair of paper plates off a microwave in the corner of his office and two plastic forks out of a repurposed coffee mug. His office had *man* written all over it. An industrial metal desk, flanked by mismatched metal filing cabinets. Gray carpet, with a plain small table and chairs in one corner. The bookcases brimmed with books of all kinds—novels, biographies, textbooks, even two copies of the Bible. The windows looked out onto the parking lot. A modest space for a man who had a modest view of his work, she'd found.

His initial joke about taking all the credit had been just that, a joke. The Roger she'd gotten to know shrugged off his own accomplishments and dished out accolades to those around him. He was kind and compassionate, honest and humble, and she liked that. A lot.

"Here you go. Would you like some coffee to go with it?"

"No, thank you." She placed her hands in her lap. "I don't drink coffee after noon."

"Bourbon, then?" He put up a hand. "Kidding, kidding." He reached into a mini-fridge beside him and pulled out two iced teas. "Better option?"

She accepted one, unscrewed the cap, and took a long drink. "Thank you."

He held his fork, poised over his slice of pie, and looked at her. "Aren't you going to eat?"

"I will. After you take your first bite." He gave her a quizzical look. She blushed and shook her head. "It's a silly thing, I suppose, but I love to watch people take their first bite of one of our desserts. I like to watch their reactions. I can tell the instant the bite hits their tongue, and if they smile, I know I've done my job well. My eldest daughter, Bridget, does the same thing." She dipped her head. "It's silly, I know."

She'd said that twice. Goodness, what was wrong with her? She was as chatty as a schoolgirl.

"Not at all. It's sort of like how I go to every move-in. I

like to be the one who hands over the keys and watch the family's eyes light up when they realize they finally have a place of their own. There are a lot of times when those moments make this old softie choke up." He patted his heart. "Okay, on to a bite of the best apple pie in the world."

Colleen laced her hands together and waited. For the first time she could remember, a flutter of nerves ran through her. Roger closed his mouth around the bite, and—

Nothing.

The nerves turned to a churning. Never had she seen anyone have no reaction to her baking. Roger took a second bite, chewed it with thought and reached for a third bite. He paused, looked up at her, and grinned. "I got you there, didn't I?"

It took a few seconds for her to realize he'd been teasing her. She laughed and swatted at him. "That was terrible."

"Ah, but I bet it's a reaction you've never seen before." He wagged the fork in her direction. "Now you will remember me."

He held her gaze for a moment. Colleen forgot her pie. Forgot her iced tea. Forgot where she was. Then someone down the hall coughed, and that drew her attention back. She got to her feet, fast, and clutched her purse to her chest. "I should go."

"Already? You haven't even had a bite of your pie."

"I...I shouldn't be late for Mass." A riot of emotions ran through her, emotions she hadn't felt in two decades.

She didn't know whether to embrace them or run for the door. In all these years, she'd never desired another man. Never looked at one's mouth while he ate a bite of pie and wondered what it would be like if he kissed her.

Roger rose and put a hand on her arm. Colleen's pulse tripped, and her gaze darted to his. "Stay, please. Mass will be there tomorrow. Have some pie with me."

TWENTY-FIVE

Dozens of photo albums lay in a circle on the Berber. Nora, Bridget, and Aunt Mary sat cross-legged in the center of the circle, sipping wine and nibbling on pepperoni pizza. An oldies station played James Taylor on the living room stereo. In the end, Nora had opted to hire a babysitter, and Abby had canceled last minute, saying something came up. The three of them had an easy dinner of delivered pizza and salad. Then, as the memories began to flow into their conversation, Bridget dragged out the photo albums.

She slid a photo out of the album's protective sleeve and held it up to the light. The image had faded some over the years but still showed the four girls standing on the front porch of the house on Park Street, dressed in matching plaid jumpers and Mary Jane shoes. Abby pouting at the forced dress, Magpie caught mid-spin to make her skirt swirl, Nora posing like a model, and Bridget, slightly off to the side, like she was ready to bolt. Ma and Aunt Mary

267

stood in the back, each with a hand of caution on the girls. "When was this?"

Nora leaned over her shoulder. "When we went to Easter at Gramma's house. I was...five? So you must have been nine. Dad must have been behind the camera."

"Oh yeah, I remember. That was the year you got cranberry juice on your skirt and spent the whole day crying." Bridget laughed and handed the photo to Aunt Mary. "Look at you and Ma. You can really see the resemblance in your eyes and smile."

Mary gave the picture a passing glance. "We always did look alike. I'm just a little taller." She took a long sip of wine.

Bridget flipped a couple pages and tugged out another picture of a tall, lanky, dark-haired teenage boy with an attitude and a leather jacket. "Oh my God, it's Charlie Phillips!" Her old boyfriend, who had dumped her just before prom, a heartbreak her teenage heart was sure would never heal.

Nora let out a squeal. "God, he was hot back then. I wonder if he still is."

"Only one way to find out." Bridget scrambled to her feet and retrieved Jim's laptop from the kitchen. Hers was upstairs, charging, and with a couple glasses of wine in her, she didn't feel like going up there to get it. For a second, she hesitated—*Jim's laptop*—but the feeling of invading his world had disappeared, and she saw the computer as just that—a computer. The laptop powered on, Windows chimed to life, and she opened up his browser, directing it to Facebook.

Bridget logged in with her name and password, and her page popped onto the screen. She hadn't posted anything since Jim's death, and the page was still filled with condolence messages. Bridget ignored them for now and clicked on the search bar. "Charles Phillips, Dorchester, Class of 2004."

"Oh my God, is that him?" Nora pointed at the first result. "He got bald!"

That made the three of them break into gales of laughter. Bridget clicked on the profile and they all spent a couple minutes determining that Charlie hadn't aged well, which served him right for breaking up with her in eleventh grade.

"Oh, I have an idea," Bridget said, and clicked on the search bar again. She typed in "William Donnelly, Dorchester." She turned to Aunt Mary. "What year did he graduate?"

"Oh, I don't think—"

"1958!" Nora crowed. "Man, I can't believe I can do complicated math after a couple glasses of wine."

Bridget added the year and clicked the magnifying glass. Facebook thought for a second, and then spit back three possibilities. "Look, Aunt Mary, I think this might be him."

Aunt Mary sat stiff-legged beside her, clutching her wine. "We don't need to look him up, Bridget. I'm sure he's just fine."

"Don't you want to see if he got fat and bald?" Nora said. "Come on. It's sweet justice for dumping you all those years ago."

Bridget clicked. The profile filled the screen, but it was

269

the cover image that her eyes went to first. A group of people arranged in staggered seating on the steps of a beach house. A family photo. Ironically reminiscent of the Easter one she'd just seen of her own family.

The hairs on the back of Bridget's neck tingled. She leaned in closer. "Oh my God. That woman looks just like Ma."

"Let me see." Nora zoomed in on the cover image and let out a low whistle. "No lie, they could be twins, just a few years apart. Isn't that weird, Aunt Mary? They're like eerily similar. Why would Billy's kid look like Ma?"

The girls glanced over at their aunt. She opened her mouth and closed it again. Her skin was flushed, her eyes wide.

"Aunt Mary? Are you feeling all right?" Bridget reached for her aunt, but before she could touch her, Mary braced herself on the arm of the couch and got to her feet. She swayed a bit, and her hand trembled when she pressed it to her heart.

"I...I need a glass of water." She sank into an armchair. Sweat beaded on her forehead.

Oh God, was Aunt Mary having another heart attack? She looked pale and trembly and not at all like the calm, happy woman Bridget knew. Did Bridget even know what to do if it was a heart attack? Nora had her phone out, her finger on the call button, a mirror image of Bridget's worry. "Aunt Mary?" Nora said. "Are you okay?"

"I just need...some water. Please." She started to rise, but Bridget waved her back into the chair.

"Sit, sit. I'll go get you the water." Bridget dashed into the kitchen and returned with a glass. She pressed it into her aunt's hands. "Here. Drink this."

Aunt Mary held the glass with both hands, steadying the tremors a little. She took a long sip, then stared at the image on the computer that was still sitting on the floor by her feet. The color returned to her face and she nodded toward Jim's laptop. "Can I . . . can I see that?"

"Sure, sure." Bridget got the laptop and put it on her aunt's lap. She stepped back and shared a glance with Nora. Her sister shrugged.

Aunt Mary bent toward the screen. "Can you make the picture bigger?"

Bridget clicked on the zoom and expanded it until just the faces filled the screen. Again, that sense of this moment being something more than just looking up an old love tickled at Bridget's mind. "Is that good?"

"Yes. Thank you." A long moment passed, and then Aunt Mary reached out and touched the image, her finger sliding along the face of the woman who looked like their mother and then along the photograph of the man she had once loved. Melancholy filled her eyes, and when she spoke, her words held a soft, sad note. "I never thought he'd do it."

"Do what, Aunt Mary?" Bridget lowered herself onto the arm of the sofa.

"Settle down and have kids." Aunt Mary studied the picture for a while longer. Then she set the laptop on the side table and turned the screen away. The sadness had disappeared, replaced with a hard, cold edge in her eyes. "And never ask about the one he already had."

❧❧

Aunt Mary went to bed a few minutes later, without saying anything more. "What do you think that was about?" Bridget asked Nora.

"I don't know. But I'd like to find out." The whole thing had been really weird, yet clearly a subject Aunt Mary didn't want to discuss. It made Bridget think of all the whispers in the family, the sense that there was something hidden under all those secretive adult conversations.

"Yeah, I'd like to find out too." Bridget started to close the lid of Jim's laptop but stopped. She was holding the one piece of electronics that could deliver the answers she needed about her marriage. About the money that had been spent, the bills that hadn't been paid, the things that Jim had kept to himself. Lies and secrets—it seemed to be a part of her family heritage.

Maybe now was the time to find out some of those answers, emboldened by some wine and Nora's presence. The last thing Bridget wanted was one more surprise from Jim's legacy. If he'd been gambling or something, there'd surely be evidence on his laptop, right?

She clicked on Windows Explorer, running the mouse over the different folders, first in Documents—where she didn't see anything unexpected—and then in Pictures.

"What are you doing?" Nora asked.

"Looking for...something. I don't really know what." She scrolled down, past pictures of the house, of his parents, of them together. There was a folder labeled Honeymoon, another labeled Wedding, and then right after the W, close to the bottom of the list, one labeled simply X.

"X? That's weird. Maybe it's a typo." Nora handed Bridget a refilled glass of wine.

"Maybe." But when Bridget clicked the folder and watched it open, blooming into thumbnails of color photographs, her chest tightened. She opened the first photo, enlarging it on the screen. A tall, thin blond woman, with her arm around Jim. A younger Jim—she could tell by the length of his hair and the goatee he had thought was a good idea when they first met—but still Jim.

Her Jim.

Abby's words on the day of the wedding came back to her. How she'd seen him having lunch with another woman. A friend from work, Jim had called her.

But given the possessive hand on Jim's chest, the woman was something more than a friend. Bridget clicked the next picture, another, all of them taken at the same time, the dates saying it was a few months before she met Jim. Most of the photos were labeled with the default of numbers and letters the camera generated, but one was named Jennelle at Beach.

"That's his ex-wife," Bridget said. So, not a big secret after all, she told herself. Though why he wouldn't have told her he'd been having lunch with Jennelle, she didn't know. Maybe he'd thought she would be jealous.

"Jim had an ex? You never told me."

"He said it was just one of those crazy mistakes. Over almost as fast as it began. I think they were married for maybe six months total. He was already divorced when I met him. I just figured he'd been young and stupid." Bridget shrugged. "I didn't ask much about it."

"Then why does he still have her pictures?"

"Maybe he just never got around to deleting them." Except the folder was filled with dozens of pictures, arranged chronologically, and she'd only made it through the first few, which meant he had stored an awful lot of memories for something that hadn't mattered much to him. Why?

Bridget clicked the arrow to go to the next one, and a new, unexpected image filled the screen, and she gasped.

An image of a baby, hours, maybe days, old, in Jennelle's arms. Jim posing behind her, a tight smile on his face, his body not touching his ex-wife's.

Jim. With his ex-wife. With a *baby*.

"Is that...," Nora said, "his kid?"

Jim didn't want children. He'd made that clear, over and over. If he already had one, he'd have mentioned it, she was sure. "I don't think so. He would have told me, right? Maybe he was just visiting her." But the explanation didn't ring true.

She checked the date. Three months after her wedding. They had been living in a tiny apartment, looking for the house where they would start their lives. And Jim hadn't said a word, not about seeing his ex, not about her having a baby, not about saving these photos.

She could count on one hand the number of conversations they'd had about Jennelle. He'd never mentioned a child. In fact, he'd never mentioned his ex again after he'd married Bridget.

Bridget clicked again. The baby, a little older now, smiling for the camera. Then one of the same baby, crawling. Then the baby, standing, clearly a girl, dressed in a dark blue dress with a pink ribbon in her dark brown hair, so like Jim's. Eyes the same color as her husband's staring into the lens.

"For a kid that isn't his"—Nora leaned in—"it sure looks a lot like him."

Bridget stared, her emotions flat. If Nora hadn't been sitting beside her, she would think she had imagined the whole thing. "He said he never wanted to have kids. He said he didn't want to be tied down."

"Wait, what? I thought you guys were going to try to have a baby."

"When I told him I wanted to start trying, he told me he never really wanted kids. That he hoped someday I'd come around and feel the same. But this…" She clicked again, and there was a second family picture, Jennelle holding a party-hat-wearing one-year-old, Jim standing to the side, that same forced smile on his face. "He had a child with *her?*"

The betrayal sliced through Bridget. Her throat closed, and tears burned her eyes. Her stomach turned, and her every cell wanted to escape to the bedroom, burying her head in the sheets and Netflix and pretending she'd never seen any of this.

"Is that...is that where the money went?"

Nora's question sent dominoes tumbling in Bridget's mind. The cash withdrawals, twice a month. The extra money he'd taken out of the retirement account. Just enough money for...

A down payment on a house. The next picture showed it, a tidy Cape on a tree-filled street, with Jennelle and their toddler standing on the stoop.

Bridget opened his email program, frantic now, clicking and typing as fast as her fingers could move. She ran a search for Jennelle and came across dozens and dozens of sent emails. Jennelle's to him, in caps, telling him he needed to step up and be a father, that he couldn't ignore his responsibilities. Jim's replies, measured and distant, telling her he provided financially for his child and that was all he would ever do.

He had a child. With Jennelle. How could he? And how could he hide it?

"He never told me. Never said a word."

"Maybe because he thought you'd leave him?" Nora asked.

Bridget shook her head. All these months, she'd kept feeding herself a fiction about her marriage. Trying to convince herself it hadn't been as bad as she thought. That if they'd had more time, maybe they could have somehow salvaged something. "No, Nora. Jim never told me because he knew, if he did, he wouldn't have had a reason to deny me the one thing I wanted." Tears filled her eyes and blurred the image of Jim's child. "A child of my own."

TWENTY-SIX

The darkness of early morning wrapped around Abby like an old friend. The July morning was warm enough not to need a hoodie, but she slipped into one anyway. Something about the anonymity and shield the fleece offered made her feel protected.

A second later, she saw a familiar bike coming down the road. A newspaper hit a stoop, then another, then Joey stopped. He held up a folded bundle. "Got your paper, Ms. O."

"Throw it."

Joey arched his arm back and made a quick, hard, overhand pitch. She caught it in one hand. He let out a low whistle. "Wow, I'm impressed."

"Four years of high school softball. Guess I haven't lost my touch." Abby lowered the paper to the stoop and came down the sidewalk. "I'm sorry, Joey. I don't have any cookies for you this morning."

"Whoa. No cookies? I think that's the first sign of the

Apocalypse." Joey leaned over his bike, his brown eyes wide and shiny in the glow of the streetlamp. "You feeling okay?"

"Yeah." She blew out a breath. Why bother pretending? "No."

"Wanna talk about it?"

She snorted. "Don't tell me you're now a part-time therapist too."

He laughed. "Nah. Just someone who observes a lot. I'm out here, before the sun rises, while the rest of the world is just starting to wake up. People are...vulnerable then, you know? And I don't mean that in the creepy Ted Bundy way. I mean, they're more themselves, grumpy or happy or sad, as they start to wake up and ease into the day."

Abby thought of all the lives she glimpsed on her early morning walks, the snippets of life she spied through the frames of windows and doors. "And what do you see about these people?"

Joey propped a foot on the center tube of his bike and rested his elbow on his knee. "That most people are sad, when they have no reason to be. The mom standing by the window with a cup of coffee, looking lonely and depressed, not even realizing that her husband is standing behind her, looking like he hit the lottery when he married her. Or the little kid who wakes up from a bad dream and runs into his dad's arms, and suddenly everything's okay." He thumbed behind him. "There's a little old lady one block over who sits alone in her kitchen every single morning and never realizes that two of her neighbors are doing the same thing, all of them needing some company. I told her one day, and now, when I go by, I see them all having coffee together in her kitchen. If people just looked around, they'd see their lives are a lot richer than they realize."

For being so young, Joey really was a smart guy. Simple but kind, and more thoughtful than most people twice his age. "How'd you get so wise?"

"Watching *The Walking Dead*." When Abby laughed, Joey shook his head. "No, I'm serious. That's a show about life and death, you know? How you never know when your ticket is going to get punched. How you need to look around you, at the people and the stuff you have, and use all that to survive. How the petty crap that we let eat up our minds—fighting about who said what and when and with what tone—doesn't matter there. They care about the family they have created and about appreciating life for as long as they have it." He shrugged again. "Or at least, that's what it seems to mean after I've smoked a bowl and binged on Netflix."

Abby laughed again. Despite everything, she felt lighter, maybe a tiny bit hopeful—and all from hanging around the paperboy. "I'll bring you some cookies tomorrow."

"Double the amount." He wagged a finger at her. "No, make that two and half times as many."

"Are you charging me interest on my tip? I thought you were all about the experiences, not the money."

"Cookies aren't money, Ms. O. They're *life*." He tipped the brim of his ball cap and rode off. Every few seconds, she heard the thud of another paper hitting its target.

Abby started walking, taking the same route she took every morning and paying more attention to the people she passed. She rounded the corner and faced Maistranos' bakery, expecting to see Mrs. Maistrano, her hair piled atop her head, working magic with dough.

The bakery was dark.

Abby checked her watch. They should have opened a half hour ago. In all the years she had been coming here, she'd never known Maistranos to be closed, except for during one blizzard when the entire city of Boston had shut down. She jogged across the street and noticed a sign tacked to the front door.

closed indefinitely. death in the family.

Abby swayed on the sidewalk. One of the Maistranos? She couldn't imagine either of them being gone. Of rounding this corner and not seeing the wizened Mr. Maistrano or his perpetually smiling wife behind the counter. Her heart seized.

Death in the Family.

Abby traced over the letters on the note and knew, with a heartbreaking certainty, that she had just lost something very important. Then she turned on her heel and started to run.

Bridget and Nora arrived at work at the same time, parking side by side in the dark back lot. "Great minds think alike," she said as she got out of her car.

"Or can't sleep for shit." Nora yawned. "I think it was the wine that had me tossing and turning. Either that or what Aunt Mary said. Or what you found out. Geez, I'm starting to feel like we're living in the middle of a soap opera."

"Except it's my real life. And a shock I didn't expect." Bridget leaned against her Toyota and waited for Nora to grab her purse out of the backseat. It was still early in the morning, the rest of Dorchester quiet and still. None of the people outside this parking lot had any idea that Bridget's world had imploded last night.

"So...what are you going to do about Jim's kid?" Nora asked.

Bridget had thought about it most of the night, absorbing the information, processing it. Trying to square it with Jim's absences, the bank balance. She'd expected it to hurt more, but maybe she was numb. Or maybe a part of her knew all along that Jim wasn't the dream she'd imagined, and this secret child was just the final nail in that coffin. "I don't know. There's no life insurance, which means he didn't just let me down, but he let his own daughter down too. I can probably split the retirement check when I get that, but other than that...I don't know."

Did she want to meet Jennelle? The child? Maybe someday, but for now, no. That was a bit more than she wanted to deal with.

"How are you feeling about the whole thing?" Nora asked.

"Betrayed. Pissed. And...not surprised." Bridget sighed. She'd read the rest of the emails late last night, and it had been clear Jim had never wanted Jennelle to get pregnant and had been angry when he found out she was. He'd done his part financially but had maintained an emotional distance that Jennelle had resented. Bridget didn't understand that—how could anyone not want to connect with their own daughter? What kind of man could let her grow up with a father who was always on the sidelines? If she and Jim had had a child, she had no doubt he would have been the same, and as much as she grieved never having a family, she realized no baby should be brought into a home where only one parent wanted him. "I think I always knew Jim wasn't quite what I thought. But I was so caught up in the wedding and being married, and every time we fought, he would convince me that we were happy, and I pushed all those worries and doubts to the side."

"Just like you pretended it didn't bother you that he gave you a hard time about the fucking bananas."

"Yeah, like that." The more time she put between herself and Jim's death, the clearer the picture got. It wasn't an image she liked to look at, because she had deluded herself for so long. The day she planted the primroses was the day she finally realized Jim had only been paying lip service to the idea of a baby. That the future she dreamed of was never going to happen with him—and the only way to have the life she wanted was to leave.

Nora fiddled with her keys. "Wasn't that whole thing with Aunt Mary and Billy weird too? Especially how much alike those photos were? Do you think she's hiding something?"

"Nothing would surprise me at this point." Bridget sighed. That laptop had opened up a big can of worms. A necessary one, but still, a part of Bridget wished she'd never lifted that lid. "Maybe Aunt Mary had a baby and gave it up for adoption? That would explain why that woman looked like Ma, if Billy's family adopted the baby."

"Yeah, but wouldn't someone have said something about that long before now?"

"I don't know, Nora. I've discovered it's pretty easy for people to keep secrets from those they are closest to. Even someone they have slept beside for three years."

"Aw, Bridge. I'm sorry. I shouldn't even have mentioned it. Jim was—" Nora halted. From this angle, they could see the front side window of the bakery. "Is that a light on inside the bakery?"

A soft glow through the window cast a puddle of light on the alley. "Maybe Ma got in early?" Bridget glanced at the parking lot. "Her car's not here, though. Or maybe one of us forgot to shut off the lights."

"Well whoever forgot last night is gonna be on dish duty today." Nora unlocked the back door and held it for Bridget.

She took a cautious step inside and stopped. "Abby? What are you doing here?"

Abby was up to her elbows in bread dough, pressing

and kneading the pale ball with constant, smooth motions. She glanced up and blew her bangs off her forehead. "Baking bread."

"But we get a delivery from Maistranos every morning," Nora said. "Not that I don't love your bread way more, but I don't want you to do unnecessary work."

Abby stopped working the dough and stepped back from the counter. Bridget noticed her sister's eyes were red and swollen. "There's not going to be a delivery today. And not in the immediate future. There was a sign on the door this morning." Abby sniffled and bit her lip. "Mrs. Maistrano died. I found her obituary in the online edition of the *Globe*."

Bridget drew in a sharp breath. She'd known Mrs. Maistrano was old—hell, the Maistranos had seemed old even when Bridget was a little girl—but had never really thought about how someday they would die. They'd been such friendly people, part of the same church that Ma attended and always willing to lend a hand during busy season, and vice versa. "Oh, that's terrible. She was a wonderful woman," Bridget said.

"Still baking every day at eighty-five." Abby shook her head. "I'm going to miss her."

"I think we all will," Nora added. "Remember how much Mrs. Maistrano loved Ma's carrot cake? And every year, Mr. Maistrano would buy one for her birthday. They were such a sweet couple."

Bridget looked around the kitchen, at the stacks of baked bread, the new loaves ready to go in the oven.

"Abby, did you come in today to fill our bread order until we find a new baker?"

"Partly that, yes. I came in today because"—Abby pressed her hands onto the counter—"I needed to work. To get my hands in some dough. To...create again." She lifted her gaze first to Bridget, then to Nora. "But more than that, I needed my family."

"Oh, Abs, we need you too." Bridget drew her sister into a tight hug.

"You all have to quit making me cry before nine a.m." Nora threw her arms around the two of them, and in that embrace, tears began to flow, and old wounds began to heal. The scent of fresh-baked bread danced in the air, and in that moment, it was as if they'd all come home.

Nora drew back first and swiped the tears off her face. "Okay, okay. Enough of that. We all need to get to work because the world needs more chocolate cake."

"And challah bread." Bridget grinned at Abby. "Think we still got it? We can all work together in this little kitchen as a team again?"

"I don't know about you," Abby said to Bridget, "since you're the old one—"

"Hey!" Bridget flung a handful of flour at her sister, who retaliated with a flour bomb of her own.

Abby swiped the flour off her cheeks and laughed. "It's good to be back with you guys. Real good."

In the first hour, there were a few missteps and hip collisions, but then the girls settled into a routine as familiar as their own names. Abby baking loaves, biscuits, and bagels while Nora transformed triple-stacked tiers into elaborate white wedding cakes with black trim and incredibly realistic red roses. Bridget churned out cookies, pies, and brownies. As they worked together, the bakery filled with the sweet scents and even sweeter laughter.

Abby slid a half dozen loaves into the oven, then stepped back and wiped the sweat off her brow with the back of her hand. "I forgot how much work this is. I kinda miss my cushy job at Williams-Sonoma."

"That was me, my first week back. I went home every night completely exhausted." Bridget turned off the stand mixer and then wheeled the stainless steel bowl over to the counter. "Hey, can you help me fill these cake pans?"

"Sure. I finished all the bread orders, so we're good to go for a few hours." Abby lifted the mixing bowl while Bridget scooped the batter into rectangular pans. When they were done, Abby pulled her phone out of her pocket and checked the screen. With a sigh, she slid it back into her pocket.

"It's like the tenth time you've checked that thing this morning. Is everything okay?" Bridget asked.

"No. Not even close to okay." Abby swallowed hard and toed at the floor. "Jessie broke up with me yesterday. She called off the wedding, went to her mom's, and isn't answering my calls or texts. She was mad—and rightly so—when I told Ma she was my friend." Abby cursed under her breath. "Why am I so damned scared to stand up to her?"

Bridget and Nora exchanged a glance. "Because we all

286

feel that way," Nora said. "I try never to rock the boat. It's a lot easier than having that battle of wills."

"Yeah. Ma can be...forceful," Bridget said. *Like drag you out of bed, put you in a dress you hate, and haul you off to church when you're a grown woman forceful.*

"Forceful?" Abby poured herself a cup of coffee and leaned against the counter. "That's just code for controlling."

"And whatever other synonyms Roget's has for that word." Nora stepped back to assess her work, spinning the cake left, right. As with all of Nora's creations, this cake was elegant and simple. The roses could have been plucked directly from their stems, and the intricate lace work rivaled any found on a wedding dress.

Abby grabbed a cloth and started wiping the countertops. "I'm tired of being afraid to be myself and I'm tired of feeling...like I don't have a home," Abby said.

Bridget thought of the beautiful house she'd bought with Jim—a house far bigger than what she had wanted and far more expensive. They'd lived there for three years and never had it truly been *home*. It had been a castle built on shifting sand. How much of it had been real? How much had she imagined to fill in the gaps?

"Remember that Children of Lir thing?" Abby asked.

"Yeah, with Mr. O'Donnell at the candy store." Bridget nodded. "Though I look back now and wonder if he made that up just to sell us extra candy."

"Ha, maybe he did. I never thought of that." Abby washed her hands and dried them on a towel. She was quiet for a moment, her head down, that wing of black hair hiding her eyes. "Do you know why I kept hiding the candy and toys in the yard?"

"Because you thought those children might find it?"

"Because I hoped they'd find *me*." Abby raised her gaze, and in her eyes, Bridget saw so much of herself. A woman who had felt alone, even with another person standing right beside her. A woman who had been lost and struggling to find her way, her place. "Even when I was little, I never felt like I was me. You know what I mean? I was different from all of you, and especially from Ma. After Dad died, it was like I lost my anchor in the family. And then when I realized I was gay, I felt even more excluded. Every time I went to church, every time I listened to Ma criticize someone who was gay, it was like she was attacking me. So I withdrew more and eventually..."

"Withdrew altogether."

"Yeah." She wrung the towel over and over again. "I'm sorry."

"No, *we're* sorry," Nora said, closing the distance with Abby. "We all let you down, let you go. It's no wonder you didn't feel included. I know I got caught up in my own life, my own bullshit, and wasn't there for you."

"Well, I didn't make it easy," Abby said.

"Ha. None of us make things easy," Nora said. "We're all a little stubborn."

"A little?" Bridget laughed. "Try a lot."

Nora put an arm around Abby's shoulders. "You're here

now, and just so you know, you're always gonna be one of us, whether you like it or not."

Abby grinned. "Riding the crazy train with all of you?"

"Oh God, I'd forgotten all about that," Bridget said. When they were girls, there was a traveling carnival that came to Dorchester every summer. One of the rides was a train that circled around and around in a figure eight. It had a clown head mounted on the front and an elephant mounted on the back. The girls had dubbed it the crazy train the first time they rode it, and every year after, they made it a point to go to the fair and ride the train, until they got far too old and the ride operator refused to let them on. The shared memory warmed the space between the girls.

"Of course. Who else would you ride it with?" Bridget grinned.

"Thank you, guys, for having my back," Abby said.

Bridget gave her sister a squeeze. "Anytime, Abs. I should have done it all along."

The back door opened, and Ma strode into the kitchen, shedding her purse and barking out orders. "We need to get the Kimball cake done today. The hall needs it by six. Also, we have to find another bread source. Maistranos' is closed. I think poor Mrs. Maistrano died. I don't know what we're going to..."

When she saw Abby, the sentence trailed off. Ma stopped moving.

"We already found another bread source," Bridget said in a bright, happy, isn't-this-awesome voice. "Abby is back. For the time being anyway."

"Well...good." Ma slipped an apron over her head and swept her auburn hair off her face with a barrette. "Why are you all standing around? We open in an hour. Surely you girls know that. Abigail, I expect we won't have any dramatic interruptions today?"

Abby's face reddened. "Dramatic interruptions?"

"From your"—Ma waved a hand in the air—"friend."

Abby glanced at Bridget and then at Nora. A storm brewed in Abby's eyes, and Bridget stepped forward to stand by her sister. Nora did the same, sisters flanking her on either side. "Jessie isn't my friend, Ma—"

"I should hope not," Ma said, already immersed in flipping through the order sheets, "given the way she disrupted din—"

"She's my fiancée. Or she was, until she broke up with me yesterday."

Ma froze. The clipboard shivered in her hands. For a long second, there wasn't a single sound except for the ticking of the clock and the faint sound of a siren somewhere in the city.

"I'm sorry," Ma said. "I think I misheard you. Did you say...*fiancée?*"

"Yes, I did. I'm in love with her, and I'm going to marry her, if I can get her to work things out after what happened last night." Abby glanced at her sisters. Bridget nodded and placed a hand of support on Abby's back, just as Nora did the same. It made Bridget think of that Red Rover game they'd played in gym. Everyone linking arms, trying to stand strong against whatever the other team sent their way.

Ma stared at her. "Are you...did you...does this mean...?"

"Yes, Ma, this means I'm a lesbian," Abby went on, her voice picking up steam. "You can call me a freak of nature or tell me I'm going straight to hell. But you know what? I don't care. I love Jessie, and I'm going to marry her, because"—and now Abby's voice caught, choked a bit—"I have finally found someone who accepts and loves me exactly as I am."

Silence. The clock ticked. The siren came to a halt.

"I...I...I can't have this conversation right now." Ma pulled down a set of cupcake pans. They clattered against the metal counter. "There are things to...to, uh, bake and orders to...fill."

Abby gaped at her mother. "You're really going to work right now, while I'm telling you the most important thing in my life?"

Ma reached for the container of cupcake liners. She fumbled them, and they spilled on the stainless steel. She scrambled to restack them. "Work doesn't wait for conversations that can be had another time."

"In other words, you're just going to ignore it and hope it goes away. Maybe I'll meet the right man this afternoon and suddenly realize I was straight all along? Well, Ma, that isn't going to happen. I met the right one for me, and I'm marrying her, as soon as I can." Abby drew her shoulders back and raised her chin. "Either you're there with me or you're not."

Ma kept her head down while she dropped liner after liner into the pan. "I have to get these cupcakes made."

Abby shook her head. "Of course. Why am I not surprised you're not talking to me now? You never understood me. You never even tried."

She hung up her apron, grabbed her car keys off the shelf, then pushed on the back door. Sunlight burst into the kitchen for a moment, then the door shut, and both Abby and the bright day disappeared.

TWENTY-SEVEN

Nora hurried outside after Abby. Bridget wheeled around and faced her mother. "You're going to let her go...just like that?" Bridget said.

"I have work to do." Ma abandoned the cupcake tins and started wiping counters that were already clean, moving in fast, furious circles along the stainless steel surfaces, her head down, her body language screaming avoidance.

Bridget bit back her frustration. She could, after all, understand avoidance, because she had been the queen of that for a long time. But this wasn't ignoring a bill or procrastinating on calling the lawn service. This was a child who needed their mother to understand, to accept, to open her arms. "Work, huh? That's more important than a daughter who is hurting?"

Her mother finished the first counter and attacked the second one, faster and harder. "Work...keeps me busy," she said between breaths. "You would do well to do more of it yourself."

Meaning Bridget should bury herself in baking and cleaning and not in what her family wanted or needed. She was done doing that. She had buried her head in the sand for three years, and in the end, she'd ignored the truth about her marriage, and she'd almost lost her sisters. Never again. "When are you going to stop telling me what to do? I'm not a child, Ma."

"Then stop acting like one and get to work."

"No." Bridget crossed her arms over her chest, realizing in that second that she did, sort of, look like a child staging a protest. Maybe that was the only way to get her mother to listen. To really hear her. "I'm done working here. Working for you."

Colleen looked up, shook her head and got back to the countertop cleaning. "Oh for goodness' sake, Bridget, stop throwing a tantrum."

"This isn't a tantrum. This is me finally realizing that I married a control freak"—she paused a beat—"because I grew up with one."

"I am not—"

"Ma, I love you, but you are a total control freak, and you know it. You've been telling us all what to do for years. Which was fine when we were seven but not now, not when we're all adults." Bridget took the rag out of her mother's hands, forcing her to listen. Ma got the deer-in-headlights look, as if she'd rather be anywhere but here, discussing the underpinnings of her family. "Every time any one of us tries to have a serious conversation with you, you blow us off."

"I don't see the point in rehashing old history. I had a difficult childhood, but you don't see me blaming every little thing on it." Without the rag to clean the counters, she leaned against the wall, her body tense and coiled, ready to get busy with some other meaningless task.

"History isn't old if it keeps impacting the present. All your bluff and bluster, Ma, is so you don't have to talk about the hard stuff like Dad dying and how much that hurt. Hurt you, hurt all of us." Emotions long dormant, like frozen weeds in winter ground, creeped into her voice. Bridget saw it now, saw the domino effect from that moment twenty years ago when their father died and their mother had buried herself in everything but her family. "My God, where were you when we needed you?"

"Where was I? I was right here, working in this bakery, trying to keep a roof over our heads." She picked up the cleaning cloth where Bridget had put it down and threw it across the room. It hit the sink with a solid *thunk*. "You think I didn't hurt? You think I didn't cry every single day after I lost your father? You think I never got weak, that I never lost myself and made mistakes?"

Bridget couldn't remember a solitary second when she'd seen her mother cry. Never a moment of weakness. Only work and expectations that were foisted on the girls.

"I think you thought you were doing us a favor by keeping all that to yourself." Bridget took a step closer to her mother and leaned on the counter. "You were *wrong*, Ma. We needed someone there to let us know it was okay to cry. To fail. To be messy and imperfect, and that you would love us just the same."

"What is this nonsense?" Ma threw up her hands. "Of course I love you girls."

"Regardless of who or what we are? Whether our hair is brushed or we're quiet in church or we fail algebra? Or we make choices that don't fit your prescription for our lives?" Bridget scoffed and pointed toward the back door. "Try telling that to the daughter you hurt so badly. We may never see her again."

"Abigail? She'll be back. It's just a—"

"Tantrum? No, Ma, it's not." Frustration bubbled inside Bridget. All these years, her mother had controlled and judged—and never understood. "And you are too blind to what is going on with all of us to even see that."

Ma turned away. She checked the loaves in the top oven and inserted the cakes into the bottom oven. She trembled, grabbed the edge of the counter, then straightened and began tipping the loaves out of the pans. "I'm working, Bridget. I'll talk to Abigail later."

Bridget sighed. Why did she stay here and keep arguing? It was like trying to convince a wall to bend. "This bakery matters more to you than your children."

Ma put a loaf of bread onto the counter and reached for a bread knife. Steam wafted off of the warm surface. "It does not."

"Oh yeah? Then prove it." Bridget waited a moment but her mother kept busy slicing the finished loaves, her back to her daughter. "That's what I thought. I'm done here."

Bridget ripped off her apron, threw it in the corner, and walked out of the bakery. The back door shut with a heavy slam. It was the second time she'd quit the bakery in three years, except this time the decision had been entirely hers and entirely about family.

She found Nora in the parking lot, leaning against her car, arms crossed. She was still wearing her bakery apron and had a smudge of flour on her nose. "Abby left. I tried to get her to stop, but she hailed a cab and was gone."

"We'll talk to her later." Bridget tipped her head to the sun and let out a long breath. "I just told Ma off and I quit."

Nora arched a brow. "You did? For real?"

"For real. I think I'm definitely out of the will now." She tossed a grin at Nora. "Those Hummels are all yours, sis."

Nora wagged a finger at Bridget. "Not so fast. I'm joining the O'Bannon Girls' Revolution and quitting too."

Nora, the responsible, practical, dependable one, was the last person in the world she could imagine quitting the bakery. Bridget had always thought Nora would be the only one of the girls to take over when Ma retired. "You? Why would you quit?"

"Because I think it's high time we all took a stand. And supported Abby."

On the other side of the heavy metal back door, chances were good that Ma was inside, muttering about her ungrateful daughters. Bridget was stunned that her mother hadn't come out after any of the girls, that she hadn't even tried to get them to stay.

Abby's strength and confidence had been contagious. Bridget used that to fuel her own words and to stand her ground here, with Nora, rather than going back inside and making peace. Abby needed them—and Bridget was done letting Abby down.

"I think it's about time everyone in this family got honest," she said. "With themselves and with each other. Listening to Abby talk about Jessie and how much she loved her and how Jessie made her feel..." Bridget shook her head. "I never had that with Jim. I kept telling myself I did, but it was just to keep myself from realizing that I had made a colossal mistake. You all were right about him, and I didn't realize it until I was already married. In fact I was..."

"What?"

"Leaving him. I had made plans to walk away that week because I didn't see how we could fix the problems we had. And good Lord, I was only seeing the tip of our problems. Turned out things were far worse than I knew." She leaned against the hood of her car. Getting honest felt like shit when you were doing it, but as soon as the truth left her, a sense of freedom and liberation filled the space left behind. "I felt so guilty about him dying that day, and because of that, I've been drinking too much wine and putting off decisions I should have made long ago. He was never the husband I thought he was, and I don't have anything to feel guilty about. I'm moving forward, and if that means leaving this place, then that's what I'm going to do."

Nora let out a low whistle. "Wow. You really have changed, Bridge."

"In good ways, I think." The sun above them was bright, the day open to possibilities and new ventures. Bridget had expected to be panicked about the loss of full-time income, but instead, she felt...peace. Because what she was finding instead was so much sweeter than any paycheck could ever be. She was finding her family, her sisters, and for that she was grateful. "Come on, sis, let's ride the crazy train with Abby."

TWENTY-EIGHT

Colleen sank onto the carpeted kneeler, clasped her hands together, lowered her forehead to her steepled fingers, and tried to pray. For the first time in her life, no words came to mind, no solace. Nothing but an aching pain that filled her chest.

She had lost her girls. Three of them, walking out of her life at once. She had no doubt Magpie would do the same once she talked to the others. The four girls had always had a bond as strong as superglue. Something Colleen had encouraged—

Until it came back to haunt her.

She prayed to a God who wasn't listening, asking Him where she had gone wrong, how she had failed as a parent. How she could undo all of this and go back to the days when they'd all been happy.

She raised her head and watched the flicker of the prayer candles. The church was quiet—nearly empty in the middle of the day, and only a handful of candles were lit, two of them by Colleen. One for her dear Michael and another for her girls. The light danced before her eyes, and the votives began to melt to their quicks, but nothing changed.

Bridget was right. She *had* turned away from her children when Michael died. But the girls didn't understand—they'd been too young, too confused—to see that Colleen's grief had been a constant tsunami, threatening to swamp her every waking minute. As soon as she woke up in the morning, all she saw was four mouths to feed, a mortgage to pay, food to buy...the list never ended. She'd had panic attacks that launched her out of bed at three in the morning, nights when she'd paced the floors trying to balance an upside-down budget, drinking wine just so she could feel some measure of peace, and so many days when she'd forgone a meal so her children would have enough.

Work had been her salvation. When Mary had found out how much Colleen was drinking, she'd encouraged Colleen to put that stress into work. It had taken a while, but eventually she stopped thinking about the bottles under the sink and began to see her life ease up. The repetition of mix, bake, serve, had numbed her mind, subdued her pain. Church had given her the forgiveness she needed and eased her guilt over spending all those hours earning money instead of being with her girls. But now those two things no longer worked, no longer quieted her mind. She found the remorse creeping into her thoughts, felt the weight of her busy life on her shoulders, and she craved...peace.

When she'd been a little girl, she'd begged her father to let her get on a ride at the fair that spun in a circle. From the outside, it hadn't looked so bad, or very fast. But as soon as the carney started the motor, she realized she'd underestimated the ride.

The curved seat looped back and forth, then swooped around as centrifugal force propelled it faster on the track. She'd gripped the metal bar so tight that she could no longer feel her hands. All she wanted to do was get off the ride, get back to solid, stable ground, but she knew the second she moved, the ride would pitch her into the air. So she held on tight, closed her eyes, and prayed. When the ride finally came to a stop, she'd still been so sure she would tumble to the ground that she didn't move. Her father had to climb onto the metal platform, pry her hands from the silver bar, and lead her back to the fair.

That was what her life had become in the last two decades—a spinning dervish she didn't know how to get off of. She couldn't make it stop, couldn't slow it down. So she lowered her head again and whispered prayers into the dim cavern of the church.

A light touch on her back. Colleen turned to find Father McBride beside her in the pew. "Oh, hello, Father."

"Is everything all right, Colleen? I never see you at church in the middle of the day."

"Just a tough day at work." She started to add that she was fine and stopped herself. She thought of the hundreds of times she had refused help or feigned happiness, when inside, she felt like she was falling apart. All those lies, to protect...what? Her girls were gone, driven away by the very rigidity that Colleen had used to get through twenty tough years. "It's more than that. I had a disagreement with my daughters and...all three quit working for me today."

Father McBride's brows rose. "Oh my. That must have been quite an argument."

"It was." She drew in a deep breath and decided if she couldn't be honest with the man who had heard her confessions for four decades, who could she be honest with? "And on top of that, my daughter Abigail told me she is marrying a woman."

Father McBride nodded. "Okay."

Colleen had braced herself for a long, stern lecture. Father McBride's easy acceptance of the news surprised her. "And that is a sin against the church. How can I support her and still come here to worship?"

Father McBride pushed his glasses up on his nose and turned to face Colleen. His blue eyes weren't as bright now, forty years after he'd joined their church, and his face was thinner, more lined, but his voice still held the same calm wisdom. "She is your daughter, Colleen. While the church decries gay marriage and homosexual acts, it also recognizes that all people, regardless of their race or sexual preference, deserve to be loved." He covered the back of her hand and gave it a squeeze. "She is your daughter. Accept her. The rest is up to God."

"That's it?"

Father McBride smiled. "Well, there are many complicated layers to this issue, but in the end, they all boil down to the same thing. Love each other. I happen to think the world is a much better place when we do that. Don't you?" He got to his feet and gave her shoulder a pat. "Please do pass on my greetings to Bridget. Tell her if she ever wants to go on a mission trip, we'll have a spot on the bus for her."

Colleen would bet dollars to donuts that Bridget was never going to sit on that bus. "Thank you, Father, I will."

He gave her a nod and walked away. Colleen remained in the pew a while longer but the peace she had always found in church remained elusive.

❧❧❧

The next morning, Bridget stood on the back deck, doing the math in her head. If she was careful with the retirement check, she could pay off the funeral home, give half to Jennelle for Jim's daughter, and have a small, very small, cushion in the bank. There was still the mortgage to consider, which was more than she could handle alone.

Which meant selling the house.

Moving. Changing. Starting over.

She also needed to find a new full-time job, but the retirement check would buy her a little bit of time to get there. The thought of a new future, one she created herself, still scared her a little. It had been so long since she had done anything like this that she wasn't sure where to start.

The sun began to rise over her backyard, waking the grass with a touch of gold and then kissing the shrubs and the primroses. Bridget lowered herself onto the top step and hugged her knees to her chest. Part of her wished Jim was still here. Someone else to make the decisions, call the Realtors, figure out what to pack, what to donate.

But if Jim had been here and they'd still been married, there never would have been a family dinner this week or pizza and wine with Nora and Aunt Mary last night. He would have made all the decisions, controlling every facet of her life. As terrifying as it used to be for her to step up and be in charge, now there was a sense of excitement and reinvigoration running through Bridget. Maintaining a budget. Selling the house. Moving...somewhere. Finding a job. All major changes—

But good ones.

Decisions she was making on her own, for better or worse. Decisions that put the control in her hands again.

Her life had upended in the last few months, but that fear of the future had begun to abate, and she was starting to feel like she was getting a handle on things. Selling the house didn't frighten her nearly as much as she had thought it would.

The back door opened with a squeak, and Aunt Mary came out onto the porch. Pedro trotted along beside her and then climbed into Bridget's lap and curled into a tiny furry ball. "Looks like you made a friend," Aunt Mary said.

Bridget had gotten used to the dog and had to admit she liked him. Maybe after Aunt Mary left, Bridget would get a dog of her own. She'd never had one—Ma had always said she had her hands full enough with the bakery and four daughters—and it might be nice to, as Garrett had said weeks ago, let something living depend on her again. Of course, she hadn't had great luck with the hummingbird, so maybe that was a sign she should wait on pets.

"He's a good dog." She rubbed Pedro behind his right ear, and he curved his body into hers and let out a little groan. "I've liked having him around more than I expected."

"Well, don't get too used to it." Aunt Mary smiled. "I'm feeling much stronger, and soon, I think, I'll be off on another adventure."

"Already? Why don't you stick around a little while longer? We've loved catching up with you." Although Aunt Mary did look better now than when she'd first arrived. She had more color in her cheeks, a bigger spring in her step. She'd been more active and even started doing some of the cooking and housework.

"It's . . . difficult to be here," Aunt Mary said.

"If I've made you feel unwelcome—"

"No, no, that's not it at all." Aunt Mary sat down on the step and ran her hand over the dark wood decking. "There are . . . issues between your mother and me that we can't seem to resolve."

"Welcome to the club."

Aunt Mary cocked her head and studied her niece. "That sounds like something more than the normal family squabbles. What happened?"

"Long story short? A nuclear meltdown in the O'Bannon family." Bridget explained about Abby and

Jessie and how she and Nora had quit after Abby had walked out. "We had it out with Ma in the bakery. Then when I realized she wasn't going to try to fix things with Abby, and she was just going to go on being the same stubborn person she always was, I told her I didn't want her controlling my life anymore."

"Wow. How'd she take that?"

"I don't know. I left, and she didn't follow." Bridget shrugged, as if the lump of disappointment in her gut didn't grow with every passing second of no texts, no phone calls from her mother. How could she let all three of them leave?

"Well, I won't say I'm surprised. Just surprised it took this long to come to a head." Aunt Mary rested her arms on her knees and drew in a deep breath. "There's something you should know about your mother. About why she is the way she is. She had a tough childhood. I know you all loved your grandmother, and she was a wonderful woman—when she was older. But when we were kids, she was...tough. She had to be. Your grandpa was a bit of a drinker, and your grandmother had the responsibility of raising the children, running the bakery, and cleaning up any messes your grandfather left behind."

"I never knew any of this. Grandma never said a bad word about Grandpa." The grandfather she remembered had been kind, quiet, a man who liked to putter in his garden and play solitaire.

"Well, he eventually got his act together, but in those days, he was a mess. Most weeks, your grandpa would spend his entire paycheck at the bar. He couldn't even make it the four blocks home with some money left in his pocket. That left Gramma pretty much always stressed and on the edge. She would bark at us, and if we were too slow or too messy or too anything, she'd get us back in line quick."

"Sounds familiar."

"Well, your mom learned it firsthand. And like you girls, we each took different paths. My brothers went to college. One became a doctor; one became a scientist. But me...I started acting up when I was fourteen. I think she gave up on me. I was the wild child, and after working all day and trying to take care of my brothers, she just didn't have the energy to look after one more."

"Until Ma came along, right?"

"Well...Grandma didn't exactly ask for your mother to come along. She did as best a job as she could, but honestly, it was never really her job to raise your mother."

Never really her job to raise Ma? How could that be? The only reason raising a child would be someone else's job would be if—

Then it hit Bridget. The conversation about Billy Donnelly The offhand comment about abandoning the child he already had. The family pictures that so resembled her own. "Wait...is Ma"—she hesitated—"is she your daughter?"

Aunt Mary didn't say anything for a long time. The neighbor started up a lawn mower, and that sent a flock of birds scattering into the sky. A slight breeze whispered along the grass, tickling at their feet. Pedro buried his head in the crook of Bridget's knee and went to sleep.

"Aunt Mary? Is Ma your daughter?"

"Yes," Aunt Mary said after a long pause. "She is."

Wow. Bridget absorbed that information and filled it in with all the blank spaces that had been in the O'Bannon family over the years. Apparently her late husband wasn't the only one keeping secrets about a baby. "And you never said anything?"

The birds did a U-turn and came to rest on another tree. The lawn mower kept up its steady drone, the sound receding, growing, receding, growing. Pedro whimpered in his sleep and kicked one leg out.

"Back then, girls didn't have babies out of wedlock," Aunt Mary said. "Billy broke up with me as soon as he found out I was pregnant. We were in high school, and he was scared that his life would be over. He'd have to drop out, get a job, support the two of us. He wasn't ready for that, and honestly, neither was I. I went to stay at my aunt's for a while and came home with this beautiful baby and no idea what I was going to do."

"That must have been terrifying," Bridget said.

"It was. I didn't know anything about babies or child-birth, or anything. My mother immediately said, 'I'll raise it as my own, and you will be her sister.' At first I liked the idea because I still got to be a teenager, but the first time Colleen called your grandmother Mom, it almost broke my heart. I'd see her run to my mother at the end of the day and call for her when she was scared . . ." Aunt Mary's voice broke, and her lower lip trembled. Even now, sixty-two years after she'd given birth, it was clear she still felt the same pain and loss. "She *never* called for me. Never even knew how much that hurt. So I left home and went on adventures and tried to forget."

Bridget thought of all those whispers within the O'Bannon family. The way Grandma had always seemed a little harder on Ma than anyone else—something Bridget chalked up to the two of them working together. The way Aunt Mary would flit in and out of their lives, never here for a holiday or family occasion, because that surely only drove home the point about her relationship with Colleen.

Years of heartbreak, buried in the O'Bannon genes. And no one had known or said a word.

"But you never forgot you were her mother, did you?" Bridget took Aunt Mary's hand in her own. Pedro woke up and snuggled into the space between their hips. "I can't even imagine how hard that was for you."

Tears glistened in Aunt Mary's eyes, held back for so many years, and even now, still unshed, a secret Mary had had to bear alone. "Your mother never knew. Not until a few years ago, after your grandmother died. I decided it wouldn't harm anything to tell her but she...wasn't very happy to hear it. I thought I'd lost her forever, and it damned near broke me."

Five years of silence. Five years of distance.

"Maybe she just needs more time," Bridget said, even though she didn't believe it.

"And maybe she just needs me to go away." Aunt

Mary got to her feet. Pedro popped his head up and scrambled over to his mistress. "That's why I'm leaving as soon as I can."

Bridget ignored her aunt's words. Aunt Mary had always run from the family—like Bridget had done, and Abby too. Maybe even Magpie. But running hadn't done anything but fracture the fragile bonds between them, and Bridget was tired of that happening.

As her aunt turned to go, Bridget said, "You know what I see when I look at my yard, Aunt Mary?"

Her aunt looked confused at the change in subject. "Uh...grass?"

Bridget drew in a deep breath of the sweet summer air and let her gaze roam over the lush green space before her. "Possibilities. The yard was the only thing I really liked about this house when we bought it. When we first moved in, all that was back here was grass. I planted the shrubs over there, the primroses at the back, that Japanese maple in the corner. Some of the things I planted didn't take, and I had to learn my lesson and start over again. But some of them flourished and bloomed and now, every time I come out here, I see something that has...hope."

Aunt Mary sank back onto the step. Pedro let out a long-suffering sigh and lay beside her. "This whole yard thing is some kind of metaphor for my relationship with your mom, isn't it?"

"Would I be Irish if I didn't have at least one allegory for life?" Bridget laughed. "Seriously, though, I've had a lot of time to think over the last few months and a lot of these things are starting to make sense. Like the yard—I've watched it morph into a place that brought me…peace."

Aunt Mary propped her elbows on her knees. "That's something I've been looking for my entire life. I've been all over the world and never found it."

"Maybe—and here's your lesson—it's as simple as looking in your own backyard. And not being a *sabhaircin*."

"The fairies that come in and ruin your garden when you're sleeping?" Aunt Mary rolled her eyes and dismissed that with a wave. "My mother talked about them all the time. But what do the *sabhaircin* have to do with anything?"

"Grandma said they were destructive little things sometimes," Bridget said. She could remember sitting on her grandmother's lap while they decorated cookies, listening to her tell Irish tales in that slight, soft brogue of hers. For all her faults, her grandmother had loved her granddaughters and left them with hundreds of sweet memories. She'd taught them how to turn flour and sugar into masterpieces and how to remember their heritage. "You know, I haven't seen a single fairy since I planted the primroses."

Aunt Mary laughed. "I'm thinking that has more to do with the fact that fairies don't exist." She glanced at the sky and crossed herself. "Sorry, Mom."

"Maybe. Either way, I didn't set out planting the primroses to scare off mythical fairies." She thought back, remembering the hours of digging in the garden, nestling each plant into its new home, gently nudging dirt around the roots. Jim had told her they were a waste of time, that that part of the yard got too much sun. In the end, he had helped her plant the last of them, laughing at Bridget's *sabhaircín* superstitions. "I did it as a last-ditch effort to save my marriage. I kept talking to Jim about how, if we had a baby, the baby's room would face the garden and the baby would see them. I tried to get him to see my dream, to believe in it. But by the time the last primrose was in the ground, I realized he was never going to want children. And that the relationship I thought I had with him had deteriorated over the years we'd been married. Now I've found out that he lied to me about dozens of things, and that I was like the *sabhaircín*, only seeing what I wanted to see, thus creating havoc in my own life."

"Another metaphor. Grandma taught you well." Aunt Mary smiled. "And now? What do you see now when you look out there?"

The lawn mower had stopped, leaving only the bird songs as music for the day. It seemed appropriate, Bridget thought. She inhaled again, a breath of summer happiness and hope. "Now I look at those primroses and see them as a chance to begin again. They bloom, they die, and then they come back. Sometimes weaker, sometimes stronger, but always one more time. They're not going to give up, no matter what comes at them." She drew her knees to her chest. The discovery of Jim's child, the truth about the missing money, were all storms that had tried to uproot her. But she was still here, and still moving forward. "And neither am I. And neither are you."

Aunt Mary drew her niece close. "Ah, Bridget, how did you get so wise?"

Bridget leaned into her aunt—*grandmother?* It didn't really matter; Mary was family. And for Bridget, that had become the most important thing, the garden she intended to always nurture. "Easy, Aunt Mary. I have great genes."

TWENTY-NINE

Colleen sought solace in the bakery. After running to church, she'd gone back to Charmed by Dessert and stayed long after closing, baking treat after treat and freezing cakes, cookies, pie, brownies, anything she could create. Her back ached, her feet hurt, but she kept working. Idle hands gave way to an idle mind, and an idle mind dwelled.

But no matter how many cakes or tarts she made, her mind kept circling through her life, like a movie that started with her earliest memory and spiraled forward. When she'd been a little girl, her mother's words had felt like harsh stones. *You don't sit up straight enough. Can't you do something with your hair? Were you dressed by a band of baboons?* She'd never understood what she had done that had made her mother so angry, so strict. She'd started working in the bakery because it was the only place she found praise from her mother. Here, she could create things people loved.

Her sweet Michael was the only man to love her just as she was, bristly and stubborn. He'd been the light to her dark, bringing laughter into her life. When he died, it was as if the entire world deflated. Colleen had lost that spark, that laughter, and for a time, she used alcohol to forget. Then she replaced that with burying herself in the only thing she could count on to be the same day after day—the bakery.

Because of that, the girls had suffered, even though she had never meant for them to live the life she had. She'd been too hard on them, too difficult, and now...

They were gone. The only thing she'd ever feared had come true.

Colleen O'Bannon was alone. Utterly, completely alone.

She said a silent prayer, whispering the words into every stir of the spoon. *Please let me make it right with my daughters.* She added chocolate chips, folded the batter over the little dark chunks. *Please show me how.* She sprinkled in chopped walnuts, giving the batter a few more gentle turns. *Please help me find my way back to them.*

There was a knock on the glass door. Colleen abandoned the cookie dough, washed her hands, and then crossed through the darkened bakery. Mary stood on the other side of the door, one hand cupped over her brow, trying to peer into the dim interior.

A little wave of happiness ran through her, but Colleen tamped it down. Her sister—her mother, she couldn't decide which was easier to think—was one of those people

Colleen had always loved to talk to when she was young, and still did, even though they were now talking about things that opened old wounds.

She unlocked the door and opened it to let Mary in. "What are you doing here?"

Mary propped her hands on her hips. "I should ask you the same thing."

"I'm working."

"Working at avoiding things. Am I right?"

"Of course not." Colleen tried to draw herself up in righteous indignation, but her aching muscles protested and instead she sank into a chair. "Okay, maybe I am."

"Oh, Colleen, you silly, stubborn woman. You're going to work yourself into an early grave." Mary sat in the opposite chair and shook her head. "All this avoiding isn't good for you. Eventually it all boils over, like an untended pot on the stove."

"It already has." Colleen let out a sigh. She wasn't just tired from working for several hours straight; she was exhausted to her core. Her heart was tired, her mind, everything inside her. If she went home, she would probably sleep for a week straight. "I don't know what else to do, Mary. How to fix this. How to get my girls back."

"Talk to your family." Mary's hand covered hers. "Talk to *me*. Please."

"I...I don't know how." All her life, she'd had this complicated relationship with Mary, and now she knew why. There were no defined roles for them, no guidelines to follow. "I mean, are you my sister? Or my mother? Or what?"

"How about just Mary?" She gave Colleen a lopsided smile. "We're too old for labels, don't you think? All I want is a relationship with you, Colleen. You set the parameters. However little or much contact you want will be...a blessing to me."

In Mary's voice, Colleen heard the same pain that was in her heart. Was this how God wanted to communicate with her? By bringing in the one woman who understood what it was like to have your daughter shut the door in your face?

But Colleen had gone so long in this same mode, this solo path, she wasn't sure she could pave a new road with Mary, with her daughters, with herself. "It's hard for me to accept change."

Mary chuckled. "Tell me something I don't know."

"But I'm going to try. I have to." She sighed and gazed out the window, into the dark outside the shop. Somewhere out there were four O'Bannon girls, each of them incredible in their own way, but right now, so very, very far away. If she closed her eyes, she could still hear the slam of the door, the finality of that act. She could still hate herself for staying in the kitchen and mixing cupcake batter instead of running out the door and begging them to come back. "I'll lose my daughters for good if I don't."

"They'll still be there. You just need to be easier on them and on yourself. And admit to them that you are just as fallible as they are. Be honest, Colleen."

She shook her head. "They'll judge me. And rightly so. I should have been there for them when they were younger and so grief-stricken, instead of rushing them off to bed so I could drink away my pain."

Mary covered Colleen's hand. "You fell into a pit for a time. It happens to all of us."

"I would have still been there if you hadn't shown up." Mary had come to stay one Christmas and stood beside Colleen as they poured every single one down the drain and then stayed with her for weeks, until she got her life back on track. "I never really thanked you for that."

"You don't have to. I did it because I love you. Because you're my daughter. Just as you would do the same for your own children." Mary gave her a soft smile. "So talk to them. Let them see you, really see you. They love you, you know."

Colleen fiddled with the place mat on the table. A part of her wanted to run back into the kitchen and start whipping up some brownies or a complicated torte, just to avoid this conversation. But she knew if she did that, it was only a matter of time before she circled right back to this place, these same arguments. That was the funny thing about getting older—you realized how much of life was a circle. You were destined to travel the same bumpy road if you didn't see the hazards and chart a new course.

"I don't know how to be easier and softer," she whispered. "When Michael died, I felt like, if I fell apart, the rest of my family would too. I've gone twenty years holding on to that thought, and holding on to myself by a thread. Making sure everything was ordered and neat and perfect became a way to control what was uncontrollable."

"And putting your life on hold in the process. Your girls are grown. They don't need you to brush their hair or make them eat their vegetables. They just need you to be"—a bittersweet smile crossed Mary's face—"their friend."

In the soft hitch of that word, Colleen heard longing. For a do-over for all those years she'd kept Mary at a distance. When she was young, the space between them had been a by-product of Mary's constant travel. She'd barely known her sister. But after Mom's death—and it was still weird dealing with this who's-your-mother thing—Mary had come around more. At first, Colleen had loved the time with the sister she had missed so much.

Then Mary dropped that bombshell in Colleen's lap, and her first reaction had been to shut it out. Shut her out. To use the shock and betrayal as an excuse to avoid the truth and, in the process, avoid Mary.

She thought of how much it had hurt to hear that door shut behind her daughters today. Her girls—her heart. If she ever lost them for good, Colleen knew she would curl up into a ball and die.

Mary must have felt the same thing when Colleen had walked away five years ago and cut off all contact. She could see that pain echoing still in Mary's eyes and in that little bit of hope she'd heard in the words *talk to me*.

Maybe it wasn't too late for them to figure out how to be...friends, or whatever this was going to be. Maybe it wasn't too late for Colleen to learn how to do the same with her own daughters.

"Will you..." It took a bit to push the next words out,

to admit maybe she didn't have it all together like she thought she did. "Help me?"

"Of course." Mary squeezed Colleen's hand. "That's what I'm here for, Colleen. What I've always been here for."

The two them sat in the dim bakery for a long time, talking like friends, like family, and, finally, like mother and daughter.

THIRTY

Abby stood on the front porch of Jessie's parents' gray saltbox house in a tony neighborhood of Newton, clutching a bouquet of daisies and trying not to sweat. She'd rehearsed what she wanted to say thirty times in her head on the drive over, but every time, the words had sounded hollow, cheap. Like she was trying too hard.

She blew out a breath and pushed the doorbell. A series of gongs bellowed inside. She waited, counting the beats in her head. One. Two. Three. Four. Five. Just as she raised her hand to ring the bell again, the door opened. And there was Jessie.

Abby's heart hitched. She tightened her hold on the flowers and tried not to be an idiot who burst into tears.

Jessie's hair was in a messy ponytail. She had on an old T-shirt of Abby's—Bruce Springsteen's faded image filled the front—and a pair of sweats. Her feet were bare, the polish chipped. And Abby thought she'd never looked more beautiful.

She sucked in some courage and moved forward, thrusting the flowers in front of her like a knight's lance. "First, these are for you, and if I don't give them to you now, I'll crush them because I'm so nervous. I know daisies are your favorite, and I hope you like them. Second, before you say anything at all, please let me explain."

Jessie took the flowers, but the look on her face was pained. "Abby—"

"Jessie, please." Abby drew in another breath. The second she opened her mouth to say her practiced speech, the entire thing flew out of her mind. There was no right way to undo all the damage of the last few weeks. Not enough words in the world to tell the woman who had saved her when Abby had gone off the rails—drinking too much, cursing too often, hopping from job to job and relationship to relationship looking for what she had lost the day of Bridget's wedding—that she owed her life to Jessie. That she was Abby's whole world, and nothing felt right without her in it. "I know I'm not going to say this right, and not at all like I practiced in the car, but let me just start with— I was wrong. So, so wrong to not tell my family about you. I knew they would judge you and judge me, and I was trying, in my own weird way, to protect you from that. I didn't want them to hurt you like they've hurt me."

"Oh, Abs." Jessie took a step forward but didn't touch Abby, didn't completely close the gulf between them. "It would have been okay."

"No, it wouldn't. You are the best thing that ever happened to me, and they should know that and respect it.

You take my wild and crazy and tame it, and you make me want to be a better version of myself." She ran a hand through her hair and searched for the words she needed. She'd never been good at this part. Put a lump of dough in front of her and she could form a wreath of bread. But give her a bunch of words and Abby felt like she was grasping at straws, trying to fashion them into a house. "What I mean to say is that when I'm with you, I feel...safe."

Tears welled in Jessie's eyes. Inside the house, someone was watching *Wheel of Fortune*. Pat Sajak's voice floated on the air, celebrating the award of another trip to Switzerland, which seemed so alternate universe right now. Abby stood on the porch while the sun beat down on her and tried to remind herself to breathe.

"Oh, Abs, damn it, I can't stay mad at you. Because...because I feel the same with you. Safe. Loved. Needed," Jessie said. But still she didn't move any closer. The gap between them remained, maybe too wide to traverse.

Abby plowed forward, a jumble of what was in her heart and what she had rehearsed. "I don't care what my family thinks anymore. I told my mother I was in love with you and that I was going to marry you. Then I walked away from her, from the bakery." Abby shrugged. "If she can't accept us, accept me, then I don't need her in my life."

Jessie shook her head. She laid the flowers on the table inside the door. "You can't just walk away from your family. I mean, they're *family*, Abs."

"*You* are my family. And, God, I need you, Jessie. Today, tomorrow, forever. I want to marry you, and I don't want to wait for a hall and a DJ. I want to marry you now. Today. Tomorrow. Whenever you say. Just please, please say yes."

"Today?"

"Sure. Why not?" Abby waved toward her car. "Let's go run down to city hall and grab a judge or city clerk or whatever it is we need and get married."

Jessie shook her head again, and for a second, Abby's heart fell. All this had been for nothing. She was too late, had done too much damage. The door was going to close, and Jessie was going to disappear from her life. Jessie's gaze dropped to the floor.

Then Jessie looked up, and the tears had been replaced with laughter, joy. "You're crazy, you know that?"

"Crazy about you." Abby reached for Jessie and took her delicate hands in her own. She'd always liked Jessie's hands, how they moved when she talked, how her fingers curled around Abby's when they were sitting together on the sofa. "Come on, let's get married and have the expensive party later."

"You really want to do this?"

"More than anything in the world. I love you, Jessie. I really, truly do."

Jessie reached out and hauled Abby against her. In an instant, the nerves in Abby's chest disappeared. She inhaled the fruity scent of Jessie's shampoo, and leaned into her soft embrace, and thought to herself, *This is what home feels like.*

"I love you, Abby O'Bannon." Jessie pressed a kiss to Abby's hair. "Let's get married."

Someone on the television won a new car, and the audience erupted into applause and wild whoops. Abby held on to the one person in the world she couldn't live without, a gift so much better than any Honda sedan.

THIRTY-ONE

B ridget stood in the stark gray hallway of Boston City Hall, wearing a pale pink dress she had found in the back of her closet. A long time ago, it had been her favorite, but Jim had hated the pale color on her and the dress had gathered dust. She vowed to wear it more often going forward, a lot more often.

She'd swept her hair into a loose chignon, added a spray of baby's breath, and slipped on a pair of nude pumps that fit so well, she could have worn them for days, unlike those mean black shoes from the funeral. When she got home, she was throwing those damned things away. In fact, she was throwing away anything that didn't make her happy. Didn't fit the new and improved Bridget.

She had arrived at city hall a good half hour early. After getting Abby's text last night, she didn't want to risk missing this wedding. Magpie and Nora were on their way—Magpie flying in from Texas, and Nora grabbing her from the airport just in time. Aunt Mary had said she'd meet Bridget at city hall, saying she had an errand to run first.

"My God, you are stunning and a very nice surprise to see."

Bridget spun around and found Garrett standing behind her. A part of her had hoped she'd see him at city hall, even though she hadn't told him she'd be here today, and his work didn't take him up this way very often. She smiled and felt a blush creep into her cheeks. "Thank you."

He glanced over at the city clerk's office door. "Please tell me you aren't here to marry somebody?"

Bridget laughed. "No. Just to watch my sister get married."

"That's great. And I mean that on multiple levels." He took a step closer and reached up to twirl a loose tendril of hair gently on his finger. Bridget had to remind herself to breathe. "I like your hair like this. I like your dress. I like the whole package."

"Thank you again." She couldn't remember the last time she'd been complimented that much. It was heady, intoxicating. As was the way he looked at her, the same way some people looked at the cookies in the case. That made her think about him taking a bite—

Not appropriate. She was in a government building, waiting for her sister's wedding. There was undoubtedly some ancient Puritan law on the books outlawing such a thing. "What are you doing here today?" she asked Garrett.

"One of my clients is trying to get a new building approved, so I'm here to throw myself on the sword of the mayor's mercy so we can get the permits taken care of."

Men in suits and clerks with loaded arms scurried past them, breaking like the Red Sea around the two people in the middle of the hall. A sullen boy stared at them as he walked by, his father keeping a directing hand on the boy's shoulder. Any second now, her family was going to get off the elevator, and Bridget would have to explain Garrett. But that was okay. It was about time she explained him. She was ready to make him a part of her life, her world.

"So...what are you doing after the wedding?" Garrett asked.

"Going back to my house. We're having the reception there."

"Am I allowed to say I'm disappointed?" He shifted closer to her. She caught the dark, masculine scent of his cologne, and it made her want to kiss his neck, to follow the trail of that scent. "Because I'd love to take you out in this dress."

"I'd like that." She inhaled. "Very much."

A smile curled across his face. "God, I like you, Bridget."

The busy city hall seemed to disappear. All she saw, all she knew, was the way this man was smiling at her. Her breath hitched, her pulse raced, and she wondered—no, hoped—he would kiss her. "I like you too."

His smile widened and lit his eyes. She loved his smile, how it seemed to take over his whole being. "Then maybe we should do something about that."

Her heart stuttered. "Maybe we should."

Very slowly, Garrett leaned in, his green eyes locked with hers. At the last second, she closed her eyes and surrendered to the kiss. His lips drifted across hers with a feather touch at first, and she let out a soft mew of anticipation and the kiss deepened. Electricity lit every nerve in her body, and when his hand cupped her jaw, his thumb tracing a seductive line beside their lips, she almost melted.

Too soon, Garrett pulled back. "Damn. I'm supposed to be at work. And be all professional lawyer-guy right now." He lowered his voice and brought his mouth to her ear. "But all I can think of is taking you out of here and to somewhere private for one very long, very nice afternoon."

The deep growl of desire in his words made her wish she could take him up on that offer. Right now. "Let's, umm...start with dinner and see where that goes."

"Tomorrow night?"

"Actually, tonight." Why put one more element of her life on hold? Things were changing, and this new Bridget, the one who had been stifled for too long, was embracing those changes. "Why don't you come over and meet my family? If you still want to stay after that, then we'll see where this"—she pressed a finger to his lips, repeating his words with a flirt in her voice—"goes."

"Deal. I'll bring the wine."

She gave him her address and a time to be there. He left her with a quick kiss on the cheek and a song in her heart. She glanced over her shoulder after he left and caught him looking at her too.

Bridget blushed and turned back. But not without a small smile of satisfaction. He really did like her—and she really did like him.

The elevator opened, and a second later, Nora and Magpie came down the hall, Nora carrying several bouquets of flowers. Magpie had her professional Nikon around her neck and was wearing a blue floral patterned dress that swirled around her knees. Nora had opted for something more conservative—a light coral dress with a scoop neck. She had on low heels and had pushed her hair back with a sparkling headband. "Are we late?" Nora asked.

"Nope. The brides aren't even here yet." Bridget glanced at her watch. "We have ten minutes."

"And Ma?"

Bridget shook her head. She hadn't heard anything from her mother since the fight in the bakery yesterday. No texts, no phone calls, nothing. Abby told her she'd invited Ma, but there'd been no response.

The other girls sighed. "I'm not surprised," Nora said, "but I am disappointed."

"Me too. I was hoping she'd be here. I even left her a voice mail with the time and place, but..." If Ma missed this wedding, she'd be carving a wound in this family that might never heal.

"Yeah, I know," Nora said, reading what Bridget left unspoken. Nora separated the simple, ribbon-tied bouquets of daisies and lilies, handing one to Magpie, another to Bridget. "I've got ones for Abby and Jessie, too, though I wasn't actually sure which one of them wanted a bouquet. God, I hope I didn't screw that up. There should be a how-not-to-offend-your-sister's-new-wife book out there. I'm not quite sure how to act."

"Act like Abby is marrying the person she loves. That's all." Bridget put a hand on Nora's shoulder. "I don't think either of them are going to care about flowers or ribbons or whether the sky is gray today. I think Abby's just going to be thrilled we are here, and everything else is just..."

"Gravy," Magpie finished.

"Exactly." The elevator at the end of the hall dinged, and the doors slid open. The conversation halted, and all three women turned.

Abby and Jessie stepped off the elevator, holding hands and wearing similar versions of the same knee-length white dress. Jessie's had a sweetheart neckline and a dark blue ribbon around the waist while Abby's had a simpler scoop neckline. No veils or tiaras, just simple elegance, which seemed to fit both of them perfectly.

Magpie shoved her bouquet into Nora's hands and ran forward and drew them both into a hug. "Oh my God! You both look gorgeous! Happy wedding day, both of you!"

Abby stepped back and smoothed a hand down the dress. "Thanks. Though I'd be a lot more comfortable in a hoodie and jeans."

"After the wedding, you can wear whatever you want." Jessie kissed Abby's temple. "But for now, let's at least look bridal. Okay?"

"Okay." Abby drew in a deep breath.

"Are you ready?" Magpie asked. "Bridge says we have ten minutes until your appointment with the clerk."

Abby exhaled, clenching and unclenching her hands. "I'm nervous. This is a big deal."

"Look at me, Abs." Jessie caught Abby's gaze and brought their foreheads together. "It's gonna be fine." They stared into each other's eyes for a long, tender moment while people hurried through city hall in a constant wave. Bridget could see her nervous sister gaining strength, calm, from Jessie's touch. Her shoulders relaxed, her frown lines eased, and her breathing slowed.

"Yes, I'm ready," Abby whispered. They exchanged a soft, gentle kiss, and then a smile meant only for Abby spread across Jessie's face.

"Me too," Jessie whispered.

"God, I hope I meet someone who loves me like that," Magpie whispered. "That is just too damned sweet."

Bridget grinned at her little sister, usually the very vocal anti-commitment and anti-settling-down one. "Are you getting sentimental on me?"

"Hell no." Magpie dabbed at her eyes. "I just watched too many sad movies on the plane, and now I'm all sappy. It'll wear off soon."

Nora leaned in and gave Magpie a wink. "Don't bet on it. Now that you're all softened up by a real-life love story, maybe there's some guy out there who can tame the last O'Bannon girl."

"Good Lord. I have to get away from you two before you grab some stodgy lawyer and make him marry me. I'm just saying that was a sweet moment, not a reason for me to jump off the marriage cliff too." Magpie grabbed the extra bouquets from Nora and strode forward. She handed Abby and Jessie each some flowers. "Hey, guys, it's time. Are you ready?"

"Yup." Abby took Jessie's hand, and they started toward the city clerk's office. Just before they reached the door, the elevator dinged again. Abby froze in place for one long second. Then slowly, she pivoted back.

Hope was written all over her face, in the way she leaned toward the elevator doors as they shuddered open, the way she held her breath. Bridget whispered a prayer that the person getting off the elevator was the one person they all wanted to see. She watched her sister's face, watched the hope begin to slide away, and then a light in her eyes—

And a smile wider than Boston Harbor. "Ma. You came."

Ma and Aunt Mary, complete with a bow-tie-wearing Pedro, walked down the hall toward Abby. Aunt Mary's bright, floral maxi dress skimmed the floor and showed peeks of sparkly sandals. Ma was wearing her church clothes, a dark blue button-front knee-length dress along with her sensible black shoes. She held her purse in both hands in front of her, her knuckles white. Here, but clearly not comfortable with it.

"Would you look at you girls? Oh my goodness, you all look so beautiful," Aunt Mary said, greeting and hugging each of her nieces in turn. She stopped and turned to Jessie. "So nice to see you under happier circumstances, and without mashed potatoes on the floor. I'm Abby's aunt Mary, by the way. Welcome to the family."

Jessie shook hands with Mary. "Thank you. Thank you so much."

They all waited to see what Ma would say. Bridget

was pretty sure every single one of them was holding their breath at the same time.

The world of city hall kept moving forward, people rushing off to hearings and meetings, security guards making the rounds, snippets of arguments escaping whenever a door opened. The plain, ancient building stood strong and cool, as if saying it had withstood hurricanes and floods and battles and would withstand this small family war too.

"Congratulations to you both," Ma said with a little nod. "You both look...lovely."

Abby stood beside Jessie, a protective hand on her fiancée's waist. She reached for her mother's hand and tugged her closer. "Ma, I'd like you to meet Jessie, my wife-to-be."

Colleen hesitated for a split second. The air stilled, but then Colleen's face relaxed and she reached out to draw Jessie into a hug. It wasn't a warm, known-you-all-your-life hug, but it was a start. "Welcome to the family, Jessie. Take good care of my daughter."

"I will, Mrs. O'Bannon. I promise." Jessie wiped a tear away from the corner of her eye. "And thank you. It's an honor to marry Abby."

Ma drew back and turned to her middle daughter and cupped her face with both hands. Ma's eyes filled, and her lips trembled. "Oh my, you are a beautiful bride, Abigail. But...you aren't quite...all together."

Abby sighed and tried to turn away. "Ma, come on—"

"You still need something borrowed." She reached in her pocket and pulled out a pressed square of linen with two letters embroidered in dark blue on the corner. She closed Abby's hand over it. "This was your father's hand-kerchief. I thought you'd want a little piece of him here today. Because I know he'd want to be here, and if he was, he'd be so proud of you."

Abby pressed the handkerchief to her nose, inhaling the long-ago scent of the father they all missed. "Thank you, Ma. This is...perfect."

"He loved you, Abby, and he understood you." Ma bit her lip and dropped her gaze to the tile floor. Bridget could see her struggling with the words, with the chore of talking about something deeper than how much yeast to add to the sourdough bread.

"It's okay, Ma," Abby said. "Let's just go inside the office."

"Wait. Please. Let me say one more thing." Ma brushed a lock of hair off of Abby's forehead, the move full of tenderness and love. "You were always so...strong and determined and tough. I never knew what to do with you or how to connect with you. Some of that was my fault, I know, and I'm sorry, Abby. What do I need to do so we can...try again?"

"Just accept me as I am, Ma." Abby caught her mother's hand in hers. "That's all you have to do."

"I will, because I don't want to lose you." Ma looked at her other girls, and the tears in her eyes carved a fissure in the steel armor Colleen O'Bannon wore every day. "I don't want to lose any of you. I've made some terrible mistakes, things I'm not proud of, things that drove you girls away, and I'm...I'm sorry. I truly am."

"Aw, Ma, come on. I didn't want to cry today. I forgot to wear waterproof mascara." But Magpie was already crying, heedless of the makeup blurring under her eyes.

"Me too. I'm so sorry, girls. I love all of you. I always have." Ma drew Magpie into a hug and then grabbed Nora and Bridget too. The four O'Bannon girls and their mother stood in the middle of Boston City Hall, crying and hugging, and beginning to erase years of hurt.

The city clerk's office door opened, and a short elderly woman poked her head out. "Miller and O'Bannon family? Are you ready to get married?"

❦❧

The primroses had died back, their happy white faces gone until next spring. Bridget stepped out onto the deck and caught the scent of summer in the air. Soon it would be too hot to stand out here in the middle of the day, but for now, she was going to enjoy the gentle sun and soft breeze. Behind her, the post-wedding party was in full swing, but at this family gathering, instead of dour black and soft tones, the O'Bannon girls were loud and happy and singing. It was a good sound, one she hadn't heard in years.

Bridget kicked off her shoes, placed them on the top step, and then walked down to the grass. She'd gotten the lawn mower out herself last night and mowed the yard—twice—because it had grown so long in the weeks since she canceled the lawn service. There'd been a certain satisfaction in cutting long, straight lines up and down the yard. It wasn't perfect, but it was a job she'd done all on her own. And that felt good. Really good.

There were also new flowers—bright red geraniums that ringed the edges of the lawn. She'd planted six dozen of the annuals yesterday and watered them twice, giving them a head start for the warmer days ahead.

"You must have given that plant I bought you one hell of a lot of Miracle-Gro."

Bridget turned at the sound of Garrett's voice. He still wore the same dark suit from earlier today—dark pants, dark jacket, white button-down. He'd forgone the tie he had on this morning and left the top two buttons of his shirt undone. Heat curled inside her, a desire for this man, for his touch, his kiss, his voice. "I cloned it in my spare time."

He chuckled. "A woman of many talents."

"Oh, you have no idea." A throaty laugh escaped her, a flirty sound she almost didn't recognize. It felt...liberating to flirt with him, to tease him. To see his eyes widen and his gaze drop to her lips for a moment.

He cleared his throat. "So, I met your family a second ago."

Oh good Lord. She hadn't thought of that when she'd gone outside. After meeting her family, it was a wonder the man was still here. She never should have left him alone with them. She could only imagine what her sisters and mother had said. "I'm so sorry. I didn't know for sure when you'd be arriving and I shouldn't have left you—"

He put up a hand to stop her. "They're *nice*, Bridget. I liked them. Your mother tried to load me up with a plate of food, but I told her I wanted to see you first." He brushed a tendril of hair behind her ear and let his touch linger. She wanted to lean into his hand and stay there for hours. "I know I said I wanted to take things slow, but ever since that kiss, I haven't been able to stop thinking about you."

"Same here." God, she felt as giddy and shy as a teenager. She liked his eyes, the way they crinkled at the corners, the light reflected in them. Being with Garrett was so...easy. With Jim, she'd always felt like she had to try, as if there was some test she needed to pass. Garrett took everything in stride, and she found herself more drawn to his laid-back spirit every second. "It's getting harder and harder to remember why we were taking things slow."

"That's good to hear you say," Garrett said, and leaned in and closed the distance between them. "Real good." The words skimmed her lips, and the heat in his breath made her edge closer.

Garrett cupped her face with his hands and kissed her. Not the easy, sweet kiss they'd shared in the hall, but a deeper, slower kiss that awakened her in waves. Tender then hot, gentle yet sensual.

Damn. The man knew how to kiss. And that told Bridget there was a good chance he knew how to do everything else just as well. Anticipation for more coiled inside her.

How long had it been since she'd been with a man? At least six months. Jim hadn't touched her in two or three months before he died. And now the want for Garrett measured on a Richter scale. Especially given how damned good he kissed.

His hands slid down to her waist, thumbs resting in the divot above her hips, and she wondered vaguely if there was another spot on her body quite that sensitive. She pressed into him, and his kiss deepened, hotter now, faster, the waves becoming a rushing surf. Finally, he pulled back, the two of them breathless. "If I don't stop now, I'll be doing things I definitely shouldn't be doing in your backyard during your sister's wedding reception."

"That's okay," she said, leaning against his chest, listening to the thudding of his heart. Happy to hear it racing as fast as her own. "It gives us something to look forward to later."

"I have a thousand things I'm anticipating with you, Bridget." He placed a gentle kiss on the top of her head and then wrapped his arm around her waist and drew her even closer. They stayed there for a long while, letting the breeze dance in their hair, listening to the strains of music coming from the stereo inside the house.

Something flickered in the shrubs at the back of the yard. Bridget leaned forward and looked again. Another movement, a shadow, and then she saw it again. "Oh my," Bridget whispered. "I think it's back."

"What's back?" Garrett said.

"The hummingbird." She pointed across the yard just as the tiny bird darted out of the shrubs and hovered over the bloomless primroses. He zipped back and forth, maybe looking for the primrose flowers, then flitted away. "Oh no. He left."

"Shhh," Garrett said. "Give it a minute."

Just when she was about to give up, the hummingbird returned, his body riding the slight breeze, past the primroses, over the shrubs, bypassing the geraniums, and then straight across the lawn. He darted past the kitchen window, overshooting it, and for a second she thought he was going to leave again. Then at the last moment, he U-turned and zipped back around and up to the feeder. He lifted his long beak, wings beating so fast they looked like they weren't moving at all. He hovered for a moment and dipped his beak in to taste the red nectar.

"Hey, he likes the feeder," Garrett said. "Can I say I told you so?"

"You can." The hummingbird darted in for a second drink, backed up, then in again, and back, over and over. It was such a silly thing to get so excited about a visit from a bird no bigger than her palm, but it gave Bridget a sense of satisfaction. This one living thing had depended on her, and she'd come through after all. "Did I ever tell you how I first found him?"

"You found him?"

She nodded. "On the day of the funeral, I was sitting on the deck. Mostly avoiding my mother." And the expectations and the quiet and all the sadness in her house, but she didn't add that. Bridget pointed toward the flowers at the back of the yard. "I saw something moving in the primroses, and as I got closer, I realized it was the hummingbird, caught in a spiderweb. He was smaller then, probably just a baby. I cleaned the web off his body, and he sat on my hand—for just a second—and then he flew away. I always felt like..." She shook her head. "This is going to sound crazy."

"No, it won't." He took her hand in his. "Tell me."

She looked into his eyes and took a leap in trusting him. Garrett seemed genuinely interested, and she got the sense he wouldn't tease her for believing in the impossible once in a while. "I always thought that the hummingbird was a sign. Or a messenger, you know? My grandma believed in those kinds of things, and I could just hear her telling me to pay attention to whatever message he was bringing."

Garrett watched the hummingbird make his rounds of the yard before returning to the kitchen window feeder. "Makes sense. I believe in that kind of thing. There are those little whispers in the back of your head that make you turn left instead of right, and you end up avoiding a five-car pileup. Or the letter that comes at just the right time, encouraging you to take a chance on that new job. There are signs and messages all around us, if we're willing to listen. Even if they come in the form of hummingbirds. So, what message do you think he was bringing you?"

She thought about that question for a long time, watching the hummingbird skip from hole to hole on the feeder. She could see her sisters inside the kitchen, watching the bird too. They were smiling and pointing, clearly enjoying the up-close look at Mother Nature.

The first time she'd seen him, her husband had just died, and her world had come to a screeching halt. The second time she'd seen him, she'd been wallowing in her grief and fear, afraid to leave her bed, her house. And now the hummingbird had returned on the very day her family had come back together, this time in celebration, not sadness. The little guy wasn't caught in a dangerous web this time but had returned stronger and happier.

That sure as hell seemed like a sign to her. And maybe that was why she hadn't seen him for so long—he was waiting for her to be ready too. For her to be untangled and ready to move on to new things.

Bridget thought of how her life had changed in these months. How much it was going to change in the months going forward. "I think..." She could hear her grandmother's voice whispering to her, *He brought you the signs you needed when you needed them, dear Bridget.* "I think that the hummingbird was meant to show me that I could escape my own web. I felt caught for so many years, and I didn't even know it. Not until one giant life event changed everything."

"Sometimes we need a big wake-up call." Garrett raised her hand with his, gesturing toward the tiny bird filling his belly with sugar water. "You know what I think that is over there? That's hope. That even in the darkest times, life prevails and finds a way."

"Even when it seems like the path you need to take is impossible to find?"

"Even then." Garrett turned and took her in his arms. "I have been there, Bridget, in that dark, impossible place. You just have to keep fighting to see the light. And be brave enough to step out into it."

"To move on, and move out." She stepped out of his arms and spun a slow circle in the yard. She would be leaving this space behind, but she would find another place, with another yard, and plant geraniums and primroses there. "Tomorrow, I'm putting this place on the market. I have to find someplace else to live, someplace I can actually afford."

"I can help you with that."

She cocked her head. "You're not offering to marry me, right? Because I am definitely not ready for that."

"No." He chuckled. "I do own some rental properties, remember? And I have a tiny little Cape that's going to be available next month. It's maybe a half mile from here, and a few blocks away from the bakery. And it has a great yard that's sure to attract lots of hummingbirds."

"I'm...I'm not sure I'll still be working at the bakery." She hadn't talked to her mother yet. She glanced at her family, now no longer in the kitchen watching the hummingbird but instead standing on the deck, pretending to talk but really making no secret of watching her with Garrett. Always in her business, but this time, Bridget didn't really care.

"Well, keep it in mind. Keep me in mind."

A little Cape-style house. She closed her eyes, and she could imagine it. See herself sitting on the front porch, hanging white lace curtains in the kitchen windows, maybe planting a little garden out back. "Do you allow pets? Like a little dog?"

He smiled at her. "I think we can work something out.

I love dogs, and I don't have one of my own right now. So maybe I could waive the pet deposit in exchange for some fetch time."

"I think that can be arranged. I'd like to take a look at the house as soon as possible, Garrett." She plucked a leaf from one of the geraniums and rubbed it between her fingers until it released a lemony green scent, fresh and bright. "For the first time in years, I don't know what my future is going to hold, and that's exciting and scary, all at the same time. All I know is that I'm in control of every decision I make going forward. I only hope I make the right ones."

"There are no right decisions, Bridget," he said. "There's only the one that feels best at that moment in time. Look at him." Garrett pointed at the hummingbird. "He isn't thinking too much farther down the road beyond fattening up for his long journey south in a few months. What happens next season or the one after that is too far away for him to think about. All we have is right here, right now."

She looked up at the women on her deck, the women who had helped shape her and mold her, in good ways and bad. They were a pain in the ass, but she loved them, and she was damned grateful to have every single one of them here. "Right here, right now, is pretty damned good if you ask me."

THIRTY-TWO

The next morning, Bridget scribbled out a note for Garrett. She'd left him, still asleep in her bed. He'd stayed last night, sitting in the kitchen with her and her sisters, playing cards for hours. When everyone else had finally gone home—with Aunt Mary taking Ma up on her offer to stay at her house for the night, Garrett had remained. They'd sat outside and talked until the wee hours. Then she'd led him into her bedroom and found out that, yes, he did do *everything* as well as he kissed. He was a generous man in bed, giving so much more to her than he took for himself, leaving her sated in a thousand different ways. Even now, operating on just a handful of hours of sleep, Bridget was still smiling.

She propped the note beside a blueberry muffin and a brewed pot of coffee, and then got in her car and wound her way through the crowded streets of Dorchester. It was still dark out but already warmer than yesterday. She could smell fresh tar, newly laid in yet another road-improvement project on her way to work that had tied up traffic and diverted the growing number of commuters into neighborhoods, filling the narrow side streets like water trickling into a pipe.

Two detours later, Bridget parked in back of the bakery. Nora's car was already in its customary space beside Ma's. Bridget shut off her car, pocketed the keys, and went in through the back door, a little hesitant because she wasn't sure what kind of reception she was going to receive. The last time she was here, she'd read her mother the riot act and stormed out, vowing never to return.

A Meghan Trainor song was playing on the kitchen radio—and Ma, Nora, and Magpie were all humming along with the catchy tune as they worked. Bridget stopped and gaped at them. "One, music while we work, and two, all of you are humming it?"

"I thought maybe we could stand to change a couple things around here." Ma shrugged and went back to pressing a rolling pin against an oval of pie dough. "It's about time you got here, Bridget. We need four vanilla sponge and two chocolate within the hour. No time for chitchat."

Guess that meant she didn't have to worry about her job, or that everything would change overnight. In a way, that was kind of comforting. Bridget slid her apron over her head and tied it behind her back. "Magpie, what are you doing here?"

"Thought I'd spend a couple days with you misfits, helping out at the bakery. Like old times."

"Meaning you're going to burn the muffins and forget to add sugar to the brownies?" Nora teased.

Magpie flicked a towel at Nora's hip. "Hey, there's a reason they pay me to write, not bake."

Bridget laughed. Damn, it was good to have her sisters back. Even Ma was smiling as her hands made quick work with the piecrust dough.

"So...Bridge, you want to tell us about this new guy? A guy who was still there when we all went home, I might add," Nora said.

Magpie started pouring brownie batter into a waiting pan. "Oh, and in case he didn't tell you, there was a quiz when we met him, and he passed with flying colors."

"As he should. Any person who wants to marry one of my daughters better treat them right," Ma said.

"He's nice, and he does treat me right, and...that's all I'm going to say about Garrett right now." Things with them had only just begun, and she wanted to hold that sweet newness to herself a little while longer. Bridget grabbed the clipboard, flipped through the orders. She looked up when she heard the back door open again and Abby entered. Everyone stopped working, and a hush fell over the bakery.

"Good morning," Abby said. She parked a fist on her hip and glared at her sisters. "Quit staring at me like you've never seen me before. God, I was just in here two days ago."

"Yeah, but aren't you supposed to be on a beach in Key West somewhere?" Nora twisted the icing bag, pushing a thick wad of buttercream to the tip. She leaned over and began adding delicate pale pink flowers to the edge of a sheet cake.

"I will be—on Friday. Jessie and I changed the plane tickets. I told her I needed some time to"—Abby looked at her sisters and her mother—"get caught up. She understood. Plus, I couldn't leave you guys to bake the bread. You all are amazing at cakes, but your sourdough skills are sorely lacking."

"You're going to be here all week?" Magpie said. On the radio, Meghan Trainor yielded to an Adele ballad. "Me too! Which means there's going to be trouble in the bakery."

Ma wagged a finger. "There better not be any shenanigans here. We have work to do."

"Ah, but, Ma, what's life without a few shenanigans?" Magpie nudged her mother and gave her a grin. Ma pursed her lips but couldn't hold the feigned disapproval, and her face dissolved into a smile.

"Just don't burn anything, Margaret. We're already behind from the last two days."

Abby grabbed her apron and slipped it on. She dipped into the storage room, grabbing a small container of yeast as she talked. "You will need to find another bakery to supply the bread by this weekend, Ma, but hopefully me being here for a few days gives you some time to do that and keeps you from getting further behind."

Ma spun the piecrust circle a quarter turn and rolled it again, repeating the turn and roll as the circle widened.

"I'll make a few calls later this morning. I appreciate the help for now, Abigail. We have missed your breads. No one is as good as you."

"You know...me being here doesn't have to be a temporary thing." Abby leaned against the counter and toed at the tile floor. "If you want...I can come back to work after I get home from Key West. I have really, really missed working here and working with all of you."

The rolling pin stopped spinning. Ma held it over the crust, frozen for a moment. Then she nodded, and when she spoke, her voice was thick. "I'd love it if you came back, Abigail. We need all the help we can get, especially since we just landed that order with the organic food emporium. And especially since Bridget's newest cake is getting a write-up in *Boston* magazine."

"My newest cake?"

Ma nodded. "Remember that chocolate peanut butter one you sold to those women a few weeks ago? Turns out, they worked at the magazine and gave the food editor a slice. They called me this morning and asked if they could do a piece on it. You'll need to make another one—"

"Maybe a lot of other ones, if we get that kind of publicity," Nora said. "That's the kind of thing that could really turn things around for this bakery and put us back on the map."

"It could," Bridget said. "Which means we're going to need a lot of help."

"Good thing Ma had a lot of daughters," Abby said with a grin.

"Wait, are we bringing the old gang back together again?" Nora asked. "Because I don't know if that's a good idea."

"Why not?" Bridget dumped butter and sugar into the giant stand mixer, turned it on, and let them blend before sliding in the eggs, one at a time.

"Because whenever all the O'Bannon girls are together, there's trouble. Like food fights and screaming arguments and—"

"And I wouldn't have it any other way," Ma said.

"Me neither," Magpie said. "That's what makes us O'Bannons. For better or worse."

Abby poured warm water in with the yeast and watched it begin to bubble and foam, working together to form the basis of all she would create today. "From here on out, I'll gladly take the better and leave the worse behind."

"May the saddest days of our futures be no worse than the saddest days of our past," Bridget said softly, reciting the toast she had heard her father make dozens of times at weddings and birthday parties and Sunday dinners.

"Indeed," Nora whispered. On the radio, Adele's voice drifted away, replaced by "Best Day of My Life" by American Authors. One by one, the O'Bannon girls began to sing along, the harmony rising and falling as cakes baked and tarts were filled and the bakery woke from its nighttime slumber.

Bridget watched the pale yellow blend of butter, sugar, and eggs accept the new additions of flour and baking soda, incorporating them until all those disparate ingredients merged into one. Alone, none of these ingredients did a thing, but once they were brought together, they created magic.

Just like her crazy, complicated family.

READING GROUP GUIDE

Dear Reader,

I grew up in a small town outside of Boston with a family who believed food was part of the glue keeping us all together. When I was a little girl, my mom and my grandmother ran a donut shop out of our repurposed front porch. Even after the shop closed, my mom and my grandmother baked often.

I can still remember coming in from playing outside and being greeted by the sweet, tempting scent of fresh-baked bread. My mom would butter the hot loaves, making them glisten. Many times, she'd cut me two slices of hot fresh bread for a quick peanut butter and jelly (or peanut butter and Fluff, a Massachusetts lunch staple). To this day, I miss those loaves and wish my mom was around to bake them for me.

Families, I have found, are messy. They fight, they make up, they hate, and they love. My own was no different. But when things were at their worst and I needed to call someone, my family has always been there, always had my back. There's something comforting in that, and it was the starting point for writing THE PERFECT RECIPE FOR LOVE AND FRIENDSHIP.

I added several Massachusetts-unique things to this book: The gas tank with the rumored image of Ho Chi Minh that you can still see as you drive into the city on I-93. The strong delineation between neighborhoods outside of Boston, and the pride they have in being their own special places. Wollaston Beach, a place I went to more than once when I wanted a moment to clear my head. For me, writing about those places is almost like going home again, and for those few pages, I'm back in that kitchen with my mom and my grandmother.

I hope you find the same solace in this book, that sense of family and community that we all crave. And that you grow to love the O'Bannons, in all their messiness, as much as I did. This novel is my tribute to my own family and to the memories that linger in my mind, as sweet as that first bite of fresh, warm bread.

DISCUSSION QUESTIONS

1. The hummingbird appears at the beginning and the end of the story. How does the hummingbird help Bridget cope with her grief? Do you think it was a symbol, as she does? Do you have things in your life that are symbols or messages?

2. *The Perfect Recipe for Love and Friendship* is filled with secrets and devastating revelations. What was the most shocking secret?

3. Each of the women is hiding a secret. Some seem to believe that keeping a secret is wrong while others appear to feel that keeping a secret may be the right thing to do to spare others' feelings. Do you believe that family secrets should be revealed or hidden forever? What do you think is most important in a relationship, total honesty or sensitivity to the other's feelings?

4. How much of a marriage's success or failure do you think can be attributed to the love between husband and wife and how much to external factors, such as jobs, finances, location, and other people? Do you think that Bridget and Jim loved each other enough to get married? What was the biggest factor in the failure of their relationship? Could their marriage have been saved?

5. Shirley Jump has often been praised for writing stories that pull at readers' emotions. Looking back on the story, discuss the moments that were the most emotional for you. What moments made you cry? What moments made you laugh?

6. Who is your favorite of the four sisters: Bridget, Nora, Abby, or Magpie? Why?

7. Discuss the roles of sisterhood and friendship in the novel. Are the four sisters also friends? Which character proves to be the greatest friend to one of her sisters? Does the way Bridget values sisterhood and friendship change as a result of her husband's death?

8. Baking is a creative and therapeutic activity for Bridget. How do you think baking alleviates her grief? Does Colleen have a similar experience with baking? Does Nora? Does Abby?

9. Why do you think Colleen is so controlling and critical of her daughters? What was your impression of Colleen at the beginning of the book? What about at the end? Over the course of the novel, how does she change and what does she learn about herself?

10. Each of the women struggles with religion throughout the story but Colleen has the closest relationship with God, so she has the most conflict. Do you think it's possible for Colleen to resolve her issues with faith and religion? Do you think she can accept Abby and Jessie's marriage?

11. If you had to reinvent yourself the way Bridget did after her husband's death, what would you do? Was Bridget right to go back to the family business or should she find a way to strike out on her own?

12. At one point in the story, Bridget and Nora fight about bananas. Nora feels that Jim was being too controlling but Bridget says that she would be happy just to have Jim back to complain. Who did you side with? Have you lost someone and would you be willing to take the bad along with the good to have them back? If Jim were still alive, does the story about the bananas make you think that Bridget should try to make her marriage work? Do you think this event was one that made Bridget finally start seeing how deep the problems went in her marriage?

13. Bridget meets Garrett soon after her husband dies but several months pass before she is ready to go out on a date with him. If they had met sooner or later, do you think Bridget and Garrett's relationship would have evolved differently? Would they have even struck up a friendship without Bridget's grief? Will they get married or is this just a rebound relationship for Bridget?

14. When Bridget looks out at her yard, the primroses bring happy and sad memories. Are you a gardener? What brings you joy about gardening? Do you use gardening to reduce stress?

15. Aunt Mary is a colorful character with an interesting past. She is a bit of a loner and has missed out on a lot of family events due to her travels. Do you have an unconventional person in your family? Do you envy their freedom or do you think that they have wasted their life?

Everyone thinks there's nothing Nora O'Bannon can't do. In reality her picture perfect family is on the verge of falling apart. She can't imagine life getting worse—until she is forced to make a decision that could cost her everything she holds dear...

A preview of *The Secret Ingredient for a Happy Marriage* follows.

From the street, Nora O'Bannon Daniel's life looked almost perfect. The quintessential three-bedroom, two-bath house in a decent neighborhood, with a wooden swingset in the backyard and a pink bike leaning against the garage. The cornflower blue Dutch Colonial sat a hundred yards back from the sidewalk on a leaf-covered quarter-acre lot of weedy grass peppered with the detritus of two kids. A trio of pumpkins marched down the stairs, still whole and uncarved. The brick stoop had weathered from the harsh winters, and the black paint on the railing had peeled down to gray metal, but the house had that air of well-worn and loved.

If her life had been a TV show, there'd be some quirky, close-knit family on the other side of the front door, a family whose biggest problem was a lost set of keys. Within thirty minutes, the keys would be found, and the family would be sitting down to a dinner where they'd laugh and hug and pass the creamed corn.

But when Nora parked her aging sedan in the driveway, the grumpy engine ticking as it cooled, she could see the truth she'd been avoiding for months. She didn't live in a sitcom, and there wasn't going to be a life-saving solution in the next half hour, punctuated by commercials for Geico and Smucker's jam on either end.

No, in Nora's world, life pretty much sucked. She hadn't thought that the bank would actually do it—some unrealistic part of her had been hoping for some last-minute sympathetic, divine intervention—but the threatened end had finally arrived. While she was at work, a bright yellow sheet of paper had been tacked to her front door, its message stamped in black block letters underscored with a paragraph of red warnings.

NOTICE OF AUCTION

On the welcome mat sat a cellophane-wrapped orange chrysanthemum topped with a mylar balloon. The balloon waved back and forth in the fall breeze, screaming Happy Birthday in neon green letters.

Happy birthday, Nora O'Bannon, you've lost your house. Your family is now homeless.

Not exactly the way she'd wanted to turn thirty. The irony of it all would have made her cry, if she'd had the energy to work up some tears. For a year, she'd argued and prayed and strategized and negotiated, so sure she could head off this disaster. Her husband Ben had done what he always did, buried his head in the sand and left her to handle the incessant phone calls and letters. Nora, who had always been told she could do anything she set her mind to, had failed. The faceless person on the other end of the phone had no interest in letting them skate on the mortgage. No heart for the two children she was going to have to uproot. And no solution that Nora could actually afford.

Nora got out of the car, carrying a takeout pizza in one hand and a bag of fabric in the other. Madeline wanted to be a princess for Halloween, and in a thick cloud of denial, Nora had bought yards of pink tulle and dozens of sparkly rhinestones. She figured she could whip out the old Singer and stitch up something that would pass for a princess, all in time for Madeline to go trick-or-treating on Friday night. Jacob was still wavering between being a pirate and a ninja, so Nora had grabbed a couple yards of black fabric.

Ben pulled in behind her and climbed out of his ten-year-old Toyota. Every time he got out of the sporty little two-door, Nora wondered how he fit inside. Ben towered over her, a lean but fit six-foot-three man with soft brown eyes, dark wavy hair that curled against convention, and a ready smile. She'd fallen in love with that smile at a party one stormy winter night twelve years ago. She'd been a senior in high school, Ben a college freshman, the two of them on Christmas break and crammed into Tommy O'Brien's basement while Aerosmith thudded from the speakers.

"Hey," Ben said. "They finally did it."

"They told us they would." Nora sighed. "I don't know what I'm going to tell the kids."

"Easy. Don't tell them anything." Ben jogged up the stairs, ripped the yellow notice off the door and stuffed it into his interior jacket pocket.

The exact way Ben always lived his life. If he didn't say it out loud, it wasn't real. "That doesn't make it go away, Ben. We've lost the house. There's no going back, no passing Go again, no deal to work with the banker."

"There's always a deal, Nora. Just give me a chance—"

She wheeled on him. "You are the reason we're in this mess. You're the reason our kids are being evicted. You—"

"I didn't get here on my own, Nora." He waved at the pizza and the bags. "Takeout? Shopping? What happened to 'we've got to buckle down so we can get caught up'?"

He was really going to compare twenty dollars' worth of pizza and fabric to what he had done to them? "We are three hundred thousand dollars in debt, Ben. I could buckle down until I'm a hundred and ten and still not pay that off."

"I, me. What about *we*, Nora? Till death do *us* part?"

"That ended the day you walked into Mohegan Sun and blew your paycheck at a roulette table. And then did it again two weeks later, and a month after that. Chasing a stupid white ball."

Ben shook his head. "You're never going to let that go, are you? Fuck it. I don't need to listen to this." He slid his key into the door and went inside.

Nora grabbed the plant and balloon—a gift from her sister Abby—bumped the door open with her hip before it could close and then dumped the pizza on the hall table and the flowers and bag of fabric on the floor. "Our kids don't have a home, Ben. You don't get to be selfish now."

"Nora, let it go." He took out his phone. "I'll fix this."

She snorted. "I've heard you say that twelve thousand times, Ben. And all you've ever done is make it worse." Her gaze skipped over the kitchen, half painted, still missing three upper cabinets, a renovation started four years ago. Yet another of Ben's promises that had been broken the second the work got hard, inconvenient. Once upon a time, she'd thought she could create a home here. Now some other family would stand on the front lawn, hold up a hand, and buy the house she loved for pennies on the dollar. "I'm going to pack some things and take the kids to my mom's until I find a better solution."

"You're leaving?"

"Yeah, Ben, I'm leaving. And I don't want to argue about it or cry about it. Let's just be adults here and admit we screwed this up. We," she waved between them, "screwed us up. This whole thing with the house is a sign. We should go our separate ways and start over."

Silence. She'd finally spoken the words both of them had danced around for two years. Ben's gambling had taken a toll on their marriage, damage they'd never recovered from. They'd gone through the motions for the sake of the kids, but the death knell had sounded the night they'd moved into separate bedrooms.

Ben crossed his arms over his chest. "You're not taking my kids from me, Nora."

"You already did that yourself, Ben." She turned on her heel and walked out of the kitchen. If she stayed there for another second, her foolish heart would cave to the haunted look in his eyes, the pain etched in his forehead.

How many times had she done that? How many times had she believed things would change?

All staying with him had done was cost her the only home her children had ever known. In the back of her bedroom closet, she found a trio of suitcases. She threw them open on the bed—the bed she had stopped sharing with her husband over a year ago—and started stuffing clean laundry inside. Enough for a few days. She'd figure out the rest later.

Ben leaned against the door, watching her without a word for a long time. Finally he said, "Nora, don't go."